A Moment of Madness

Michael Chalk

Copyright © Michael Chalk 2024

First published in Australia in 2024
by Michael Chalk Author & Publisher
ABN 16 077 772 457
https://www.authormichaelchalk.com

ISBN 978-0-6458464-4-7 (paperback for IngramSpark)

Cover design and execution by Simon Chalk

Disclaimer

This novel is a work of fiction set in a historical time period. While every effort has been made to accurately represent the events, people, and culture of the era, certain elements have been fictionalised or adapted for the purposes of storytelling.

Apart from historical characters, events, and dialogue already in the public domain, all other characters, events, and dialogue are products of the author's imagination. Any similarities to actual people, places, or events are purely coincidental.

For clarity, it should be noted that the character Jonathan Khumalo is a fictional creation. However, the surname Khumalo, is derived from the historical figure King Lobengula Khumalo (1845 to circa 1894), who was the second king of the northern Ndebele people.

Dedications

This book is dedicated to the following people:

Firstly, to my beloved wife, Barbara Chalk. Your unwavering love, support, and patience have been my anchor throughout the nine months of writing *A Moment of Madness*. During the times when I was deeply immersed in my work and less present, your encouragement and constructive feedback were invaluable. For this, I am profoundly grateful.

Secondly, I would like to thank those who have helped me prepare this book for publication. This includes my son, Simon Chalk, whose exceptional design and execution of the book cover continue to impress me. I also extend my gratitude to Wally, Brian, and Nigel for their assistance with proofreading and fact-checking.

Thirdly, to the many Zimbabweans of all backgrounds who remain deeply connected to their country's beauty and potential. Despite the economic, political, and social challenges, your dedication to staying in Zimbabwe allows visitors like me to experience its unique wonders and charm.

Finally, this book is dedicated to the millions of ordinary Zimbabweans who have been let down by their leaders since independence in 1980. From the late President Robert Mugabe to his successor, President Emmerson Mnangagwa, you have been promised much but received little, while enduring significant suffering. Your patience, resilience, and abiding hope for a better future are remarkable.

Please know that many people around the world share your aspirations and remain hopeful for a new dawn of equality, opportunity, and prosperity in Zimbabwe, bringing an end to your prolonged period of hardship and despair.

TABLE OF CONTENTS

Road Map of Zimbabwe

The town names shown are the post-colonial names.

Prologue

This book is a sequel to *The Unravelling*, a work of historical fiction published in August 2023, which vividly chronicles the downfall of Rhodesia, now Zimbabwe, in the late 1970s and early 1980s.

On one level, *The Unravelling* depicts the military, political, and tribal intrigue that led to the collapse of a prosperous and sophisticated country with immense potential. The disenfranchised black population, vastly outnumbering the ruling white minority, took up arms in a bid to escape their colonial past. Their struggle was supported by the global superpowers, China and Russia, whose strategic interests had little to do with the political and economic freedom of the black population.

On another level, *The Unravelling* is a multifaceted love story.

Firstly, it explores the deep bond between two young men, Nick Sinclair and Sipho[1] Pukelo, who share a profound love for their homeland and its endangered wildlife. During the Rhodesian Bush War, both men served and fought with distinction in the 3rd Battalion of the Rhodesian African Rifles (3RAR), becoming comrades-in-arms. After Zimbabwe's independence in April 1980, Nick was demobilised, and the country began its reintegration into the international community.

Secondly, it is a love story between Nick Sinclair and Rachel Dixon. Rachel, the only daughter of the controversial but successful English businessman Stuart Dixon, had collaborated with Nick's father, Matthew Sinclair, on tobacco sanction-busting deals. Following his demobilisation, Nick attended the University of Edinburgh, where he met and fell in love with Rachel, a student at Oxford University. Their relationship flourished, and in July 1981, Nick brought Rachel to Zimbabwe for a month-long visit.

---

[1] Sipho is a Ndebele boy's name meaning Gift.

Thirdly, it delves into Sipho's story, a born leader from the Ndebele nation and a patriot. Sipho loves his tribal heritage, but not as much as he loves his country. He demonstrated this love and loyalty both as a serving member of 3RAR and in the new Zimbabwe National Army (ZNA) when, in February 1981, he fought with bravery and honour during the Entumbane uprisings[2] in Bulawayo, Zimbabwe's second-largest city. During this battle, the ZNA, with significant help from its former enemy, the Rhodesian Security Forces, neutralised a significant outbreak of armed conflict between the country's two main tribal militias. However, despite his loyalty, Sipho soon became the victim of blatant and shameful tribal discrimination by the senior leadership of the ZNA against the Ndebele nation.

Finally, it is the story of Johannes du Toit, a man driven by greed and power. Johannes, a callous white man of dubious character, served with the elite Rhodesian Light Infantry (RLI), the country's premier counter-insurgency unit, during the Rhodesian Bush War. However, he fled the country in September 1978 when his illegal poaching activities were exposed. Johannes returned to Zimbabwe in July 1981, shortly after its independence, to resume his nefarious poaching operations.

Fate brings Nick, Sipho, Rachel, and Johannes together at Mhuka[3] Ranch, near Chiredzi in south-eastern Zimbabwe. Here, a deadly encounter occurs, resulting in the deaths of three individuals. The truth of this tragic event remains unknown to the public but is revealed to the reader.

For more information on *The Unravelling* and its availability, visit Michael's website at https://www.authormichaelchalk.com.

---

[2] These had occurred in February 1981 in and around Bulawayo. During the uprising former ZIPRA guerrillas rebelled creating a situation that threatened to develop into a fresh civil war, barely a year after the Rhodesian Bush War. The uprising was quashed by the newly formed Zimbabwe National Army who used troops from the former RAR and other white-commanded elements of the Rhodesian Security Forces to eliminate the threat.

[3] A local word meaning animals or wildlife.

Chapter 1 – The promise

Timeline – Saturday, 7th July 1984

The afternoon sun embraced St. Saviour's Anglican Church with a warm golden glow. Nick stood at the sanctuary rail, feeling both nervous and excited. The air was filled with hushed whispers from the wedding guests seated in the church's highly polished oak-tiered pews. As stragglers made their way through the heavy wooden entrance doors, a murmur of excitement rippled through the seated assembly. They craned their necks, hoping that the new arrival might be the beautiful bride-to-be, Rachel Dixon.

This day marked one of the most significant milestones in the lives of the handsome couple, Nick Sinclair and Rachel Dixon. Their union was one they hoped would resonate throughout their lives, a bond to be celebrated for many years to come.

Nick's upright stature was touched by a beam of sunlight streaming through the stained-glass windows high up on the hand-hewn stone rear wall of the church. In a pensive mood, he reflected on the journey that had brought him and Rachel to this day.

Only four short years ago, he had first laid eyes on Rachel shortly after disembarking through Terminal 3 of Heathrow Airport. Newly arrived in England from Zimbabwe, Nick was due to be picked up by a business associate of his father. Fate, however, had other plans, as Stuart Dixon, Rachel's father, had been delayed by an urgent business meeting in London that day. Consequently, Stuart had asked Rachel to meet Nick at the airport and drive him back to their house in Guildford.

Nick and Rachel had been immediately drawn to each other. Nick was struck by Rachel's striking looks, her sparkling blue eyes, and long blonde hair. She was tall and slim, and her good looks and figure ensured she would stand out in any crowd. Her outward appeal was complemented by her good humour, easy manner, and vivacious personality.

Rachel, in turn, was drawn to Nick's handsome looks. Just over six feet tall, with an athletic build, dark wavy hair, and piercing chestnut brown eyes, Nick's youthful mannerisms, adventuresome spirit, and his outlook on life differed markedly from her English friends and colleagues. The fact that he had completed his 18-month national service as a 2nd Lieutenant in the Rhodesian African Rifles added a touch of mystique and panache to his persona, as did his distinctive clipped 'African' accent.

On the drive to Rachel's house in Guildford, Nick discovered that she had just finished her first year at the University of Oxford, where she was pursuing a four-year Bachelor of Arts degree in Classics. She had returned to spend her university vacation at her parents' home in Guildford.

Their initial attraction to one another deepened during Nick's short stay at the Dixons' beautiful home in Guildford. These intense feelings soon changed from discreet sexual liaisons between the two young people to a profound and deep love. So much so, that a short time later when Nick had to leave for the University of Edinburgh to commence a four-year degree in business and economics, the couple agreed to embark upon a long-distance relationship.

Despite the distance between London and Edinburgh, their relationship not only endured but flourished. Nick and Rachel successfully navigated the challenges of a long-distance relationship and adeptly weathered the trials of university life, thereby allowing their love to deepen into a sincere, heartfelt, and enduring bond.

A pivotal moment in their journey together had occurred in August 1981, when Nick brought Rachel to Zimbabwe for a month-long holiday. During the holiday, Rachel had found herself captivated by both the country and its people. This helped her better understand and appreciate the deep respect and affection Nick had for the land of his birth and for all its people, regardless of their race or tribe.

After their holiday, the couple had returned to their respective universities in the UK. A year later, they got engaged. For a while, they toyed with the idea of getting married in Zimbabwe, but in the end, they decided to have the wedding in the UK, followed by a month-long honeymoon in South Africa and Zimbabwe starting on 14th July 1984.

Nick shuffled his feet and looked back over his shoulder, hoping to catch a glimpse of Rachel's arrival. As he did so, he caught the cheeky grin of his best man, Russell, who was also his younger brother. Russell winked at him, saying in a low whisper, "Don't worry, mate. She will soon be here."

Nick smiled at him and gave him the thumbs-up sign. He couldn't believe how well all the wedding plans had gone. When he had asked Russell to be his best man, he hadn't really expected Russell to agree. After all, Russell, having graduated from the University of Cape Town in November 1983, had only recently started working in a wildlife conservation and management role with the Southern African Wildlife Foundation[4] based in Cape Town.

Russell had arrived in the UK a week ago. A day later, Russell and Nick's parents, Matthew and Brenda Sinclair, had also landed in the UK from Zimbabwe. During their stay in England, Russell and his parents were very kindly being hosted by the Dixon family at the guest cottage at their lovely home in Guildford.

The Dixons had also generously insisted that Nick and Rachel's wedding reception be hosted in the beautiful garden of their family

---

[4] This was founded in 1968. It later became the Southern African Nature Foundation and in 1995 was renamed the World Wildlife Fund South Africa.

home. A magnificent marquee had been erected in the garden, transforming it into a lavish festival celebration site for the 150 invited guests.

These guests included Nick's two groomsmen, Brian McKenzie and Sipho[5] Pukelo. Brian was Nick's close friend from the University of Edinburgh, while Sipho and Nick had both served with 3RAR[6] in 1979 towards the end of the Rhodesian Bush War and had become brothers-in-arms.

Sipho had been a corporal in the 3RAR platoon commanded by Nick. Their friendship had been forged in a deadly firefight between the platoon and a gang of terrorists in the Chimanimani mountains in Zimbabwe's Eastern Highlands[7]. This friendship had been further strengthened in another dramatic incident that had occurred at Mhuka[8] Ranch near Chiredzi during Nick and Rachel's holiday to Zimbabwe in August 1981.

Nick was just beginning to recall details of the incident when his thoughts were interrupted by an audible gasp that echoed around the church. Rachel had arrived and now stood at the church entrance in all her bridal glory. Her father, Stuart Dixon, distinguished looking as always, paused for a few seconds and then escorted her down the aisle.

Nick's breath caught in his chest. Rachel looked stunning. The elegance of her tailored white silk wedding gown, with a white gossamer veil trailing behind her, and the radiant joy in her bright blue sparkling eyes, created a sight too beautiful to behold.

When Stuart reached the end of the aisle, he handed Rachel over to Nick. Nick noticed a tear of pride and joy roll out of the corner of

---

[5] Sipho is a Ndebele boy's name meaning Gift.
[6] 3rd Battalion of the Rhodesian African Rifles.
[7] The Eastern Highlands is a mountainous area on the border of Zimbabwe and Mozambique. It extends for about 300 kilometres from north to south and includes the Inyangani Mountains, the Vumba Mountains, and the Chimanimani Mountains.
[8] A local word meaning animals or wildlife.

Stuart's eye. Then he stepped back into his front row seat, next to his wife, Lynne.

Nick reached for Rachel's hand and gave it a loving and reassuring squeeze as the priest began the service.

Overwhelmed by the deep and intense love that he felt for Rachel at that moment, Nick scarcely absorbed the proceedings of the service. The priest carried out the ceremony in the traditional Anglican manner. Rachel and Nick made their heartfelt and lifelong vows to each other and sealed their commitment with an exchange of rings. Then the loving couple gave each other a passionate kiss.

The priest then welcomed Mr and Mrs Nick Sinclair to the gathered assembly, amidst a spontaneous outburst of clapping and cheering. For a moment, the world outside stood still for the happy couple as the promise of their union took root, marking the beginning of the next chapter of their lives together.

Chapter 2 – The reception

Nick and Rachel exited the church, still basking in the afterglow of their recent vows. Their guests spilled out onto the narrow forecourt in front of the church and alongside Woodbridge Road, eager to congratulate the happy couple with hugs and handshakes. After these congratulations, Nick and Rachel managed to politely navigate their way through the crush of people to the waiting limousine, which would take them to the reception in the Dixons' beautiful garden at their home in Chantry View Road.

Nick opened the limousine's rear door, helping Rachel into the back seat to avoid crumpling her trailing veil. He then circled to the other door and joined her inside. Their chauffeur drove them the short distance to the Dixons' family home. They passed through the pillared gates and travelled along the oak-lined driveway that wound through two acres of beautifully manicured gardens. Meticulously clipped hedges enclosed the property, creating an air of elegance and refinement.

The limousine halted in front of the Dixons' attractive two-storey Edwardian home, which exuded luxury, style, and good taste. The photographer and the bridal party, along with both sets of parents, had arrived shortly before Nick and Rachel. The photographer efficiently shepherded them and other family members into the gardens for official photos.

Meanwhile, the remaining guests made their way to the marquee, their cars neatly parked along the driveway or on the street. Gravel pathways, lined with neatly arranged flower beds, led guests from the parking areas to the marquee alongside the house.

It was a glorious English summer afternoon. The temperature was a mild 24°C, and the sky was cerulean blue. The garden looked beautiful thanks to the extensive planning and preparations undertaken by Lynne Dixon and her team of gardeners. In the centre of the garden, a grand fountain glistened in the golden sunlight, and the sound of its cascading water mingled with the chirping of garden birds, creating a melody that would lift even the heaviest of spirits.

Many guests gathered beneath the shade of stately oak trees, sipping tea and engaging in polite conversation. Two croquet sets on the carefully mown lawns attracted the more competitive guests, whose laughter added a sense of energy to the garden's tranquillity.

Older guests found their way to stone benches tucked away in shaded nooks, where they drank chilled champagne from crystal glasses, sipped tea from fine china cups, and nibbled on canapés. Others strolled through the garden, enjoying the fragrance of rose and lavender bushes as industrious bees and delicate butterflies completed the picturesque setting.

After about 45 minutes, a clanging bell rang through the gardens, signalling the arrival of the happy couple. The smartly tailored waiters politely directed guests to the marquee, where they found their allocated seats.

The marquee had been beautifully prepared. Tables were laid with crisp white tablecloths and napkins, each place setting adorned with stainless-steel cutlery, glassware, and a calligraphed name card with a handwritten note from Rachel thanking guests for their attendance. Vases of white and pale pink roses graced the centre of each table, with other flower arrangements strategically placed around the marquee to conceal unattractive structural elements.

By now, the sun was lower in the sky, casting long shadows across the garden and marquee. The music inside the marquee quietened as the emcee announced, "Ladies and gentlemen, please be upstanding for your hosts, the happy couple, Nick and Rachel Sinclair."

Dressed in resplendent wedding attire, Nick and Rachel entered to applause and made their way to the head table. The bridal party followed, comprising Claire Illingsworth, Rachel's maid of honour, bridesmaids Sarah and Morag, both university friends, Nick's best man and brother Russell, and groomsmen Brian McKenzie, his good friend from the University of Edinburgh, and Sipho[9] Pukelo from the RAR[10].

The reception was an elegant blend of tradition, finery, sincerity, and joy. The catering company had assembled a menu rivalling those of many leading restaurants. Stuart had engaged a nearby pub, The Spread Eagle, for drinks and bar attendants, while Rachel had hired a well-known local band for live music.

Russell, Nick's best man, regaled guests with humorous stories from Nick's childhood in Harare. Claire, Rachel's maid of honour, followed with light-hearted anecdotes from their teenage years. Claire had been lifelong friends with Rachel, and her parents were close friends with Rachel's parents. This lifelong friendship enabled Claire to recount humorous stories from their school years.

Nick's reply speech was heartfelt, expressing deep love for Rachel, gratitude to her parents, and appreciation for his own parents' support. He complimented the maid of honour and bridesmaids on how beautiful they looked and managed to elicit chuckles from the guests when he expressed regret that his best man and groomsmen might not quite match up!

As the night wore on, Nick and Rachel sought out Sipho, who had seemed distracted during Nick's buck night a few days prior. Sipho saw them approaching, stood up with a big smile on his face, and

---

[9] Sipho is a Ndebele boy's name meaning Gift.
[10] Rhodesian African Rifles.

extended his hand, saying, "Good evening, *Ishe*[11]. Congratulations to you both. You are both looking so happy and very glamorous. I am very happy for you."

Nick was a little surprised that Sipho still addressed him using the term of respect that had been the norm when they had both been in the RAR. However, that had been nearly five years ago, and since then, Zimbabwe had achieved its independence and the former racial class structures had become redundant. Notwithstanding this, Nick realised that the Ndebele tradition had always been to hold their military leaders in high esteem. Nick did not want to embarrass Sipho in any way, so he let the use of the term *Ishe* go through to the keeper.

After Sipho's congratulations, they sat together to talk. Nick said, "Gee, it is so good to see you again, Sipho. Thank you so much for making the trip all the way from Zimbabwe to attend our wedding. We both feel very honoured."

"We certainly do," concurred Rachel. "And I am delighted we will be catching up with you in Zimbabwe in a few weeks' time during our honeymoon. I can't wait to be reacquainted with Mhuka[12] Ranch. There haven't been any more poaching incidents on the ranch, have there? I still thank God that He kept you and Nick, as well as Hamish and Mark, safe when we were last at the ranch[13]. All four of you were so lucky not to have been injured when the three poachers opened fire on you."

At the mention of the incident, Nick and Sipho exchanged a knowing glance. Sipho was surprised that Rachel was still unaware that the firefight in which the poachers were shot and killed had, in fact, been

---

[11] *Ishe* is a term of respect used by RAR soldiers when referring to their officers.
[12] A local word meaning animals or wildlife.
[13] Rachel and Nick had first visited Mhuka Ranch in August 1981. During their visit, Sipho had accidently stumbled upon a gang of three poachers who were planning to poach the first two rhinos which had been translocated to the ranch under a government sanctioned rhino protection and conservancy program. Sipho and Nick had hatched up a plot to eliminate this poaching threat. The execution of their plan went far better than either Nick or Sipho could have ever hoped.

carefully orchestrated by him and Nick to eliminate the poachers instead of merely apprehending them. He was impressed that Nick, like himself, had obviously not told anyone the truth of what had happened that day.

In response to Rachel's question, Sipho assured her that there had been no further poaching incidents on the ranch and that the rhino conservation and breeding programme was progressing extremely well.

However, Sipho then shared his concerns about recent events in Zimbabwe. With a worried expression, he said, "Since independence, tensions between the Shona and Ndebele have only grown. Mugabe's politics have made things worse for the Ndebeles. The new national army, the ZNA[14], which was supposed to unite the country, is now under Mugabe's control. He has even set up a special brigade, trained by North Korea, called the 5th Brigade. This brigade answers only to him, not to the ZNA. They've been sent to Matabeleland to deal with ZIPRA[15] dissidents. The situation has become very bad. Mugabe is targeting not only military dissidents but anyone who opposes ZANU-PF[16]. I fear Mugabe's real aim is to weaken the Ndebele nation."

Nick and Rachel were shocked, with Nick recalling Rachel's father's dire predictions from 1981. Rachel expressed surprise that none of this had been reported in the British press. Sipho responded, "Well, it's all quite recent, and reports are just starting to come out in Zimbabwe. The government's propaganda machine is working hard to protect Mugabe and keep both Zimbabwean and international media in the dark about these things."

Their conversation risked drifting into heavier subjects. Sipho, realising this, apologised for bringing up such serious matters on their

---

[14] Zimbabwe National Army.
[15] Zimbabwe People's Revolutionary Army. ZIPRA was the military wing of ZAPU.
[16] Zimbabwe African National Union – Patriotic Front. ZANU-PF is a political organisation that has been the ruling party of Zimbabwe since independence in 1980.

special day, and the conversation shifted to lighter topics. Rachel shared news of her graduation, job, and the charming bungalow she and Nick had recently purchased in Medstead, Hampshire, where they would move after their honeymoon.

Later that evening, Nick had another sombre conversation, this time with his father, Matthew Sinclair. Matthew voiced his concerns about Zimbabwe's future and questioned the wisdom of staying in the country. He noted increasing attempts by ZANU-PF to interfere at his workplace, TMB[17], explaining that the government was pushing to move tobacco production from large white-owned farms to smaller black-owned ones. Matthew expressed the view that these changes would lead to significant inefficiencies and doubted whether black farmers had the expertise to produce high-quality crops on a large scale.

At around 11:30 pm, the chauffeur-driven limousine returned to pick up Nick and Rachel. The couple left the reception through a human archway formed by paired guests standing opposite each other, clasping their arms overhead. Blessings, well-wishes, and the usual bawdy banter about their plans for the night in the bridal suite accompanied them as they made their way down the archway and exited the marquee.

They climbed into the limousine, which would take them to a nearby boutique English country hotel, marking their first night as a married couple. A short time later, the rest of the guests began drifting away. The crew of waiters and helpers packed up the remnants of the night's celebrations. The marquee emptied, and silence once again settled over the house and garden.

---

[17] Tobacco Marketing Board.

Chapter 3 – The morning after

Rachel was the first to awaken. Even with the curtains drawn, it was clear that the sun was shining. She hoped that the glorious English summer they were enjoying would continue.

Their first night as a wedded couple was spent at Grovefield House, an Edwardian country house in Buckinghamshire, about 30 miles from her parents' home. Being Edwardian, its architecture was similar to that of her parents' house, only on a grander scale, set in large, tranquil gardens spanning about seven acres.

Nick was still asleep. Being careful not to awaken him, Rachel climbed out of bed and quietly tiptoed into the adjacent kitchen to make herself a mug of coffee. She was wearing the sexy two-piece mulberry silk beige pyjama set that she had bought especially for their wedding night.

Despite her efforts to be quiet, Nick stirred. He sat up in their luxury king-sized bed and gazed towards the kitchen. Rachel was standing next to the kitchen windows and looking out over the garden. The early morning light streaming through the window highlighted her slim, sensual figure beneath her silken pyjamas.

"Well, that is a sight worth waking up to," said Nick in a husky voice.

Rachel looked back over her shoulder into their bedroom. "I am so sorry, honey," she said. "I did not want to wake you."

"Well, I am glad you did," he said. "Now, how about climbing back into bed with me so that I can say good morning properly?"

Rachel giggled. "Now that's an offer a well-brought-up girl like me simply cannot refuse. Especially if it is coming from her dashing husband."

With that, she skipped from the kitchen into their bedroom, diving under the bed linen into Nick's waiting arms. The two lovers embraced each other tenderly but eagerly. When they had arrived at Grovefield House, it had been well after midnight. They were both tired and wrung out after all the excitement of their wedding day. So, they had agreed not to consummate their wedding day until after a good night's sleep.

Their lovemaking that morning was passionate and considerate. Having been in an intimate relationship with each other for nearly four years now, they both knew how to please the other. And this morning, their desire to please the other overrode any selfish passion. They teased and tantalised each other without shame. There was a moment when Nick felt he was about to climax, but he sensed Rachel was still not ready. So, he pulled back and gently eased her hands away from his erogenous areas. He began to tenderly kiss her along her inner thighs. Very soon these were trembling with readiness and desire.

They cleaved themselves to each other and gently moved together in unison. Their movements quickly became more strident as they strove to please both themselves and the other. They both felt as though they were going to explode. When they could bear the ecstasy no longer, they released themselves to the other and climaxed together. Their orgasm brought them down from their sexual climax, and they crumpled back onto the sheets in exhaustion.

"That was simply wonderful," gushed Rachel. "It reminded me of when we made love at the Victoria Falls Hotel."

"Yes, that was special," Nick agreed. "I loved you back then, but today I love you even more. I cannot wait for us to discover the rest of our lives together."

Shortly afterwards, Nick and Rachel showered and then went down into the light-filled and airy dining room. They were given a cosy table close to an open window. Here, they engaged in an intimate dialogue while eating a delicious but healthy English breakfast. To achieve this, the kitchen staff had carefully followed Rachel's instructions on how to limit the fat content of a typical English breakfast.

Over breakfast, they talked about their plans for the day. Russell had kindly volunteered to pick them up from the hotel at 11:30 am. From there, he would take them back to the Dixons' home in Guildford, where a post-wedding garden BBQ had been arranged starting at about 1:00 pm. The entire bridal party, plus both sets of parents, planned to attend.

Russell arrived just before 11:30 am as planned. Nick and Rachel had checked out of the hotel and were waiting in the reception area when he arrived. When Russell saw them, he strode over to them and gave them a generous hug. He congratulated Rachel on the accuracy of her directions and also complimented her on her car. She was still driving the XJ6 Jaguar that her parents had given her in February 1980 when she turned eighteen.

Nick chucked their small overnight bag onto the back seat. Russell suggested that it would be easier for them all if Rachel took responsibility for driving back to her parents' house. She agreed and climbed into the driver's seat. At Nick's insistence, Russell got into the passenger seat while Nick sat in the back.

The ride back to the Dixons' home was short. During the trip, Russell and Rachel chatted, while Nick surveyed the passing countryside from the comfort of the back seat.

Rachel was keen to know what had happened to Russell's girlfriend, Yvonne. Russell had met her when they were both students at the

University of Cape Town. She was studying marine biology and had accompanied Russell on a trip to the UK in July 1982.

During that trip, Russell and Yvonne had spent a week with Rachel and Nick hiking in the Scottish Highlands. At that time, they both seemed committed to their relationship. However, shortly after they returned to South Africa, their relationship had ended.

Rachel turned to Russell and said, "I am so sorry that you and Yvonne split up. Do you mind me asking what happened?"

"Absolutely not," answered Russell. "As you know, she was doing marine biology at Cape Town. We both graduated in November 1983. Yvonne accepted a marine biology research position at the University of Aberdeen, while I accepted a position in wildlife conservation and management with the Southern African Wildlife Foundation in Cape Town[18]. Neither of us was prepared to forego the job offers we had received. So that meant an end to our relationship. I was pretty upset that our relationship ended up being the casualty. But the fact that neither of us was prepared to walk away from our respective job offers must have meant that our bond could not have been that strong. That's life, I guess."

"That is sad," said Rachel. "Do you know how Yvonne ended up being offered a job at the University of Aberdeen?"

"Yes, I do," said Russell. "While a student at the University of Cape Town, she became very close with one of her lecturers, a bloke called Francois Swanepoel. Anyway, at the beginning of 1982, he accepted a senior position with the School of Biological Sciences at the University of Aberdeen. Yvonne caught up with him just after our hiking holiday with you and Nick in July 1982. Apparently, he offered her this research position on that visit. And, as they say, the rest is history."

---

[18] This was founded in 1968. It later became the Southern African Nature Foundation and in 1995 was renamed the World Wildlife Fund South Africa.

"It must have been a very good position for Yvonne to decide to move all the way from South Africa to Scotland," observed Nick from the back seat.

"Well, between you and me, I now am sure that there was more to the relationship between Yvonne and him than lecturer and student. She certainly was always in awe of him," said Russell. "But that is behind me now. I have definitely moved on."

"Well, I am glad to hear that," said Rachel. "You deserve only the best. I am glad you are not dwelling on her. Anyway, let's enjoy the rest of this beautiful day. We are almost at my parents' house. I cannot wait to catch up with the bridal party and our folks again."

Chapter 4 – The confession

Rachel parked in front of her parents' house. She, Russell, and Nick exited the car. Russell headed to the guest cottage while Nick and Rachel went into the house and made their way up to the spacious guest bedroom on the first floor. After leaving their overnight bag on the bed, they joined their respective parents in the garden.

By now, it was just after 12:30 pm, and the sun hung in the cloudless sky. The day was warm, but the large trees and shrubs offered ample shady spots to escape the heat.

Three market umbrellas were set up near a massive oak tree on the front lawn, close to the fountain. Beneath the tree was a trestle table laden with salads, cold meats, and fruit. Their parents, along with Sipho[19], Brian, Claire, Morag, and Sarah, were relaxing in garden chairs arranged under the umbrellas.

Nick and Rachel, hand in hand, joined the group and were warmly welcomed. Shortly afterwards, Russell joined them.

Rachel's father, Stuart, always the impeccable host, ensured everyone knew each other and were comfortably seated in the shade. A waiter took their drink orders while Lynne fussed over the food table.

---

[19] Sipho is a Ndebele boy's name meaning Gift.

Nick stretched back in his chair, observing the scene. He had been in England long enough to know that while this setting might have been relatively common in Zimbabwe, at least among the white community, it was definitely not the case in the UK.

While the splendid summer day, meticulously landscaped garden, elegant house, table laden with food, attentive waiters, and the convivial gathering of friends and family might have been a scene from England 50 years ago, it was not representative of modern-day England. In the contemporary era, expansive homes and gardens had given way to more modest dwellings, while egalitarianism, the assertion of one's rights, and the dilution of one's responsibilities were the prevailing ethos.

Even though Margaret Thatcher was striving to restore some of the former glory of the British Empire, most Britons were in no doubt that the UK's best days were long behind her. Ruefully, Nick wondered whether the same was true for Zimbabwe. Logic and common sense suggested that this was likely to be the case.

Stuart and Sipho were engaged in deep conversation under one of the large oak trees. Nick heard his name mentioned and walked over to them.

Stuart had been congratulating Sipho on how he and Nick had eliminated the gang of three poachers on Mhuka[20] Ranch back in 1981. He was recounting the incident as it had been told to him by Nick's father, Matthew Sinclair.

With a thoughtful expression, Stuart said, "I recall Matthew telling me that the plan was for you and Nick, along with Duncan Oliver's[21] two sons, Hamish and Mark, to covertly make your way to the kopje where the three poachers were encamped. The four of you arrived at the kopje well before sunrise. Sipho, I understand that you, Hamish, and Mark silently approached the lay-up position where two of the

---

[20] A local word meaning animals or wildlife.
[21] Duncan Oliver was the owner and patriarch of Mhuka Ranch. It had been Duncan who had authorised and sanctioned the mission to capture the three poachers.

poachers were sleeping. Meanwhile, Nick went to the lookout point where the remaining poacher was on guard. The plan was that at precisely 6:15 am, you, Hamish, and Mark would capture the two sleeping poachers, while Nick would deal with the sentry at the lookout site."

"Yes, that's right," said Sipho. "The aim was to capture the three poachers, not to kill them. However, as the poachers were armed, so were we. Mr Oliver had also given us permission to use our rifles if the poachers fired upon us."

"Yes, that is as I recall it," said Stuart. "However, the mission did not play out as planned. This was because the sentry at the lookout site spotted Nick and opened fire on him. This occurred at 6:15 am. Fortunately, the sentry's shots missed Nick. Nick then moved into an offensive position and, shortly thereafter, opened fire on the poacher and killed him. The two sleeping poachers at the lay-up position had been alerted by the initial shots fired by the sentry and had naturally leapt for their rifles. Sipho, I understand you were fearful that the two poachers, who were now fully awake, were about to lay down fire against your, Hamish's, and Mark's positions. So, you opened fire on them and ordered Hamish and Mark to do the same. Is that correct?"

"That's right," said Sipho.

Nick had been listening to Stuart's detailed recall of the incident with deep interest. While he was impressed by Stuart's recollection, he felt a cold unease in the pit of his stomach and feared that the conversation was leading to a place he did not want to go.

Stuart sat back in his chair for a long time without saying anything. During this excruciating pause, Nick and Sipho exchanged worried looks but remained silent.

In a grave voice, Stuart then said, "Now, come on, lads. That story just doesn't add up. I know the police in Zimbabwe have accepted it without equivocation, but frankly, I feel there must be more to it than just that."

Nick and Sipho were both silent. Then Nick hesitatingly said, "What do you mean?"

Stuart replied, "Obviously, I don't know what actually happened, so I have no right to doubt what you have said. But I will tell you why it doesn't seem to add up to me.

"First of all, from all the evidence that the police established when investigating the incident, all three poachers were current or former members of the RLI[22] with plenty of active military experience. Given that, I find it strange that when the sentry poacher opened fire on Nick, he missed. Moreover, it seems remarkable that when Nick took counter-offensive measures against him, he was able to eliminate him so quickly and easily."

"Maybe he was just having an off day," offered Nick.

Stuart did not respond to that comment but continued, "I am also a bit perplexed about what happened at the lay-up site. Both poachers were asleep. They did not know that their position had been compromised. Your intention was to capture and arrest them at 6:15 am. Isn't it a strange coincidence that the initial unplanned firefight at the lookout site also occurred at precisely 6:15 am?"

Looking at Sipho, he continued, "I am also curious why you opened fire on the poachers at the lay-up site so quickly and ordered Hamish and Mark to do so as well. The three of you had not come under fire yet. If your intention was really to apprehend them, wouldn't you have first attempted that rather than opening fire on them?"

"Maybe I panicked," said Sipho.

"You don't strike me as someone prone to panic," retorted Stuart.

Nick and Sipho were silent for many long minutes. They looked down at their hands but briefly locked gazes. Nick raised his eyebrow, and Sipho gave him an imperceptible nod.

---

[22] Rhodesian Light Infantry. This was an infantry regiment and was one of the country's main counter-insurgency units during the Rhodesian Bush War.

After a few more seconds, Nick began to speak, hesitatingly at first but with growing confidence. "Stuart, you are a most perceptive person. You are correct when you say that there must be more to the story. There is. Sipho and I would like to take you into our confidence. It's time to shed light on this matter. The incident has been a heavy burden for us to carry over the last few years."

Stuart said, "That is good. I will obviously respect your confidence if at all possible. But that is not to be presumed. I hope you understand. A lot will depend on what I now hear."

"Fair enough," said Nick. "Would you give Sipho and me a minute or two to confer in private?"

Stuart nodded his agreement. He went to the drinks table to top up his glass. After a couple of minutes, he returned to Nick and Sipho under the oak tree.

He looked at them both, cocked his head slightly to one side, and said, "Well?"

Nick then proceeded with the explanation. "Sipho and I would like to tell you exactly what happened. As you know, Duncan Oliver sanctioned the original plan, which was for us to try and apprehend and capture the poachers. Once they were captured, Duncan wanted them to be handed over to the ZRP[23], who would fully investigate the matter and, if appropriate, take it to the courts. While Sipho and I both understood Duncan's view, we did not agree with him."

"Why was that?" asked Stuart.

"I guess there were three reasons," said Nick. "The first was to do with the competence of the police force at that time. Duncan was assuming that the police were still as competent as they had been during the Smith regime. But Sipho knew that was not the case. Even though the incident occurred just a year after independence, the police force had already begun to become incompetent and open to

---

[23] Zimbabwe Republic Police.

corruption. Moreover, as the three poachers were white, we knew they would be represented by well-qualified lawyers. We were absolutely convinced that their lawyers would shred any brief of evidence the police prepared.

"We were also very worried about corruption. It was obvious that the poachers had access to very good intelligence. After all, it was no accident that they had trespassed onto the ranch at the same time as the ranch had taken delivery of the first two black rhinos under its rhino protection and conservation programme. We figured that the poachers must have been working with well-connected persons. We were concerned that even if the police case against the poachers had been well prepared, potential corruption would mean that the case would never come before the courts, or if it did, justice would not prevail.

"Finally, we were moved by the work done by the IUCN[24]. Based on their work, the government had accepted the IUCN's recommendation that the country's rhinos were an incredibly valuable natural resource under an existential threat from poaching. Accordingly, the government had agreed to establish rhino conservancies across the country and mandated that these conservancies be safeguarded and protected. Sipho and I were determined to do whatever was needed to ensure that this national treasure was preserved for the benefit of future generations of Zimbabweans."

Stuart said nothing for a while. Finally, he said, "So then, what was the actual plan?"

"It was quite simple, really," said Nick. "The plan was for me to covertly find the sentry and move into position by no later than 5:45 am. Sipho, Hamish, and Mark needed to do likewise with the two poachers at the lay-up site. At precisely 6:15 am, I was going to shoot

---

[24] International Union for the Conservation of Nature. This is an international organization working in the field of nature conservation and sustainable use of natural resources.

and kill the sentry with a burst of fire from my FN[25] rifle. Once he was dead, I would use his gun to fire a short burst at the position from where I had shot him. This was to make it look like he had fired on me first. At the sound of my initial gunshots, the other two poachers at the lay-up site would obviously spring into action. But they would already be lined up in Sipho's rifle sights. Sipho would fire on them and give the order to Hamish and Mark to do so as well. In the hail of bullets, the remaining two poachers would be killed. The plan, if successful, would mean that all three poachers would be slain and the rhinos would be unharmed. The plan was devised by Sipho and me. Duncan, Hamish, and Mark knew nothing of it."

"Hmm," said Stuart. "And obviously the plan worked out perfectly."

"Fortunately, it did," said Nick. "The police investigated our version of events in detail and accepted everything we told them."

"You do realise," said Stuart, "that what you and Sipho actually did was tantamount to murder. You deliberately killed three men for what they might have done, not for what they did. They may have been vile persons, but you and Sipho acted as policemen, prosecutors, jury, judge, and executioner. That is not how the Western judicial system works, nor is it how the Zimbabwean judicial system is meant to work."

Sipho, who had remained relatively silent throughout, said, "What you have said, Mr Dixon, is of course quite right. But for the system to work properly, it requires the police, the government, and the judiciary to play their parts properly. This might have been the case in Rhodesia prior to independence. But I regret it is not the case in independent Zimbabwe. Therefore, in order for justice to be done, people sometimes need to take matters into their own hands."

"And that is a very dangerous position for any country to be in," said Stuart.

---

[25] This was a light automatic rifle designed in Belgium and manufactured by FN Herstal. The FN had been the standard issue rifle for the Rhodesian Security Forces.

There was another long period of silence. This was eventually broken by Stuart, who said, "Well, boys, thank you for being so upfront with me. While I don't like to admit it, now that I know what actually happened and the reasons for your actions, I think there is plenty of justification for you having acted as you did. I am not sure I would have done the same. But I am used to the way things work in the UK, not how they work in the new Zimbabwe. So please be assured that I will respect the confidentiality you have asked for. For what it's worth, I would, however, strongly counsel you not to disclose what actually happened to anyone else, not even to Rachel or to your respective parents."

Nick and Sipho looked at each other in surprise. "Is that it?" Nick said.

"Absolutely," said Stuart. "As far as I am concerned, the version of events as recorded by the ZRP is exactly how things unfolded. Now, we are being impolite. The others will wonder what we have been talking about. Let's go and join them and have something to eat."

Chapter 5 – Gukurahundi

During the wedding proceedings and lunch on the following day, a noticeable attraction became apparent between two members of the bridal party, Brian[26] and Morag[27]. Nick had first observed their chemistry during the wedding reception dinner and remarked on it to Rachel.

"Look at those two," he said. "They certainly seem to be hitting it off. It's a shame Brian is catching the train to Edinburgh early next week to get back to work. I am sure if he stayed longer, those two could easily become an item."

"Well, I am just glad they are both enjoying themselves," said Rachel. "Morag needs to let her hair down a bit. She has recently started nursing at Charing Cross Hospital in London, and I know she has been putting in long hours."

Morag had secretly hoped to meet up with Brian at a local pub later that evening. However, her plans fell through when it was decided that the male members of the bridal party would go to a pub for drinks, while the female members would gather at Claire Illingsworth's[28] house in Guildford to watch a video and enjoy a light supper. Both sets of parents were excluded as they had opted to

---

[26] Brian was one of Nick's groomsmen.
[27] Morag was one of Rachel's bridesmaids.
[28] Claire was Rachel's maid in honour.

remain at the Dixons' house for a takeaway Indian meal and a bottle of wine.

Nick suggested that the lads should go to the same pub which had done such a fine job in running the bar at the wedding reception. Just before 6:00 pm, they all jumped into Nick's car and headed for the Spread Eagle, which was about six minutes away in Chertsey Street. Meanwhile, the girls got into Rachel's car and drove to the local video store, where they rented a newly released film, ET[29], and returned to Claire's house for a girls' night in.

That Sunday night, the Spread Eagle was surprisingly quiet. The late afternoon sun was still warm, prompting the lads to go into the beer garden for drinks and pub food rather than into the front bar itself. This was despite Brian's objections. He had noticed that there was a small television set in the front bar which was screening a replay of the 3rd Test between the British Lions and Australia. This had been played the day before in Sydney, and Brian had not yet caught up with the result.

After their food and drinks arrived, Nick began commiserating with Sipho[30] about how difficult things had become for Ndebeles living in Matabeleland. He asked Sipho if he would like to tell Russell and Brian what was happening.

Sipho knew that Russell, being from Zimbabwe, already had a good grasp of Zimbabwean politics. However, this was not true for Brian, who was Scottish and had never visited the country.

Accordingly, for Brian's benefit, Sipho gave a quick overview of Zimbabwe's political landscape. He explained that the two largest tribes in the country were the Shona and Ndebele. Historically, the two tribes had often been at war with each other. During colonial rule, the influence of the white government had helped to ameliorate

---

[29] ET, or The Extra-Terrestrial, was a science fiction movie that was released in 1982. It tells the story of Elliott, a boy who befriends an extraterrestrial, dubbed ET, who is left behind on earth.

[30] Sipho is a Ndebele boy's name meaning Gift.

the relations between these two tribes. However, relations between the two tribes started to deteriorate shortly after Zimbabwe had become independent in April 1980.

Sipho explained that in the country's first-ever *one-man-one-vote* general elections in 1980, the electorate had largely voted on tribal grounds. This meant that persons of Shona ethnicity had generally voted for Robert Mugabe's ZANU-PF[31] party, while persons of Ndebele ethnicity had generally voted for Joshua Nkomo's ZAPU[32] party.

As the Shona tribe outnumbered the Ndebele tribe by about four to one, Robert Mugabe's ZANU-PF party had won 57 of the 80 common roll seats, giving Mugabe a clear majority in the 100-member House of Assembly. Joshua Nkomo's ZAPU party won 20 of the 80 common roll seats, with the remaining three going to Bishop Muzorewa's UANC[33] party. The final 20 seats in the House of Assembly, which, under the Lancaster House Agreement[34], had been reserved for the white voter roll, had all been won by Ian Smith's RF[35] party.

Brian interrupted Sipho and asked, "So why did relations between the two tribes begin to deteriorate after the elections?"

"I'm getting to that now," Sipho said. "One of the first things Mugabe did after the elections was to form a new national army, the Zimbabwe National Army, or the ZNA for short. This was meant to bring together the former Rhodesian Security Forces and the military wings of ZANU-PF and ZAPU.

---

[31] Zimbabwe African Nation Union – Patriotic Front.

[32] Zimbabwe African People's Union.

[33] United African National Council.

[34] In August 1979 the British Government invited the leaders of ZANU and ZAPU, Bishop Muzorewa, and Ian Smith to participate in a Constitutional Conference at Lancaster House in London. The purpose of the Conference was to discuss and reach agreement on the terms of an Independence Constitution, to agree on the holding of elections under British authority, and to enable Zimbabwe-Rhodesia to proceed to lawful and internationally recognised independence, with the parties settling their differences by political means.

[35] Rhodesian Front.

"But getting them to work together was impossible, mostly because neither Mugabe nor Nkomo wanted the ZNA[36] to stay neutral. They both tried to ensure that only their supporters got appointed to senior positions in the ZNA. In this, Mugabe was much better than Nkomo, even though their military forces were about the same size."

"That must have pissed off the military wing of ZAPU," said Brian.

"It sure did," Sipho said. "ZAPU's military wing was called the Zimbabwe People's Revolutionary Army, or ZIPRA for short. The leaders of ZIPRA[37] realised that Mugabe was outmanoeuvring Nkomo. They saw that very few ZIPRA soldiers were getting top positions in the ZNA. As a result, the ZNA's leadership was soon dominated by soldiers from ZANLA[38], which was ZANU-PF's military wing."

Sipho continued, "You probably don't know this, but in early 1981, there was a serious battle between ZANLA and ZIPRA troops in Entumbane, Bulawayo. This could have started a civil war, but the ZNA, using some of the former Rhodesian forces, managed to crush the rebellion."

"Wasn't that ironic?" said Nick. "Mugabe had to use former Rhodesian Security Forces, his sworn enemy, to subdue a clash between his and Nkomo's troops. And what Sipho is not telling you is that he was one of the Rhodesian Security Forces who were deployed to quell this uprising. Sipho was a damn good soldier and had served with distinction with the RAR[39] during the Rhodesian Bush War."

"Well, that's another story," Sipho said. "Anyway, after the uprising in Bulawayo, many former ZIPRA troops became so pissed off that they deserted the ZNA. They were anti-Mugabe and had lost respect for Nkomo, but they remained loyal to their former commander,

---

[36] Zimbabwe National Army.
[37] Zimbabwe People's Revolutionary Army. ZIPRA was the military wing of ZAPU.
[38] Zimbabwe African National Liberation Army. ZANLA was the military wing of ZANU.
[39] Rhodesian African Rifles.

Lookout Masuku[40]. Some of them formed gangs, while others joined up with former ZIPRA members who hadn't yet been integrated into the ZNA. They gathered near a place called the Gwaai River mine in Matabeleland.

"Mugabe became paranoid that these dissidents might try to start a rebellion. His fears were fuelled by South African spies who had infiltrated the CIO[41]. These agents planted false evidence suggesting that ZAPU/ZIPRA leaders were plotting to overthrow Mugabe's Government. Their skullduggery worked. In 1982, the police arrested Lookout Masuku and Dumiso Dabengwa[42] for supposedly planning this. Interestingly, in 1983, Zimbabwe's Supreme Court found both men not guilty, but they were still kept in detention under emergency regulations."

"This sounds like a James Bond movie," commented Brian.

"You have no idea," said Sipho. "The people I am staying with in London are extremely well-informed. South Africa was, and continues, to do everything it can to harm Mugabe's Government. At the same time, apparently there are some in the British intelligence agencies who are also trying to destabilise Nkomo and ZAPU/ZIPRA."

"That would be MI5 or MI6," said Brian. "Why would they want to do that?"

"Well, from what I've heard, it's because Russia is the main backer of ZIPRA," Sipho said. "The British intelligence services think that since Russia is communist, ZIPRA must have strong communist ties too."

Nick interjected. He looked at Sipho and said, "Why don't you tell Russell and Brian what you told Rachel and me at the wedding?"

---

[40] Lookout Masuku was the commander of ZIPRA during the Rhodesian Bush War. After independence, he served as deputy commander of the Zimbabwe National Army until his arrest in 1982 for allegedly plotting to overthrow Robert Mugabe.
[41] Zimbabwe's Central Intelligence Organisation.
[42] ZIPRA's intelligence chief during the Rhodesian Bush War and for a short time thereafter. In 1982 he was charged with treason by the Mugabe administration and arrested.

Sipho paused for a moment before saying, "Based on what I've said, it might seem like Mugabe was just reacting to recent events in Matabeleland. But I've heard that he'd been planning to target ZAPU and the Ndebele people ever since late 1978, when it became clear that Rhodesia was going to lose the war."

"That is a big statement," said Russell.

"I understand why you might think that," said Sipho. "But Mugabe knew that ultimately his and Nkomo's forces would win the war and that he would be the winner in the ensuing general elections. Also, Mugabe's military wing, ZANLA, had enjoyed a strong long-term relationship with the North Korean military well before 1980. After independence, Mugabe secretly signed an agreement with North Korea's leader, Kim Il Sung. Under this deal, the North Koreans trained a new elite unit of the ZNA called the 5th Brigade. This brigade is not meant for regular military tasks. It's a special unit for dealing with political dissidents. They wear different uniforms, with red berets, and report only to Mugabe, not through the usual military chain of command.

"The training of the 5th Brigade finished in September 1982. The brigade is mostly made up of former ZANLA soldiers. A few ZIPRA soldiers were there at first, but they were pulled out before training ended. The brigade is based in Gweru[43], and commanded by Perrance Shiri[44], a distant relative of Mugabe's.

"My sources say that in January 1983, Mugabe ordered the 5th Brigade to be deployed in Matabeleland North to crush ZIPRA dissidents. At first, they went after ZIPRA veterans, but soon they started targeting ZAPU officials and Ndebele men of fighting age.

---

[43] The name of Gweru during the colonial era had been Gwelo.

[44] Perrance Shiri was distantly related to Rogert Mugabe. After independence, he commanded the 5th Brigade from 1983 to 1984. In 1992 he was appointed the commander of the Airforce of Zimbabwe. Shiri was influential in orchestrating the 2017 Zimbabwean coup d'état which removed Mugabe from power. On 30th November 2017, Shiri was appointed Minister of Agriculture by President Emmerson Mnangagwa.

Within a few months, the 5th Brigade had created a reign of terror in Matabeleland, arresting and interrogating anyone suspected of being a dissident or opposing the government. Many detainees have been forced to march to remote camps, where they are held for months. This campaign of terror is still ongoing."

"What do you mean by a reign of terror?" asked Brian.

"I mean executions without trial, torture, and imprisonment," said Sipho. "The 5th Brigade operates without limits, and their only goal is to crush any opposition to Mugabe. At first, they mainly targeted ZIPRA dissidents, but now they go after ZAPU supporters and the Ndebele people in general. For instance, in rural areas, it's common for the 5th Brigade to round up villagers and force them to watch as one of their leaders is executed — sending a clear message to anyone else who might oppose the government."

"That sounds very serious," said Russell. "How many people have been killed?"

"No one really knows," Sipho replied. "By some estimates, the number of dead is at least 10,000, and the killings are continuing. Mugabe has given this campaign the codename *Gukurahundi*."

"Guku what?" asked Brian.

"*Gukurahundi*," said Sipho. "It is a Shona word that means '*the early rain that washes away the chaff before the spring rain.*'"

So, why does Mugabe dislike the Ndebele people so much?" asked Brian.

"That's hard to say," Sipho replied. "He probably doesn't hate them, but Mugabe is driven by politics. He believes that a new country like Zimbabwe can't afford to have opposition parties. In his mind, Zimbabwe should be a one-party state. Since most Ndebele people support Nkomo's ZAPU party instead of Mugabe's ZANU-PF, they've become a problem for him."

"I can understand where he is coming from," said Nick. "Opposition parties in Western democracies can become a real nuisance for the ruling parties. And in a relatively unsophisticated country like Zimbabwe, maybe opposition parties are a luxury. And we shouldn't forget that for the first ten years of Zimbabwe's independence, Mugabe will have a very strong opposition party to deal with, no matter what."

"How do you mean?" asked Brian.

"Well, under the new Zimbabwean constitution, for the first ten years of independence, 20 seats in the 100-seat House of Assembly are reserved for the white roll. I think it's reasonable to assume that most of these seats will continue to be held by the RF during this period. And the RF is definitely strongly opposed to Mugabe."

"I never appreciated that before," said Russell. "In that case, you're correct. The white members of parliament are experienced parliamentarians and will certainly keep ZANU-PF on their toes. But I want to ask Sipho another question." He looked at Sipho and said, "You keep mentioning the people you're staying with in London and saying they have good knowledge of what's going on in Zimbabwe. So, who are these people and why is their intel[45] so good?"

Sipho replied by telling Russell a bit about his life as a schoolboy in Zimbabwe. He had been brought up and educated at a place called Inyathi Mission. Senior teachers at the mission were often overseas expatriates. Being mission-minded, they were generally driven by a desire not only to spread the Christian message but also to improve the lives and prospects of their students. Concepts of racial separation and subjugation were frowned upon by such teachers, fostering a culture ripe for black revolutionary ideas. Accordingly, in the 1960s, Inyathi Mission had become a formidable bedrock for breeding black African nationalists.

Sipho explained that the headmaster of the mission school was a far-sighted man. He realised that some of the school's more talented pupils were destined to play a crucial role in the country's leadership

---

[45] Intelligence information (often military in nature).

once it broke free from its colonial past. He worked with the UK-based Council for World Mission[46] to ensure that talented pupils from the school were smuggled out of the country to the UK, where they were housed by sympathetic donors and exposed to Western secondary schools and tertiary universities and colleges. One of these pupils was a young man who, after settling in the UK, had adopted the name Jonathon Khumalo.

According to Sipho, Jonathon claimed to be a descendant of the royal House of Khumalo[47]. Jonathon had been secretly taken to England in 1969 when he was 13. He had attended Wandsworth Grammar School in Southfields, London. Here, he had obtained impressive A-Level[48] results, which enabled him to win a Rhodes Scholarship[49] and gain admission to the University of Oxford, where he studied law.

Jonathon had graduated from Oxford University just after Zimbabwe obtained its independence from the UK in 1980. He had planned to return to Zimbabwe at the end of 1980 to take up a senior position within Joshua Nkomo's ZAPU party. However, even at this early stage, Jonathon's advisers had become wary of Robert Mugabe's true intentions in relation to ZAPU, and he had been advised to remain in the UK until the political landscape in Zimbabwe became clearer.

---

[46] The Council is a worldwide community of mainly Protestant Christian churches. The organisation works to spread the knowledge of Christ throughout the world and to strengthen their members in their mission work by sharing their resources of money, people, skills, and insights. It was formerly named the London Missionary Society.

[47] The House of Khumalo is the continuing royal family of the former Mthwakazi Kingdom (modern day Matabeleland). The Mthwakazi Kingdom was founded in 1823 and ended in 1894 with the First Matabele War. However, The House has endured to the present day.

[48] A-Levels were the Advanced Level of school examinations. It was conferred as a school leaving qualification to senior school pupils as part of the Cambridge International General Certificate of Education.

[49] The Rhodes Scholarship was founded by Cecil John Rhodes. It is an international postgraduate award for students to study at the University of Oxford, in the UK.

Jonathon had heeded this advice and remained in London. He was currently working as a human rights lawyer with Amnesty International[50].

Russell was incredulous. "Are you saying that this Jonathon fellow claims to be a direct descendant of King Lobengula Khumalo and that he is living here in the UK, waiting to return to Zimbabwe at some time in the future?"

"Yes, that's right," Sipho said. "I've met him twice since I arrived in London. He seems like a decent bloke — smart and charismatic. He's determined that when the time is right, he'll go back to Zimbabwe and restore the House of Khumalo as its king. But his claim isn't without challenge — some say he's not the rightful heir. And proving royal heritage is tough since much of the history of the House of Khumalo isn't written down."

"How fascinating," said Nick. "I would never have guessed it. I suppose he maintains close links with Zimbabwe?"

"Yes, that's right," Sipho said. "There's a group of Africans in London who see themselves as Zimbabwe's future government in exile. Most are Ndebele, but there are also some prominent Shona among them. They have strong connections with Zimbabwe's major political parties and seem to be funded by unhappy business people in Zimbabwe and some big South African companies."

"Hell, that is impressive stuff," exclaimed Brian. "Although I am a merchant banker and know very little about Zimbabwe, Mugabe sounds like a complete arsehole to me. Any organisation which stands up to him will have my support. However, right now, I would like to see how the British Lions fared against the Australian Wallabies. Let's move back into the pub."

---

[50] Amnesty International is an international non-governmental organisation focused on human rights, with its headquarters in the UK. It was founded in 1961 with the mission of campaigning for a world in which every person enjoys all of the human rights enshrined in the Universal Declaration of Human Rights and other international human rights instruments.

Chapter 6 – Nick joins Stuart's business

Nick and Rachel got engaged in September 1982, a year after they first met. Prior to their engagement, Nick had met Rachel's parents, Stuart and Lynne Dixon, on several occasions. These meetings took place at Stuart and Lynne's home in Guildford when both Nick and Rachel were on vacations from their respective universities. They had also met in Zimbabwe in August 1981 during Nick and Rachel's month-long holiday when Stuart and Lynne took the opportunity to add a short visit to Zimbabwe to one of Stuart's many business trips to South Africa.

Right from the start, Nick had made a favourable impression on Rachel's parents. They were both delighted when Nick and Rachel commenced a long-distance relationship shortly after their first meeting in September 1980.

Following their engagement, Nick's visits to the Dixons' home became more frequent. During these visits, Nick continued to charm Lynne, who was delighted with the thought of Nick becoming her son-in-law. This was also true of Stuart. Stuart had become impressed with Nick's astute business sense and his savviness when it came to world affairs. So much so that he began to sound Nick out about him joining Stuart's extensive business interests after completing his four-year business and economics degree at the University of Edinburgh.

Initially, Nick did not pay much attention to Stuart's overtures. However, as he grew to respect Stuart and understand his expansive business interests, Nick began to seriously consider Stuart's propositions.

Stuart was the managing director of a family company which he had formed many years ago. The company was called Rare Quest Imports Pty Ltd (RQI). This was originally an import and export business that specialised in sourcing, importing, and exporting items that were 'hard to get'. These comprised a diverse range of items including high-value antiques, relics, and artworks, rare earth elements, armaments and explosives, and tobacco and related products. However, in more recent times, the company had begun to invest in high-value tourist facilities in parts of Africa and Asia.

Notwithstanding these wide business interests, Nick realised that at his core, Stuart was a philanthropist. He was particularly driven to ameliorate abject poverty in Africa and Asia and to help conserve and protect southern Africa's rich wildlife resources.

Stuart was acutely aware of how the wildlife resources in many Asian countries had been decimated by the loss of their natural habitats due to the pressures of population growth. He was fearful that, without proper management and custodianship, the same fate could easily befall the treasure trove of southern African wildlife. He was also convinced that if these wildlife treasures could be protected in a sustainable manner, this would not only provide considerable financial benefit to national economies but would also provide employment opportunities and modest income streams to local communities.

To achieve these benevolent ambitions required money, and plenty of it. Initially, Stuart had diverted profits from his considerable business interests to help fund these pursuits. But the needs were so great that Stuart's financial contributions hardly scratched the surface. He realised that he needed to appeal to the philanthropic instincts of his wide network of business connections. Gradually, he had been able to attract seed funding from a number of his closest business colleagues in London. Using these funds, in 1972 he had established a foundation called the Afro-Asian Humanity and Wildlife Foundation (AHWF). The Foundation had grown exponentially since its establishment and currently was attracting considerable financial support from leading individuals and corporations in the UK, South Africa, and Hong Kong.

Stuart was Chairman of AHWF[51] and Managing Director of his family company, RQI[52]. As AHWF had grown, the time that Stuart needed to devote to its activities had increased, and this meant that he was finding it difficult to devote sufficient attention to his company. He was hoping that by bringing Nick into the family business he might be able to better manage his significant workload.

Nick had returned to Guildford in April 1984 to spend some time with Rachel over the Easter holiday period. During this visit, Stuart approached Nick with a definitive proposal whereby, once he had completed his university degree, he would take up a financial role in RQI. In addition, and assuming Rachel was interested, Stuart also proposed that Nick and Rachel take up a fundraising role with AHWF.

Nick and Rachel had discussed these proposals. As far as the financial position was concerned, Nick felt that this would fast-track the development of his financial career.

In relation to AHWF's fundraising role, both Rachel and Nick felt that such a role would be extremely interesting and would enable them to contribute to these worthy causes. Furthermore, Rachel believed that she could manage this additional responsibility without it adversely impacting her graduate management trainee program at Vivienne Westwood's[53] fashion house.

---

[51] Afro-Asian Humanity and Wildlife Foundation.
[52] Rare Quest Imports.
[53] Vivienne Westwood was one of London's leading fashion designers and businesswomen.

Accordingly, they both accepted Stuart's proposals and undertook to start in these roles in mid-August 1984, immediately after their wedding and honeymoon.

Coincidentally, shortly after their acceptance, Stuart and Lynne gave a very generous wedding gift to them. This had enabled Nick and Rachel to pay the required deposit on their three-bedroomed bungalow in Medstead, as well as paying for their honeymoon.

Prior to embarking on their honeymoon to South Africa and Zimbabwe, Stuart had arranged to meet with Nick to discuss his commencement of employment at RQI. The meeting was to take place at the offices of RQI in Belgravia, in the City of Westminster in central London, at 10:00 am on Wednesday, 11th July.

On the Wednesday morning, Rachel dropped Nick at the Guildford train station. From here he took a train to London Victoria and then a taxi to Belgravia. He arrived at the offices of RQI at 9:40 am. The attractive receptionist asked him to take a seat, which he did.

Nick looked around the reception area. It was adorned with bespoke art and plush furnishings. At the reception desk was a PC, which was a novel piece of office technology in the early 1980s. The modern office equipment seamlessly blended into the classic charm of the reception area.

Just after 10:00 am, the receptionist's telephone rang. She lifted the handset, said a few words, and then hung up. She looked across at Nick and said, "Mr Dixon can see you now. Would you care to follow me?"

The receptionist led the way to Stuart's office. His office door was open, and she ushered him in. Stuart was chatting on the phone. He covered the mouthpiece with his hand and waved at Nick. "I will only be a minute or two," he mouthed. "Please take a seat." He waved at the chair on the opposite side of his desk and signalled for Nick to sit.

While Nick was waiting for Stuart to finish his call, he looked around the office. The office was spacious with floor-to-ceiling windows, offering panoramic views of Belgravia. Mahogany furnishings, custom-designed leather seating, and subtle ambient lighting created an inviting atmosphere. On Stuart's desk, there was another PC, while a dot matrix printer sat on its own credenza within easy reach of his desk. On the desk was a beautifully carved image in ebony wood of an African bull elephant with ears flayed and trunk uplifted. On the walls were two beautiful impressionist oil paintings, one showing dark menacing storm clouds over a lake, and the other depicting the early morning sun rising over the rolling hills of the English countryside. The overall impression was one of sophistication, excellence, and professionalism.

After a minute or two, Stuart finished his conversation and hung up. "My apologies, Nick. That was an unexpected but important call which I had to take. How was the traffic this morning?"

"I actually took the train from Guildford to London Victoria and then caught a taxi to your office. It was a lovely sunny morning. I ought to have walked from London Victoria," Nick replied.

After a few more pleasantries, Stuart took him on a tour of the office. He introduced him to a number of persons in the office, all of whom were polite and pleasant. From their comments, it was obvious that Stuart had already advised his staff that Nick, his recently wedded son-in-law, would be taking up a financial position with RQI in mid-August, after the conclusion of his southern African honeymoon.

After the tour, they returned to Stuart's office. Stuart had already provided Nick with a detailed position description of his duties and responsibilities. He asked Nick if he had any questions about the document. Nick asked for clarification on a few minor issues. Stuart then outlined for him a bit about what lay ahead for RQI.

Stuart said, "Initially, you will be involved in co-managing some of the major contracts we have with our key British clients. Richard Simpson, the man I introduced you to in the staff room, will explain the accounting systems we use to manage these contracts, as well as outlining the more significant contractual terms and introducing you to the key clients. Once he feels you are ready, you will assume sole responsibility for managing these contracts under Richard's oversight. You will then move into the international department and be exposed to some of our South African and Hong Kong clients."

"That sounds great," said Nick.

"The first 18 months will serve as your induction period. After that, I have some exciting projects which I would like to involve you in," enthused Stuart.

"That's interesting," said Nick. "Are you able to give me some details?"

Stuart replied, "Certainly, but only in general terms. Over the last couple of years, my analysts have been conducting a detailed risk analysis of southern Africa. From what we can determine, we believe that southern Africa — particularly Zimbabwe, Mozambique, Zambia, and possibly South Africa — is going to face significant political, economic, and social challenges."

"These challenges are going to spook current investors in those countries. So much so that we believe there is going to be a significant flight of capital from these countries as investors seek less risky places to invest their money. This flight of capital is going to create rare opportunities for smart entrepreneurs. I want RQI to capture a big portion of those opportunities, and I want you to play a leading role in helping us do that."

In anticipation of Nick's queries, Stuart continued, "That challenge may sound daunting to you right now. But don't worry. You are smart, good with people, and seem to have your father's knack for reading the political winds of change. I have a great team of analysts on board, and they will be invaluable to us as we forge our way ahead. I know we will be successful. And this success will augur well for us in the next fifteen years, especially in Hong Kong."

"Did you say Hong Kong? I don't understand," said Nick.

Stuart replied, "Well, the British and Chinese Governments are currently negotiating the end of British colonial rule in Hong Kong. Our best estimate is that this will occur around the turn of the century. When that takes place, Hong Kong will be transferred from British to Chinese sovereignty. The period leading up to the transfer of such sovereignty, and for at least a decade afterwards, will be full of uncertainty for current investors in Hong Kong. Once again, I am predicting a significant flight of capital from Hong Kong. If this flight of capital occurs, as I am sure it will, the opportunities for smart entrepreneurs will be simply enormous."

Nick was gobsmacked. He was smart enough to understand that he was being offered an opportunity of a lifetime, and at a very young age. He had every intention of grasping it with both hands.

He was also pleasantly surprised that Stuart had not mentioned the 'confession' that he and Sipho had shared with Stuart a few days earlier.

By now, it was 11:00 am and Stuart had other meetings to attend. However, before they ended their meeting, Stuart said, "We haven't yet spoken about your and Rachel's fundraising role with AHWF. Rachel needs to be present for those discussions. I know that this Friday you are both travelling to South Africa and Zimbabwe to begin your honeymoon. So, I suggest we defer those discussions until you return."

"That is fine with me," said Nick. "I am sure Rachel will feel the same, but I need to check with her first."

"Sure thing," said Stuart. "And there is one final thing I would ask you to think about while you are in Zimbabwe. From what I understand, it seems that your parents have decided to remain in Zimbabwe. If this is correct, Lynne and I are both extremely worried about them. I don't want to be a pessimist, but I sincerely believe the new Zimbabwe is not going to be a country in which your parents will be able to enjoy their retirement. Would you be able to tactfully discuss this matter with them? Lynne and I obviously do not want to interfere, but we have always been terribly fond of them. And now that you and Rachel are married, we regard them as part of our extended family. As such, we will do whatever we can to help them if they decide to leave Zimbabwe."

Nick was stunned. Stuart's foresight, generosity, and sincerity were rare indeed. He thanked Stuart for his concern and promised to sensitively discuss the matter with his parents when he and Rachel were in Zimbabwe.

Stuart took his leave from Nick. Nick returned to Guildford via the same route he had arrived. However, this time he chose to walk from Stuart's offices to London Victoria and make the most of the glorious sunshine, rather than catching a taxi.

That afternoon, Nick and Rachel were due to pick up a car hire from Avis Car Rental. The vehicle was a Ford Transit passenger van, which they would use to take Nick's parents, Matthew and Brenda, his brother Russell, and Sipho[54], his comrade-in-arms, to Heathrow Airport.

The group of four were all flying on a British Airways flight to Johannesburg which was due to leave at 6:20 pm. They were due to land at Johannesburg's Jan Smuts International Airport early the following morning. From Johannesburg, Matthew, Brenda, and Sipho would be catching an Air Zimbabwe flight to Harare, while Russell would be catching a South African Airways flight to Cape Town.

Rachel used her XJ6 Jaguar to take her and Nick to Avis's offices in Guildford. They left her car in Avis's car park, took delivery of the Ford Transit, and returned to Rachel's parents' house in Chantry Road. There, they picked up Matthew, Brenda, Russell, and Sipho, who had made his own way to the house, and then drove all four to Terminal 3 at Heathrow. They said their farewells at Heathrow, drove back to Avis's offices in Guildford, collected Rachel's car, and drove back to the Dixons' house, arriving just in time for dinner.

The next two days sped by as Nick and Rachel prepared themselves for their trip to South Africa and Zimbabwe. They were flying with British Airways to Johannesburg Jan Smuts International Airport on the evening of Friday, 13th July.

---

[54] Sipho is a Ndebele boy's name meaning Gift.

They would be arriving in Johannesburg on Saturday morning. From Johannesburg, they were catching an internal SAA[55] flight to Pietermaritzburg. From here, they were picking up a hire car and driving to the Sani Pass Hotel in the Drakensberg mountains where they would be staying for four nights. On Wednesday, 18th July, they would be driving back to Pietermaritzburg and then catching an internal SAA flight to Johannesburg. From Johannesburg, they were catching an Air Zimbabwe flight to Harare which was scheduled to depart just after 1:00 pm. They were expecting to arrive at Harare's airport at 3:20 pm, where Matthew and Brenda would pick them up.

---

[55] South African Airways.

Chapter 7 – The making of Tawanda Nyati

Timeline – 1972 to 1984

The renowned British philosopher Bertrand Russell once said, "War does not determine who is right, only who is left." This adage could easily be applied to Tawanda Nyati[56], a ZANLA[57] field commander.

Tawanda was born in the small rural village of Mukumbura in the north-east of Rhodesia, close to its border with Mozambique. He was the youngest of seven children. The family lived in a mud hut comprising two rooms. It had no running water or electricity. Fortunately, the village had a perennial well with a hand-operated water pump.

His father was a labourer on a farm owned by a white farmer named Boss Millman. Boss Millman was a hard man who never cared much for his black labourers, whom he regarded as lazy and stupid. Tawanda's mother looked after the children, tended their small subsistence maize crop, and fed the six chickens they owned.

Life was hard and money was scarce. Tawanda was afraid of Boss Millman, who reminded him of a nyoka yemhumgo[58], ready to strike

---

[56] The name Tawanda Nyati loosely translated means Young Buffalo.
[57] Zimbabwe African National Liberation Army. ZANLA was the military wing of ZANU.
[58] Cobra snake.

if disturbed, especially by a stupid black boy. He assumed all white people were similarly inclined. As a young boy, he soon learned that if he did not look after himself, no one else would.

In 1972, at the age of 17, he dropped out of school and joined the armed liberation struggle against the white Rhodesian Government, which he regarded as a den of snakes, led by Ian Smith.

Tawanda travelled by bus from Mukumbura to the border town of Chirundu, about 400 kilometres west of his hometown. From there, he illegally crossed into Zambia and caught another bus to Kafue, where one of his uncles lived and worked. His uncle, who was well-connected with exiled members of ZANU[59] living in and around Lusaka, managed to get Tawanda accepted into a military transit camp at Nampundwe, about 40 kilometres west of Lusaka. Here, Tawanda received basic training in guerrilla warfare before being transferred to a new joint ZANLA/ZIPRA training camp called Mwembeshi.

Mwembeshi was about 20 kilometres north of Lusaka. This new training camp had been formed in an attempt to unite ZANLA and ZIPRA at the insistence of the Organisation of African Unity (OAU), who had become frustrated with the continual bickering and infighting between ZANU and ZAPU[60].

Tawanda's guerrilla warfare training continued at Mwembeshi for another six months. During this time, he impressed his instructors to such an extent that, in 1973, he was selected, along with another 94 recruits, to go to a military training camp, named Morogoro, in Tanzania, some 1,800 kilometres north-east of Lusaka.

The recruits were taken to Morogoro in a convoy of OAU[61] trucks. The trip was long and arduous, taking four days due to the poor state of many of the roads. The rigours of the trip and the new sights he

---

[59] Zimbabwe African National Union.
[60] Zimbabwe African People's Union.
[61] The Organisation of African Unity was in existence from 1963 to 2002. In 2002 it was superseded by the African Union.

saw in Tanzania frightened Tawanda. But he calmed his thoughts by reminding himself that if he were ever to crush the head of the white man's snake, completing his training in Tanzania was necessary.

At Morogoro, Tawanda and the other recruits underwent an intensive four-month training course covering both guerrilla and conventional warfare. Their course trainers were from ZANLA and ZIPRA, supplemented by senior secondees from the North Korean People's Army. Instruction was often difficult due to language barriers. However, the effective use of interpreters enabled the recruits to overcome these challenges, and by the end of the training course, the squad of recruits had been honed into an efficient and dangerous fighting unit.

While at Morogoro, Tawanda experienced firsthand the deep political divides between ZANU/ZANLA and ZAPU/ZIPRA[62]. On one occasion, a dispute arose between ZANLA and ZIPRA recruits about rations.

This dispute simmered below the surface for a couple of days. Left to itself, it might have blown over. However, one of the ZANLA senior instructors, a man named Perrance Shiri[63], became aware of the dispute and immediately incited the ZANLA recruits to teach their ZIPRA counterparts a lesson they would never forget. Soon, a pitched battle involving sticks, stones, and knobkerries[64] broke out. Eager to impress Comrade Shiri, Tawanda fought fiercely. Using the knobkerrie he had brought with him from Mwembeshi, he inflicted serious injuries on at least three ZIPRA recruits. Fortunately, the

---

[62] The military wing of ZANU-PF was known as ZANLA (Zimbabwe African National Liberation Army) and the military wing of ZAPU was known as ZIPRA (Zimbabwe People's Revolutionary Army).

[63] Perrance Shiri was distantly related to Rogert Mugabe. After independence, he commanded the 5th Brigade from 1983 to 1984. In 1992 he was appointed the commander of the Airforce of Zimbabwe. Shiri was influential in orchestrating the 2017 Zimbabwean coup d'état which removed Mugabe from power. On 30th November 2017, Shiri was appointed Minister of Agriculture by President Emmerson Mnangagwa.

[64] A knobkerrie is a wooden club with a large knob at one of its ends. Traditionally, they were used by South African tribespeople for throwing at animals or for clubbing an enemy's head.

armouries were locked, so rifles were not used. Even so, at least 20 recruits were injured, some seriously. The fighting was only quelled when the North Korean secondees intervened.

Following the completion of Tawanda's training in August 1973, he returned to Lusaka. Here, the ZANLA hierarchy informed him that he would be infiltrated back into Rhodesia along with other ZANLA cadres. Tawanda's section of eight cadres was transported by an armoured personnel carrier from Lusaka to a Zambian town called Luangwa. From here, they crossed the Zambezi River at night in an inflatable rubber dinghy at a crossing point near Luangwa. The night crossing terrified Tawanda, who was not a good swimmer and had heard that the Zambezi River was infested with crocodiles.

The cadres landed at a covert location on the Zimbabwean side of the Zambezi, near the town of Kanyemba. There, they rendezvoused with local sympathisers who guided them on foot to Mukumbura in the Mount Darwin district of Zimbabwe.

In late 1973, the Rhodesian Security Forces were facing an increasing number of guerrilla incursions into the north-north-eastern part of the country from Zambia. The tactics of the guerrillas had also significantly changed. Instead of engaging with the Rhodesian Security Forces, they now tried to avoid them at all costs, instead adopting Maoist principles of indoctrinating and politicising the local population.

In an attempt to control the situation, the Rhodesian military introduced the concept of protected villages and began a propaganda programme to control the hearts and minds of the local population. Although the rationale given for this policy was to help safeguard and protect the villagers, the real reason was that gathering the villagers into protected villages afforded much greater control to the Rhodesian Security Forces.

By the end of 1974, about 4,500 local villagers from Mukumbura and surrounding areas were gathered into protected villages. Yet this had done little to hinder the widespread indoctrination of the local tribespeople against the Rhodesian Security Forces.

The mission of the ZANLA section to which Tawanda had been assigned was to store arms and ammunition along the northern bank of the Mukumbura River. These arms caches were used to resupply large gangs of insurgents that had infiltrated the Mount Darwin district to such an extent that the more remote and rural areas were now under the effective control of the guerrilla forces.

Over the next four years, Tawanda's ZANLA missions evolved from resupply operations to intimidation and retribution against recalcitrant tribespeople, to lethal attacks on isolated farmsteads, the laying of mines on roads used by the Rhodesian Security Forces, and setting up ambushes against Rhodesian troops and civilians. In all these tasks, Tawanda performed admirably and with great success. He discovered a penchant for inflicting harm on others, especially white farmers and any black sell-outs who supported them.

Tawanda's exploits brought him to the attention of ZANLA's military hierarchy, who then leveraged his considerable skills to intensify the harm ZANLA was inflicting on Rhodesia.

His most notorious action during the Rhodesian Bush War was his involvement in the Elim Mission Massacres, which occurred in June 1978, by which time he had ascended to the rank of senior field commander within ZANLA.

By this time, Mozambique was governed by FRELIMO, which was favourably disposed towards ZANLA and actively collaborating with it in the armed liberation struggle against the Rhodesian Government. With Portuguese troops no longer present in Mozambique, Rhodesia's eastern border had become porous to guerrilla incursions and difficult to defend. Consequently, ZANLA relocated most of its Zambian-based training and transit camps to Mozambique and established numerous infiltration points into Rhodesia. Thus, ZANLA incursions into Rhodesia were predominantly from Mozambique, while ZIPRA continued to favour infiltration from Zambia.

In June 1978, Tawanda was in command of ZANLA troops operating in the Vumba mountains near the Mozambican border. He received orders from the ZANLA leadership in Mozambique to assault the Elim

Pentecostal Mission, located at a remote site known as Eagle School. The ZANLA guerrillas seized control of the school, isolating the white missionaries and their families from the rest of the camp. The troops then axed, battered, or bayoneted them to death. In total, twelve individuals were slaughtered, including three couples, two single women, three children, and a three-week-old baby.

The brutality of the attack appeared to have little effect on Tawanda and his men. Following the carnage, Tawanda instructed the traumatised school staff to supply his forces with chibuku[65] and food. They then made their escape back into Mozambique, taking these provisions with them to further enhance their victory celebrations.

It later emerged that all the white victims from Elim Mission were British citizens. Intelligence reports indicated that the British Prime Minister at the time, James Callaghan, had received credible reports that ZANLA troops were responsible for the massacre. However, the British Government chose not to make a diplomatic issue of the murders due to the sensitive multi-party peace talks that were then underway.

After Zimbabwe obtained its independence in April 1980, Tawanda was integrated into the 3rd Infantry Brigade of the newly formed Zimbabwe National Army, based in Mutare[66]. However, in mid-1983, he was transferred to the nascent North Korean-trained 5th Brigade to strengthen its command structure.

The 5th Brigade was the brainchild of Robert Mugabe, Prime Minister of the new Zimbabwe. Mugabe had set it up as a specialist brigade to suppress political opposition to the ruling ZANU-PF party and to consolidate his power in the country. The brigade was composed almost entirely of former ZANLA cadres, most of whom had been trained by North Korean military instructors.

---

[65] Chibuku is a traditional African beer brewed from sorghum and/or maize.
[66] The name of Mutare during the colonial era had been Umtali.

In 1983, the command of the 5th Brigade was given to Colonel Perrance Shiri, who was distantly related to Robert Mugabe and who shared a strong bond of trust with him.

Shiri had first met Tawanda in 1972 when they were both at the Morogoro military training school in Tanzania. Shiri remembered Tawanda from those days. Given his fine training record at Morogoro, his experience with North Korean military tactics and training methods, and his exemplary service with ZANLA since then, Shiri recommended to Mugabe that Tawanda be transferred to the 5th Brigade to enhance its leadership framework and help it successfully complete its mission to crush alleged military coups and political activism by ZAPU officials and former ZIPRA cadres. Mugabe had no hesitation in accepting this recommendation.

Accordingly, in August 1983, Major Tawanda Nyati was transferred as a company commander to the 2nd Battalion of the ZNA's 5th Brigade, based in Lupane, Matabeleland North.

Chapter 8 – Sipho fears for Matabeleland

Time line – mid-July 1984

The British Airways flight carrying Matthew, Brenda, Russell Sinclair, and Sipho[67] landed in Johannesburg on Thursday, 12th July 1984. From Johannesburg, Russell was due to catch a SAA[68] flight to Cape Town, while Matthew, Brenda, and Sipho were catching an Air Zimbabwe flight to Harare.

On the flight to Johannesburg, Sipho had been seated next to Russell, Nick's brother. Russell's parents were seated in the row in front of them. During the flight, Russell had started to question Sipho about the people he had stayed with in London and his meeting with Jonathon Khumalo.

In their conversation, Sipho elaborated on Jonathon's claim that he was a descendant of the royal House of Khumalo[69] and that he was intending to return to Zimbabwe to re-establish the House of Khumalo under his kingship when the time was right.

---

[67] Sipho is a Ndebele boy's name meaning Gift.
[68] South African Airways.
[69] The House of Khumalo is the continuing royal family of the former Mthwakazi Kingdom (modern day Matabeleland). The Mthwakazi Kingdom was founded in 1823 and ended in 1894 with the First Matabele War. The House has endured to the present day.

The discussion reassured Russell about the veracity of Jonathon's claims. But it also underscored Sipho's fears that Mugabe was determined to destroy ZAPU[70] as an opposition party. This could potentially lead to the ruin of the Ndebele nation. He was also very concerned for the safety of his parents who lived at Inyathi Mission, about 75 kilometres north-north-east of Bulawayo.

Sipho felt it was important for him to now consult with someone credible and well-connected in the new Zimbabwe to ensure his understanding of the military and political landscape was accurate. There was only one person he could think of who would have the right information and whom he trusted — his mentor, Emanuel Wushe. Emanuel was a member of the Shona tribe and had served with distinction in 1RAR[71], based in Bulawayo, during the Rhodesian Bush War. He had also shown Sipho around 1RAR's Methuen Barracks in Bulawayo in 1969, when Sipho was a young boy aspiring to join the army.

In his youthful enthusiasm, Sipho had initially wanted to join ZIPRA[72]. He had shared his thoughts with his parents, who were horrified at the idea and insisted he first explore the RAR[73] as a wiser alternative. Sipho had reluctantly agreed.

Sipho's father had used his connections at the Inyathi Mission school to arrange visits by Sipho to 1RAR on three separate occasions. During these visits, Sipho stayed with Sergeant Emanuel Wushe, who showed him around the barracks, allowed him to observe garrison life, and taught him about the Regiment's proud history.

These experiences convinced Sipho to join the RAR, and in 1972, he applied and was accepted.

At the end of the Rhodesian Bush War, both Emanuel, now a captain, and Sipho, now a platoon warrant officer, expected to be integrated

---

[70] Zimbabwe African People's Union.
[71] 1st Battalion of the Rhodesian African Rifles.
[72] Zimbabwe People's Revolutionary Army. ZIPRA was the military wing of ZAPU.
[73] Rhodesian African Rifles.

into the newly formed ZNA[74], which would be made up of former Rhodesian Security Forces units as well as former ZANLA[75] and ZIPRA cadres.

Emanuel, being a former member of the Rhodesian Security Forces and from the Shona tribe — the same tribe as Robert Mugabe — had no trouble securing a suitable appointment as a captain with the ZNA's 1st Brigade based in Bulawayo. His subsequent rise in rank since 1981 had been meteoric, and he was now a colonel and commander of the 1st Brigade.

Sipho, however, as a member of the Ndebele tribe, faced challenges. Despite his outstanding service with the RAR and later with the ZNA during the Entumbane uprisings[76], the ZNA hierarchy was reluctant to offer him a non-commissioned officer position within the 1st Brigade. A junior officer's rank was even more out of reach. This reluctance stemmed from Mugabe's politicisation of the ZNA, which meant that Shona ethnicity had effectively become the determining criterion for officer appointments.

Feeling uncertain about his future, Sipho had sought Emanuel's advice. Emanuel realised that Mugabe was actively politicising senior appointments in the ZNA, a situation beyond Emanuel's control. He knew that Sipho's Ndebele ethnicity would work against him within the ZNA. Consequently, Emanuel advised Sipho to explore alternative career opportunities where his excellent soldiering skills could be fully utilised, regardless of his tribal background.

---

[74] Zimbabwe National Army.
[75] Zimbabwe African National Liberation Army. ZANLA was the military wing of ZANU.
[76] These had occurred in February 1981 in and around Bulawayo. During the uprising former ZIPRA guerrillas rebelled creating a situation that threatened to develop into a fresh civil war, barely a year after the Rhodesian Bush War. The uprising was quashed by the newly formed Zimbabwe National Army who used troops from the former RAR and other white-commanded elements of the Rhodesian Security Forces to eliminate the threat.

Sipho heeded this advice and, about three years ago, resigned from the ZNA to accept a position as anti-poaching manager at Mhuka[77] Ranch.

These recollections from his youth resonated with Sipho, and he knew he again needed to meet with Emanuel Wushe upon his return to Zimbabwe for further counsel.

Sipho, Matthew, and Brenda had a two-hour layover in Johannesburg. During this time, Sipho managed to reach Emanuel by phone at the 1st Brigade's headquarters in Bulawayo. Emanuel was thrilled to hear from him and agreed to meet for lunch the following day at the Bulawayo Club.

Sipho then phoned Mhuka Ranch, and Jenny Oliver answered. She was delighted to hear from him. Sipho informed her that he would be arriving in Harare from Johannesburg later that day, and would then take the overnight train to Bulawayo. He had business to attend to in Bulawayo on Friday and planned to visit his parents at Inyathi Mission on Saturday, before returning to Mhuka Ranch around lunchtime on Sunday, 15th July. He would be staying at the Churchill Arms hotel in Bulawayo on Friday night, and asked if Jenny would be able to arrange for his Land Rover to be delivered to the hotel on the Friday. Jenny said that she and Mark would be in Bulawayo from Friday afternoon until Sunday morning and agreed to arrange for his vehicle to be parked in the hotel's car park, with the keys left at the hotel reception on Friday.

An hour later, Sipho, Matthew, and Brenda boarded their Air Zimbabwe flight to Harare. Upon arrival, Sipho bid farewell to Mr and Mrs Sinclair. He then took a taxi to Harare's main railway station and booked the overnight rail service to Bulawayo. Afterward, he visited Barbours Departmental Store in the CBD[78] to buy a gift for his parents

---

[77] A local word meaning animals or wildlife.
[78] Central Business District.

and then relaxed in the well-kept park gardens of African Unity Square[79] until it was time to return to the train station.

The overnight trip to Bulawayo was uneventful, though slow. However, with a first-class sleeper ticket, Sipho enjoyed a reasonably restful night's sleep.

Upon arrival in Bulawayo on the Friday morning, he took a taxi to the Churchill Arms hotel, about eight kilometres south on the Matopos Road. He checked into his room immediately, freshened up, and then had breakfast in the hotel's dining room. After breakfast, he relaxed in the hotel's gardens before taking a taxi to the Bulawayo Club.

Sipho arrived at the Club at 12:45 pm, having come early to avoid keeping Emanuel waiting. He ascended the grand mahogany staircase to the elegant dining room on the upper floor. The walls were adorned with paintings and photographs of historical figures, including original charcoal drawings of Sipho's ancestors, King Lobengula Khumalo[80] and Queen Lozikeyi Dlodlo[81].

While the Club's décor retained its nostalgic charm, the clientele had changed significantly. When Sipho had dined there with Duncan three years earlier, nearly all the patrons had been white males. Today, however, about 40% of the patrons were black, and the gender split had changed, with females now making up around 25% of the customers.

Sipho ordered a beer and reflected on his last visit to the Club, shortly after his resignation from the ZNA on Tuesday, 30th June 1981. Duncan Oliver had taken him there to celebrate his acceptance of the anti-poaching manager role at Mhuka Ranch.

The Club's colonial décor and furnishings were as Sipho remembered. The entrance still boasted a white-pillared portico, and the main

---

[79] Prior to 1981 this was known as Cecil Square.
[80] King Lobengula Khumalo (1845 to circa 1894) was the second and last official King of the northern Ndebele people.
[81] Queen Lozikeyi Dlodlo (c 1855 to 1919) was one of the favourite wives of King Lobengula and a senior queen until 1893.

lobby featured mahogany wood panelling and artefacts from Rhodesia's colonial past. Photos of past Club members, including Cecil John Rhodes, were still displayed on the wall. These were however supplemented by a recent photograph of Robert Gabriel Mugabe, the country's first prime minister following independence in 1980.

Sipho wondered if a photograph of Joshua Nkomo, leader of ZAPU, might once have been displayed when Mugabe's photo was first hung. Certainly, it was nowhere to be seen now, which was not surprising, given that in 1983 Mugabe had accused Nkomo of plotting to overthrow his government. Fearing for his life, Nkomo briefly fled Zimbabwe and sought refuge in London.

Just before 1:00 pm, Emanuel entered the dining room, cutting an imposing figure at 6'2" with broad shoulders and an athletic build. His chocolate-black skin gleamed with a healthy lustre, and he wore his working dress, with colonel rank insignias on his shoulder epaulettes. He walked towards Sipho's table, removing his green-peaked officer's hat with its red ribboned band as he did so.

Sipho greeted him with a broad smile and said, "Ishe[82], what a pleasure to see you again. You're looking well. The ZNA is obviously treating you well. Thank you so much for making the time to see me."

Emanuel replied, "The pleasure is all mine, Sipho. It has been some time since we last met. I've heard much about the excellent work you're doing at Mhuka Ranch. I've been told your anti-poaching rangers are among the best trained in southern Africa. Perhaps the ZNA should try to recruit some of them."

Sipho laughed. "They better not try. We'd be out of business if we lost our best men to the army. I'm delighted to see you too, and I trust you're enjoying your success with the ZNA."

Emanuel smiled and replied, "I am, indeed. But enough about me. What brings you to Bulawayo, and how is Mhuka Ranch?"

---

[82] This is a term of respect used by RAR soldiers when referring to their officers.

"There are many things I'd like to talk to you about," Sipho said with concern. "I've been hearing very disturbing reports about what the 5th Brigade is doing in Matabeleland. I'm very fearful for my parents, who live and work at Inyathi Mission. I've just returned from London, where I attended Nick Sinclair's wedding. You may remember that I served with him in 3RAR[83] towards the end of the Rhodesian Bush War. While in London, I met some well-connected Ndebele individuals who claimed Mugabe wants to crush the entire Ndebele nation, not just the dissidents."

Emanuel's face grew grim, and a deep furrow appeared across his brow. "Ah, the 5th Brigade. That is a difficult topic for most peace-loving Zimbabweans to discuss. I am perhaps more informed than most about what is going on there. I fear that Mugabe has unleashed a wild buffalo that will be difficult to control. It's a moment of madness that he will, I am sure, come to regret."

"Do you know what he is trying to achieve?" asked Sipho.

Emanuel replied, "At first, I think the goal was to deal with a large group of ZIPRA dissidents near the Gwaai River mine. These were the ZIPRA fighters who hadn't been dealt with after the Entumbane uprising. They had strong defences, including heavy artillery. As tensions between Mugabe and Nkomo grew worse, there were real fears that Nkomo might try to use these troops against Mugabe's Government."

"Well, we both remember the Entumbane uprisings," Sipho said. "The former RAR troops fought admirably. Without their involvement, I doubt whether the ZNA would have managed to end the uprising. Do you know why the remaining ZIPRA troops at the mine were not dealt with back in 1981?"

"That's a good question, and it's not easy to answer," Emanuel said. "This was a confusing time for the Zimbabwean Government. The Entumbane uprisings had shaken many in the government. The fear

---

[83] 3rd Battalion of the Rhodesian African Rifles.

of a civil war between the Shona and Ndebele nations was very real. A tribal conflict would have destroyed much of what was promised at independence in 1980."

Emanuel took a sip of his beer and continued, "On top of that, Mugabe was getting a lot of bad information from double agents in his own intelligence service, so he didn't know what to believe. At first, he hoped Nkomo would convince the ZIPRA troops to give up their arms peacefully. When that didn't happen, he sent ZNA troops to attack their fortified positions near the Gwaai River mine. Although the operation was a big success, it didn't fully eliminate the ZIPRA threat, as ZIPRA survivors scattered into local communities and began to terrorise them.

"Initially Mugabe thought the police could handle these gangs," Emanuel said. "At the same time, he was forming the 5th Brigade. But it wasn't until late 1982 that they were ready to be deployed. The police couldn't control the ZIPRA dissidents, as it wasn't just a law and order problem, but also a political and military one. So, once the 5th Brigade was ready, Mugabe handed over the job of controlling the dissidents to the Brigade."

"That makes sense now," Sipho said. "So, is the 5th Brigade as tough as people say? And what is its commander, Perrance Shiri[84], like?"

Emanuel looked around and spoke quietly, "The 5th Brigade's operations and firepower are kept secret. As you might know, they report directly to Mugabe, not through the normal ZNA military chain. From what I've heard, they're extremely effective and dangerous. I've met Colonel Perrance Shiri a few times—he's distantly related to Mugabe, who trusts him completely. Shiri has a ruthless reputation. He took over the 5th Brigade in 1983 and quickly

---

[84] Perrance Shiri was distantly related to Rogert Mugabe. After independence, he commanded the 5th Brigade from 1983 to 1984. In 1992 he was appointed the commander of the Airforce of Zimbabwe. Shiri was influential in orchestrating the 2017 Zimbabwean coup d'état which removed Mugabe from power. On 30th November 2017, Shiri was appointed Minister of Agriculture by President Emmerson Mnangagwa.

started cracking down on the remaining ZIPRA dissidents in Matabeleland. But now, it's turned into a wider assault on ZAPU officials and their supporters. Sadly, I think Mugabe and Shiri are using this as a way to get rid of ZAPU and push for a one-party state. It's very worrying."

"So Nkomo's life really was in danger? Is that why he briefly fled to the UK in March 1983?" Sipho asked.

"In my opinion, yes," Emanuel replied. "If he had stayed in the country, I am certain he would have been arrested. In a worst-case scenario, he could have been murdered or died in a mysterious car accident."

Both men were silent for a moment. Then Sipho said, "I am really worried about my parents. They live at Inyathi Mission. I plan to visit them tomorrow."

Emanuel nodded. "I understand your concern. I would be worried too. However, you need to be careful. There will be several roadblocks between Bulawayo and Inyathi, manned by ZNA or 5th Brigade troops. You are clearly Ndebele, and I am unsure how you will be treated, especially in the current climate."

"I really need to visit them," Sipho said. "I need to ensure they are safe."

"I understand," Emanuel said. "After lunch, could you come back to Brigade Headquarters with me? I will write and sign a letter confirming your credentials."

"That would be great," Sipho said. "You are a true friend."

Their conversation then shifted to less pressing matters. After lunch, Emanuel drove Sipho back to 1st Brigade Headquarters, where he prepared and signed the promised letter. Sipho placed the letter in his jacket pocket, and Emanuel arranged for one of his orderlies to drive Sipho back to the Churchill Arms hotel.

Chapter 9 - Sipho returns to Mhuka Ranch via Inyathi Mission

On Saturday morning, Sipho[85] woke early. After a shower, he gathered his belongings, taking special care to place the letter from Colonel Emanuel Wushe vouching for his credibility in his jacket pocket. He then went to the hotel's reception to check whether Jenny and Mark had remembered to leave the keys to his Land Rover there.

Fortunately, they had. "Those two are just the best people," he thought to himself.

He checked out of the hotel and by 7:30 am he was heading north on the Matopos Road towards Bulawayo's CBD[86]. Once in the CBD, he followed Robert Mugabe Way and then headed north out of the city towards Inyathi Mission.

Sipho came across the first roadblock when he was about 55 kilometres from Bulawayo and approaching the Turk Gold Mine. The roadblock consisted of a black-and-white-painted 44-gallon drum on each side of the road. On top of each drum was a long-creosoted gum pole which straddled to the middle of the road, where it rested on top of a pile of old tyres.

---

[85] Sipho is a Ndebele boy's name meaning Gift.
[86] Central Business District.

Sipho slowed down and came to a halt just before the roadblock. He put his hand into his jacket's breast pocket to reassure himself that the letter from Colonel Wushe was still safely therein.

He sat in his Land Rover and waited. After about 30 seconds, a figure dressed in dusty, dirty camouflaged fatigues appeared from the verge. The soldier was holding an AK-47[87] rifle over his shoulder. In his mouth, a cigarette was wedged into a toothless gap between two teeth on his lower jaw. The man's eyes were bloodshot, and his expression was vacant. It appeared to Sipho that he must have recently been smoking dagga[88] or drinking chibuku[89].

What a disgrace to the ZNA[90] uniform, thought Sipho.

Sipho had wound down his window. The soldier peered through it and asked, "Where are you going?"

Sipho replied, "Good morning. I have come from Bulawayo and am on my way to Chiredzi, where I work. I am going via Inyathi Mission to visit my parents who both work there."

The soldier took his cigarette from his mouth and deliberately blew a cloud of smoke into Sipho's face. Sipho did not react but used his hand to disperse the smoke from his eyes.

After a long pause, the soldier said, "Okay, you may proceed. Wait in your car while I lift the barricade."

With that, the soldier trudged back to the roadblock, lifted one end of the gum pole off the pile of tyres, moved it to the road's shoulder, and waved Sipho through.

"What an *isilima*[91]," thought Sipho as he continued on his way. "But at least there were no real problems."

---

[87] The AK-47 was developed by the Soviet Union and was the preferred light automatic rifle of the ZANLA and ZIPRA forces. After the end of the Rhodesian Bush War, it became one of the automatic rifles used by the Zimbabwe National Army.
[88] Dagga is a local term used to describe the psychoactive drug cannabis.
[89] Chibuku is a traditional African beer brewed from sorghum and/or maize.
[90] Zimbabwe National Army.

Approximately five kilometres further on, Sipho turned right into a minor dirt road which led to the Inyathi Mission, which was another eight kilometres away. Just when Sipho thought he was not going to have to deal with any more roadblocks, he came across a second roadblock. This one had been set up just before the low-level bridge over the Ingwingwisi river.

The roadblock was similar in construction to the one near the Turk Gold Mine. However, the soldiers manning this roadblock were very different. They were alert, well-disciplined, and had an obvious pride in their uniform. They were wearing distinctive red berets. Sipho immediately recognised these as being the distinguishing mark of soldiers serving with ZNA's 5th Brigade.

Unbeknown to Sipho, Major Tawanda Nyati had been deployed to this area of Matabeleland a couple of months earlier. Major Nyati was acting on orders received from Colonel Perrance Shiri[92]. These orders related to the expanded mission of the *Gukurahundi*[93] campaign. The expanded mission was to carry out comprehensive seek-and-destroy operations against former ZIPRA[94] dissidents and any Ndebele citizen who was, or might be, a supporter of ZAPU[95].

Intelligence reports received by Colonel Shiri had shown that many ZIPRA cadres had been educated at Inyathi Mission. Some of these ZIPRA cadres, including some senior field commanders, had been eliminated in the assaults near Gwaai River mine which had been carried out by ZNA troops over the last 12 to 18 months. However,

---

[91] *Isilima* is a Ndebele word meaning idiot.

[92] Perrance Shiri was distantly related to Rogert Mugabe. After independence, he commanded the 5th Brigade from 1983 to 1984. In 1992 he was appointed the commander of the Airforce of Zimbabwe. Shiri was influential in orchestrating the 2017 Zimbabwean coup d'état which removed Mugabe from power. On 30th November 2017, Shiri was appointed Minister of Agriculture by President Emmerson Mnangagwa.

[93] *Gukurahundi* is a Shona word which roughly translates as *'the early rain that washes away the chaff before the spring rain'*

[94] Zimbabwe People's Revolutionary Army. ZIPRA was the military wing of ZAPU.

[95] Zimbabwe African People's Union.

quite a number had escaped, and intel[96] indicated that these escapees had made their way back to the Inyathi area where they were receiving support and succour from the local community. Dawn to dusk curfews had been imposed in and around Inyathi and Major Tawanda Nyati was now questioning civilians right across the Inyathi district. All of this was unknown to Sipho.

A soldier from the roadblock walked smartly over to Sipho's Land Rover. Sipho noticed that despite the dusty location, his boots were shiny.

Sipho wound down his window.

Sipho was ordered to step out of his vehicle, which he politely did.

The soldier said, "Mangwanani Changamire. Ungada kundiudza kwauri kuenda[97]?"

While Sipho had a reasonable understanding of Shona, he certainly was not fluent in it. He understood the question but decided to answer in English.

"Good morning to you," he said. "I have come from Bulawayo and am going to Inyathi Mission to visit my parents. They both live there. From there, I am returning to Chiredzi, where I work."

By answering in English and not in Shona, the soldier concluded that Sipho must be a Ndebele, and his suspicions were immediately aroused.

"Do you know that this area is currently under a military curfew? Under the terms of the curfew, the movement of civilians is severely restricted."

Sipho was taken aback. Emanuel had not mentioned anything about a curfew to him. But Sipho was smart and intelligent and could think on his feet.

---

[96] Intelligence reports (often military in nature).
[97] This is Shona for "Good morning, Sir. Would you mind telling me where you are going?"

He replied, "I apologise. I have only just returned from the UK and was unaware of these restrictions."

The soldier seemed unmoved.

Sipho continued by saying, "I landed in Harare from London early on Thursday morning. I took the overnight train to Bulawayo. Yesterday I had lunch with Colonel Emanuel Wushe who is a friend. He provided me with a letter. May I show it to you?"

The soldier looked a little uncertain. "Yes, please do," he said.

Sipho reached into his jacket pocket, pulled out the envelope containing the letter signed by Colonel Emanuel Wushe, and handed it to the soldier.

The soldier took a minute or two to read the letter. He then said, "Please remain here while I speak with my superiors."

The soldier walked over to a small encampment just near the roadblock. He spoke to someone who then used a VHF[98] two-way radio set standing on a small camp table. After five minutes or so, the soldier returned to Sipho's car.

"Very good, Sir. That seems to be in order. You may continue. But please note that there is a strict dawn to dusk curfew in place. You are not permitted to travel between the hours of 7:00 pm to 6:00 am. If you do, you will be stopped and detained."

"I understand," said Sipho. "I will make sure that I stick to those restrictions."

With that Sipho got back into his Land Rover and continued on his way.

It was just after 10:30 am when Sipho arrived at his parents' home, Mandla[99] and Nandi[100] Pukelo. They still lived in the modest two-

---

[98] Very High Frequency.
[99] Mandla is a Ndebele boy's name meaning Power and Strength.
[100] Nandi is a Ndebele girl's name meaning Sweetness.

room concrete block house with a corrugated iron roof and concrete floor in which he had grown up. Although the house now had electricity and plumbed water, not much else had changed. However, these new utilities had undoubtedly improved Mandla and Nandi's quality of life.

Sipho parked outside on the dusty track and crossed the bare patch of red-brown dirt to knock on the front door. Nandi answered, her face lighting up in shock and delight. "Sipho, my son, what a surprise," she exclaimed. "Come inside."

Sipho clapped his hands in respect. "Umama[101], I should have let you know I was coming. I've just returned from London and am on my way back to the ranch in Chiredzi. I had no way to inform you and Ubaba[102], so I decided to take a chance."

Nandi beamed. "Well, I'm glad you did. Your father is at the school preparing the soccer pitch for a big game this afternoon. He should be home soon, and he will be glad to see you."

She led Sipho into the small front room, furnished with three chairs, a small table, and a rug. A transistor radio sat on the table. In one corner was a free-standing concrete tub with a tap, and nearby were a small electric fridge, an electric hot plate, and a kettle. Above the table were shelves with cooking utensils, and adjacent was a cupboard for groceries and crockery.

On the wall by the front door was a framed photo of Sipho in his RAR[103] uniform, taken in September 1972 after he had completed his initial training. Nandi had always proudly displayed this photo and frequently mentioned Sipho's achievements to visitors.

Nandi offered Sipho a cup of tea, and they sat down to chat. It had been about six months since they last spoke, so there was much to talk about.

---

[101] Umama is the Ndebele word for mother.
[102] Ubaba is the Ndebele word for father.
[103] Rhodesian African Rifles.

Sipho learnt from his mother that over the last six months things had become very difficult in the village. This was due to constant intimidation and harassment by soldiers. She explained that many young men from the compound had been forcibly removed, with no one knowing their whereabouts. Rumours of mass shootings in nearby villages were spreading, and the villager community was terrified.

At that point, Mandla arrived home. He, too, was surprised but delighted to see Sipho. He clapped his hands and grinned broadly, then took a seat. After some casual conversation, Sipho relayed what Nandi had said about the soldiers and asked Mandla for his perspective.

"Things are very bad," Mandla said. "The soldiers from the ZNA's 5th Brigade believe that all Ndebele people are against Mugabe and plotting against him. When we tell them we only want to live and work in peace, they don't believe us. There have been numerous beatings and some rapes. Young men are being taken from the compound by force. Rumour has it that they are being held in detention camps near Bulawayo and are being forced into denouncing ZAPU, Nkomo, and even our ancestral king, Lobengula Khumalo. They've been threatened with torture and death if they refuse to join ZANU."

Sipho was silent for a moment, then said, "Ubaba, just before you arrived, I was telling Umama that I have just returned from London. I went for a friend's wedding, Nick Sinclair, who was with me in the RAR. He is a true *induna*[104].While in London, I met a man named Jonathon Khumalo."

"I've heard you mention Nick before," Mandla said. "But who is Jonathon Khumalo?"

Sipho said, "He's a Ndebele who went to the mission school but was sent to England when he was 13. He finished his schooling there and

---

[104] In Ndebele culture, an *induna* was a title meaning a great leader, headman, or commander of a group of warriors.

then went to Oxford University. Now, he's a lawyer in London and claims to be from the royal House of Khumalo[105]. He wants to go back to Zimbabwe to restore the House of Khumalo. He was planning to join Nkomo's ZANU party in 1980, but his advisors were worried about Mugabe's plans, so he stayed in the UK until things become clearer."

Mandla thought for a moment. "He carries the well-known Khumalo name. I hope he's honest about his ancestry because the Ndebele people really need a strong leader now. I don't think Nkomo is right for us anymore. His reputation suffered when he fled the country dressed as a woman. Many Ndebele feel the same way."

Mandla went on, "I heard that until last year, Nkomo still had a large group of ZIPRA soldiers near Gwaai River mine. They were loyal to him and wanted to stand up to Mugabe, but Nkomo didn't act. Last year, those troops were attacked by the ZNA. They were outnumbered, and the ZNA had better weapons. Many ZIPRA soldiers were killed, and the survivors are now being hunted by the ZNA, including the new 5th Brigade."

Sipho nodded. "That is what I've heard. It's tragic to think that many ZIPRA soldiers who survived the Rhodesian Bush War are now being killed by the ZNA. I'm grateful I joined the RAR instead; otherwise, I might have been among those now being hunted."

Nandi, who had been silent, reached out and took Sipho's hand. "Sipho, you are a good man and a good son. We're proud of your bravery with the RAR and your work at Mhuka[106] Ranch. It's a pity that soldiers from the 5th Brigade don't behave as the RAR soldiers did."

---

[105] The House of Khumalo is the continuing royal family of the former Mthwakazi Kingdom (modern day Matabeleland). The Mthwakazi Kingdom was founded in 1823 and ended in 1894 with the First Matabele War. The House has endured to the present day.
[106] A local word meaning animals or wildlife.

"Thank you, Umama," Sipho said. "Things are different now. However, I'll do everything I can to keep you safe."

The conversation then turned to lighter topics. Sipho remembered the gifts he had brought for his parents. These were still in his Land Rover. He retrieved them — an electric food mixer for Nandi and an electric drill for Mandla. Both were thrilled, which made Sipho feel a bit guilty as the presents were modest.

For lunch, Nandi prepared sadza[107] and relish. In the afternoon, Sipho and Mandla went to watch the mission school's 1st XI soccer team play against Somvubu High School. The match was exciting, with the mission school winning 3-2. It reminded Sipho of a similar game in 1969 when he scored the winning goal. It was after that game that he first learned about Joshua Nkomo and ZIPRA.

Due to the curfew, Sipho and Mandla could not go to the local bar for celebratory drinks with other supporters. Instead, they returned home for a chicken dinner prepared by Nandi.

The next morning, Sipho left Inyathi to continue his journey to Mhuka Ranch near Chiredzi. While he was glad to have visited his parents, he was deeply troubled by the ongoing military operations in and around Inyathi.

---

[107] Sadza is a thickened porridge made with white maize meal. It is one of the staple foods in Zimbabwe.

Chapter 10 – Nick and Rachel start their honeymoon in the Drakensburg mountains

Time line – 14th July 1984

Nick fondly recalled his family's annual month-long holidays to South Africa. These annual sojourns were usually to the beachside city of Durban, Natal, where his grandparents had lived when they were still alive.

The 1,700-kilometre journey from Harare to Durban required two overnight stops. The trip was meticulously planned by their father, Matthew Sinclair. They typically left before 5:30 am while it was still dark. Their luggage always included a packed picnic breakfast, carefully prepared by Nick's mother, Brenda. It comprised ham and tomato rolls, hard-boiled eggs, and steaming coffee poured from a thermos flask. The flask had to be stored carefully to ensure its inner silvered-glass cylinder was not accidentally broken.

They usually stopped for breakfast somewhere just before the small rural city of Gwelo[108], at one of the many well-maintained lay-bys. After breakfast, their next destination was the border town of Beitbridge. The wide Limpopo River marked Rhodesia's southern

---

[108] Gwelo was renamed Gweru in 1982.

border with South Africa, and to cross the river, they had to travel across the impressive Alfred Beit Road Bridge[109].

Crossing into South Africa was always a highlight. Suddenly, everything seemed sophisticated compared to sanction-starved Rhodesia. The first town they passed through was Messina in the Northern Transvaal. This was a compulsory stop to fill up the car's petrol tank with cheap fuel, which could be bought without the irksome petrol coupons[110] that had plagued Rhodesian motorists ever since UDI[111] was declared by the Rhodesian Government in 1965. The stop also allowed Nick and Russell to buy all the Cadbury chocolate they wanted, a novelty since Cadbury chocolate was unavailable in Rhodesia due to sanctions.

Their first overnight stop was at a picturesque hotel in the Soutpansberg mountain range, about 20 kilometres before the town of Louis Trichardt, also in the Northern Transvaal. Before reaching their hotel, they had to pass through the impressive 730-metre-long Hendrik Verwoerd Tunnels[112], which always sparked much excitement. Their father would always comment on what an engineering feat the construction of the tunnels had been, reminding them that the tunnels had first been opened in 1961. There were no such tunnels in Rhodesia, hence Nick and Russell's fascination with them.

Their second overnight stop was near the charming town of Ladysmith. Once again, Matthew was quick to instruct his young sons

---

[109] The Alfred Beit Road Bridge is named after Alfred Beit, founder of the De Beers diamond mining company and business associate of Cecil Rhodes. The original bridge was constructed in 1929 at a cost of $600,000.
[110] International sanctions against Rhodesia, meant fuel was rationed by the Rhodesian Front Government. Individuals and businesses were allocated a specific amount of petrol based on their needs and circumstances. Petrol coupons were issued to control the amount of fuel each person or business could purchase.
[111] Unilateral Declaration of Independence. On 11th November 1965, the Rhodesian Government unilaterally and illegally declared itself to be independent of Britain.
[112] Hendrik Verwoerd was the Prime Minister of South Africa from 1958 to 1966. He is commonly regarded as the architect of apartheid.

about the siege of Ladysmith during the Second Boer War[113]. During the siege, Boer troops surrounded the town, trapping British troops and civilians inside. The siege lasted for 118 days and ended on 28th February 1900, when a British relief force, led by General Redvers Buller, managed to break through the Boer lines.

The third and final day of the trip was always the most exciting. Durban was approximately 240 kilometres from Ladysmith. Generally, they would leave Ladysmith early and stop in Pietermaritzburg for breakfast. Nick would always order scrambled eggs on toast with grilled tomatoes. For some reason, which Nick could never explain, the eggs in Pietermaritzburg were always a richer yellow than those in Rhodesia, while the tomatoes were a deeper red.

The final leg of their trip from Pietermaritzburg to Durban was only about an hour long. There would be a competition in the car to see who would be the first to spot the sea. For a few years, there was also a contest to be the first to smell the sea, but this was eventually abandoned as it was impossible to adjudicate.

Another game they played in the car was to be the first to spot other cars bearing Rhodesian number plates or insignia. Upon sighting such a vehicle, Matthew would flash his lights and toot his horn while Brenda and the two boys would wave madly. There was a strong bond among Rhodesian citizens at that time, which meant that the drivers of the other cars would invariably respond in kind. So, although they were in a foreign country, they always felt they were never far from Rhodesian kinfolk.

Their holidays in Durban were always memorable. As Rhodesia was a landlocked country, the joy of seeing and experiencing wide-open beaches with rolling waves, and full of families — many of them Rhodesians — enjoying themselves on holiday created lifelong

---

[113] The Second Boer War, was a conflict fought between the British Empire and the two Boer republics (the South African Republic and Orange Free State) over the Empire's influence in Southern Africa.

memories. Shopping in the sophisticated Durban stores, filled with all kinds of exotic goods unavailable in Rhodesia due to sanctions, was equally special.

Often, the annual holiday would also include a visit to the Drakensberg Mountains, where his Uncle Thomas and Aunt Janet owned and ran a highly successful dairy farm.

The Drakensberg Mountains were a particularly beautiful area of South Africa. As a very young boy, Nick's mother had told him that the words 'Drakensberg Mountains' meant the Dragon Mountains in Afrikaans. This description had captured Nick's imagination. His uncle's farm was situated near a small town called Himeville in Natal. The farm had amazingly picturesque views over that section of the Drakensberg Mountains, which formed a formidable barrier between Natal's eastern border and the inland mountain kingdom of Lesotho[114].

The farmhouse bedroom usually allocated to Nick and Russell had a window that looked directly onto the dark and menacing *Dragon Mountains*. Whenever he stayed at the farm, Nick's dreams often included terrifying images of fire-breathing dragons living in the deep mountain caves, whose favourite snacks were white Rhodesian boys.

The farm was near a beautiful hotel called the Sani Pass Hotel. The hotel was nestled in lush green gardens at the foot of the southern Drakensberg Mountains and close to a treacherous mountain pass known as Sani Pass.

The Sani Pass was a steep winding dirt road that took drivers up and over the southern Drakensberg Mountains into the small inland country of Lesotho. Nick had only once before been up the pass. This was when he was about 17, when he participated in a day-long

---

[114] Lesotho was formerly known as Basutoland. Its name changed in 1966 when it gained independence from British colonial rule.

4WD[115] return trip up the pass into Lesotho and back. This had been a wild and heart-thumping experience.

When planning their honeymoon, Nick mentioned the Drakensberg Mountains and the Sani Pass to Rachel, suggesting that they spend a few nights there before flying to Zimbabwe. Intrigued by the allure of the mountains and Lesotho, Rachel researched both in detail and was captivated by the idea of visiting that region of South Africa. So, their honeymoon was planned accordingly.

*****

They had flown out of London at 6:20 pm on Friday, 13th July, and landed at Johannesburg's Jan Smuts International Airport the following morning. From Johannesburg, they took an internal SAA[116] flight to Pietermaritzburg. There, they picked up a hire car and drove to a guest house called the Cloete Guest House, arriving in the late afternoon.

The guest house was owned by a delightful couple named Bert and Mary Cloete, both in their mid-50s. Originally a grand farmhouse in the Himeville area, Bert and Mary Cloete had purchased it in the late 1970s. It had taken them three years of dedicated work to transform the farmhouse into a luxury retreat that could accommodate up to 20 guests.

The complex comprised a collection of one- or two-bedroomed thatched cottages, each with its own unique rustic charm and elegance.

Nick and Rachel arrived in the afternoon, just as the sun was beginning to drop behind the imposing mountains. The disappearance of the sun brought a definite chill to the air. Nick and Rachel put on jumpers and then went to check in at reception. The

---

[115] This is an acronym for four-wheel drive. 4WD vehicles are typically used in off-road or other challenging driving conditions.
[116] South African Airways.

pleasant receptionist provided them with a map of the property, clearly showing their cottage, the central dining room, and the bar.

Nick drove along the pebble-covered drive and parked outside their cottage, which was about 100 metres from the reception area.

As they entered the building, they were immediately enchanted by its warm hues and subtle lighting, which created an inviting ambiance. The cottage was intimately and tastefully furnished. It seemed to Rachel that Bert and Mary had seamlessly managed to merge modern luxury with historic charm, creating a romantic space that radiated appeal and comfort.

This was further enhanced by the plush furnishings and a cosy glowing fire in the sitting room. There were two large floor-to-ceiling windows in the sitting room, which cleverly framed panoramic views of the imposing mountains outside.

The bedroom, with its king-sized bed, had a deluxe feel about it. The linen-quilted, eggshell-coloured duvet had already been drawn back, revealing luxurious white-starched sheets. The adjacent bathroom featured contemporary design and modern fixtures, including a free-standing soaking tub and a large double shower. The thatched roof, scattered soft hand-woven woollen rugs, and dimmed sconce wall-lighting added a final romantic layer to the overall feel of the cottage.

They both immediately knew that the cottage would be the ideal place to unwind and relax. Rachel was enamoured. She gave Nick an amorous hug and said, "This is absolutely gorgeous. It is so nice to be back in Africa with you. I can't wait to explore the local area and, of course, to travel up the Sani Pass into Lesotho."

By the time they had unpacked, it was quite dark. They decided to go to the guest bar for a drink and then have dinner in the central dining room.

The bar was called the Eland Bar, in recognition of the large herds of eland that roamed the southern Drakensberg Mountains. Upon entering the bar, Nick made his way to the bar counter to order drinks, while Rachel found a cosy spot near the large fireplace in the lounge area. Above the fireplace, mounted on the wall, was a magnificent trophy head of a male eland, sporting long spiralled horns. On the floor, in front of the glowing fire, was an eland hide. It was reddish-brown in colour and had a series of distinct vertical white stripes running down its torso and neck. Rachel had never seen eland in the wild and hoped she and Nick would come across them during the next few days.

A few minutes later, Nick reappeared with their drinks. He said excitedly, "I was served at the bar by the owner, Bert Cloete. He seems like a delightful person and knows my Uncle Thomas. He said he would love to meet you and will come and find us in the dining room later."

Later that evening, Nick and Rachel made their way to the restaurant. A table had been reserved for them in a quiet corner of the restaurant, which was quite full. All the patrons were white, and Rachel asked Nick why this was so. Nick explained that South Africa still had apartheid[117] laws, which made it illegal for black persons to enter the restaurant or for the restaurant to serve them.

"I am surprised that this is still the case," said Rachel. "Especially since in neighbouring Zimbabwe, all the racial discriminatory laws have now been repealed."

Nick replied, "You need to remember that South Africa and Zimbabwe are different countries with very different histories. South Africa has a strong Afrikaans heritage, and it was this heritage that was largely responsible for the introduction of apartheid laws shortly after WWII. There is no such Afrikaans heritage in Zimbabwe. While there was racial discrimination in Zimbabwe prior to 1980, Rhodesia never adopted the South African model of institutionalised racial segregation."

---

[117] Apartheid is the Afrikaans word for apartness. It was a system of institutionalised racial segregation that existed in South Africa and South West Africa (now Namibia) from 1948 to the early 1990s.

"Do you think what has happened in Zimbabwe will affect South Africa?" asked Rachel.

"Absolutely. It is only a question of time. Sooner or later, all South Africans will be given the right to vote in general elections, and eventually, apartheid legislation will be repealed," said Nick. "I would imagine white South Africans are carefully watching what is happening in Zimbabwe as it will give them some idea of what will happen in South Africa once apartheid is abandoned. But even if things do not work out in Zimbabwe, apartheid in South Africa will end. The pressures against it are just too great."

A short while later, a waiter came to their table and took their order. The menu was largely English cuisine, with a few South African dishes. After liaising with the waiter, both Rachel and Nick ordered a South African dish called bobotie[118] as their main meal, followed by another South African dish for dessert, malva[119] pudding. They also ordered a bottle of Nederberg Sauvignon Blanc.

Halfway through dinner, Bert Cloete approached their table. Nick greeted him and introduced him to Rachel, then invited Bert to join them for a drink. Bert graciously accepted the invitation but explained he could only stay for about ten minutes, as both the restaurant and bar were extremely busy.

Nick asked Bert how he had met his Uncle Thomas. Bert replied, "Your uncle is well known in these parts. Not long after Mary and I purchased the old farmhouse, we met your uncle. We have met him many times since then. In fact, he has a monthly meeting here at which he meets up with his farming friends and representatives from the South African Police to discuss the security situation in and around Himeville."

"I wasn't aware of that," said Nick.

---

[118] Bobotie is a spiced, baked minced meat dish topped with an egg-based topping. It's a Cape Malay dish with Indonesian and Dutch influences.
[119] A sweet and sticky baked dessert typically served warm and often accompanied by a creamy sauce or custard.

"Yes, unfortunately, there have been some incidents recently where isolated farms in the Drakensberg area have been attacked by politically motivated persons. Given the historical racial tensions both in Zimbabwe, pre-1980, and now in South Africa, I know the local white farming community is quite fearful that violence against white farmers may escalate."

Bert's comments reminded Nick of what Rachel's father, Stuart Dixon, had recently said about the political and economic challenges facing southern African countries and how these challenges were likely to spook current investors, sparking a significant flight of capital.

Bert then asked, "Will you be seeing Thomas during your visit?"

"Unfortunately, not," said Nick. "Thomas and my aunt are currently holidaying in Mauritius and will only be back in South Africa after we have left."

"That is a pity," said Bert. "But on another matter, what are you and Rachel planning to do while you are here?"

"The only thing on our '*must-do*' list is to travel up the Sani Pass to Lesotho. We haven't organised that yet. I will do so tomorrow. But is there anything else you would suggest we should do?"

Bert replied, "If you come to reception tomorrow, our receptionist will be able to book you onto one of the 4WD tours up the pass. There are lots of other things you can do. I would recommend a visit to the Giant's Castle Game Reserve and perhaps some horseback riding. Once again, our receptionist can help you organise those things."

"Can you tell us a bit about the Giant's Castle Game Reserve?" Nick asked.

Bert replied, "The name Giant's Castle came about because the shape of the peaks and escarpment is thought to resemble a sleeping giant's profile. The Game Reserve includes a number of waterfalls, fly-fishing, fantastic trails, walks, and scenery. There are also many ancient San[120] rock-art sites. The Game Reserve is home to a variety of smaller wildlife, including eland, baboons, and a diverse bird population."

"That sounds special," said Rachel. "I know Nick is keen to do the Sani Pass tour. Giant's Castle Game Reserve also sounds wonderful. Thanks for the info."

"My pleasure," said Bert. "Now I need to get back to the bar. It has been special meeting you both."

Bert left their table. After his departure, Nick and Rachel decided they would spend Sunday exploring the Himeville area themselves and, if possible, visit the Giant's Castle Game Reserve on Monday and do the Sani Pass 4WD tour on Tuesday.

A short time later, they walked back to their 'honeymoon' cottage, where they enjoyed an intimate shower together, followed by a passionate bout of lovemaking in their king-sized bed.

They fell asleep in each other's arms just before midnight.

*****

The following three days were wonderful. The weather was cold, but the skies were sunny and clear. Himeville itself was a pretty little hamlet with an eclectic mix of farm service businesses, arts and crafts outlets, and the usual assortment of coffee shops and cafés.

Their trip to Giant's Castle Game Reserve on the Monday was both exhilarating and educational. The scenery and hiking trails were better than anything Nick had ever experienced before, even in Zimbabwe's Eastern Highlands[121]. Rachel, too, said they were more beautiful than anything she had seen in the Lake District of England. Much to Rachel's delight, they also saw two large herds of eland,

---

[120] The San, often known as "Bushmen," are descendants of hunter-gatherers who have lived in southern Africa for tens of thousands of years.

[121] The Eastern Highlands is a mountainous area on the border of Zimbabwe and Mozambique. It extends for about 300 kilometres from north to south and includes the Inyangani Mountains, the Vumba Mountains, and the Chimanimani Mountains.

some large, graceful black eagles, and lots of baboons. They visited two San rock-art painting sites which, while impressive, were not as good as those Rachel had seen in the Matopos in Zimbabwe during her visit with Nick in August 1981.

But the highlight of their trip, without exception, was their 4WD trip up the Sani Pass into Lesotho on Tuesday.

They had been picked up at the guest house at 9:00 am by their tour operator, Elliott. They had been advised that once they started ascending the pass, the temperature would begin to drop quickly and that at the top, it would probably be snowing. Hence, they dressed warmly.

Apart from Elliott and themselves, there was one other couple on the tour with them. This was a German couple named Friedrich and Petra Weber. They were from Munich and were holidaying in both South Africa and South West Africa[122].

Elliott told his guests that the Sani Pass provided the only road link between Natal and Lesotho and was the only road crossing the summit of the high Drakensberg. He said that the pass had originally been a mule track. Over time, the track had been widened, but it was still an extremely steep and windy boulder-strewn dirt road with corrugation and potholes. The road was only nine kilometres long but climbed from a low point of 1,545 metres to a height of 2,875 metres above sea level. In many places, its gradient was one in five, and it had many 180° switchback bends.

They went through the South African border post at the foot of the pass. It was another eight kilometres to the Lesotho border post at the top of the pass, which meant that, in a sense, they were travelling in no-man's land for eight kilometres.

The dirt road was often only wide enough for one vehicle to pass. Some of the hairpin turns were so tight that Elliott needed to

---

[122] South West Africa achieved its independence from South African administration on 21st March 1990, and was renamed Namibia.

perform a two- to three-point turn in order to navigate the bend. In many parts, the road was bordered on one side by high steep mountains and on the other by deep ravines and valleys. On the ravine side of the road, there were no guardrails, meaning that if your vehicle left the road through misadventure, it would fall several hundred metres into these deep ravines and gullies. Nick and Rachel spotted a number of such wrecks at the bottom of some of the gorges.

As their vehicle snaked its way up the pass, it took them through a scenic valley and close to a crystal-clear river with breathtaking views. Nick and Rachel's eyes feasted on the natural landscape. While the ground was quite barren, the jagged mountain peaks and rocky features meant that the overall vista was captivating.

Rachel was surprised at how desolate it was at the peak of the pass. The Lesotho border post consisted of nothing more than a tin hut. As Elliott had predicted, it was snowing at the top. It was very windy and extremely cold. Rachel wondered how the officials at the border post coped.

There were no paved roads, just a jumbled tangle of donkey paths. The local Basotho people all seemed to be wearing colourful hats and blankets. Many of them seemed to be very old with missing teeth.

After looking around the sparse border post, Elliott took his four guests to visit a household in a small shepherd's village about five kilometres away. There, they tried to respectfully engage with the Basotho-speaking shepherds, all of whom were wearing their traditional hand-woven blankets. The visitors were keen to learn about the shepherds' remarkable lives at this elevation. Communications were difficult, but Elliott had a reasonable grasp of the local language, known as Sesotho. Consequently, they were able to learn a bit about life in Lesotho, which was hard and unforgiving.

After the village, they returned to the border post and went to have a beer at one of the few commercial buildings at the border post. This building was a pub named *The Highest Pub in Africa*. Here, they enjoyed a local beer, known as *Maluti*, and warmed themselves in front of the roaring fire in one corner of the pub. They spoke briefly with some other visitors before climbing back into their 4WD and returning down the Sani Pass to Himeville.

The following morning, they drove back to the local airport at Pietermaritzburg and caught an SAA flight to Johannesburg. Two hours later, they boarded an Air Zimbabwe flight to Harare, touching down at Harare Airport just after 3:20 pm.

On their flight back to Zimbabwe, Rachel said, "I loved South Africa. But I worry about its precariousness. In some ways, it seems to be rather like Zimbabwe, but just not quite as far down the path to uncertainty."

"I totally agree," said Nick. "Just before we left England, I had a meeting with your Dad about my new job with RQI[123]. Do you know what he said to me?"

"No," said Rachel.

"Well, he is predicting that most countries in southern Africa, including South Africa and Zimbabwe, are going to face significant political, economic, and social challenges. He reckons these challenges are going to spook current investors, leading to a significant flight of capital from these countries.

"He thinks that this flight of capital is going to create rare opportunities for smart entrepreneurs. He wants to make sure that RQI captures a big part of that action, and he wants me to play a significant part in helping it do that. I think he is dead right about the risk of a flight of capital. I am not sure what role I will be able to play to help ensure RQI captures a big slice of these opportunities. But I sure am looking forward to the ride."

Rachel squeezed his hand. "I bet you are," she said. "And you will be brilliant. Just wait and see."

---

[123] Rare Quest Imports.

Chapter 11 – Nick and Rachel arrive in Zimbabwe to continue their honeymoon

Nick and Rachel landed at Harare Airport just after 3:30 pm on Wednesday, 18th July. The weather was beautiful, with the temperature still hovering around 20°C despite the lateness of the day. The sky was a bright blue and cloudless, stretching from horizon to horizon like a perfectly sculpted canopy.

They disembarked onto the tarmac and walked toward the arrivals terminal. Their flight had been full, and to Nick's surprise, more than half the passengers were black. Additionally, one of the flight attendants was an attractive young black woman. This was a new phenomenon in independent Zimbabwe. Prior to independence in 1980, there would have been no black flight attendants or pilots, and the number of black passengers would have been few.

"It's nice to see so many black people on the flight," said Nick. "You wouldn't have seen that three or four years ago."

"Yes, it's good to see the emergence of a black middle class," said Rachel. "I cannot tell you how nice it is to be back in Zimbabwe. I wonder if you'll notice any changes. But one thing that hasn't changed is the weather. Gosh, it's a beautiful afternoon. As you've told me often enough, Harare's climate must be one of the best in the world."

Nick's mother, Brenda Sinclair, was waiting for them in the arrivals hall. She was thrilled to see them and gave them a warm hug.

"Good afternoon, Mr and Mrs Sinclair! Welcome back to Zimbabwe. I can't believe that only two weeks ago we were all in London for your wedding. And I cannot wait to hear about Lesotho. It was such a pity you weren't able to catch up with Uncle Thomas and Aunt Janet. They would have loved to see you, Nick, and meet Rachel," she said.

"Yes, I'm sorry that didn't work out," Nick answered. "But we loved the southern Drakensberg mountains, and the trip up Sani Pass to Lesotho was spectacular. At the top of the pass, there's even a pub. It's called *The Highest Pub in Africa*. We had a beer there."

"Really?" replied Brenda. "Matthew and I always enjoyed our holidays in South Africa, especially the ones that included a stay in the Drakensberg. You can tell me all about it in the car."

It took them about half an hour to drive from the airport back to Matthew and Brenda's house in Nigel's Lane, in the affluent suburb of Ballantyne Park. Nigel's Lane was a cul-de-sac, and Matthew and Brenda lived at number 15, which was at the end of the road. Their property was walled and gated. Brenda opened the remote-controlled gates using a control pad in her car and parked in front of the large double garage on the right-hand side of the house. The house was set back about thirty metres from the gate. Rachel immediately recognised the front garden with its large jacaranda tree and the all-weather tennis court on the left-hand side of the house.

They entered through the front door into the foyer. On the right-hand wall of the foyer was the abstract oil painting that Nick and Rachel had bought in 1981 as a gift for Brenda and Matthew. Rachel was pleased to see that Brenda had hung the painting in the foyer, which was where Nick thought it would look stunning. And stunning it was. The yellows, reds, and blues of the large oil painting were a perfect match for the décor of the foyer. Brenda remarked on how often visitors commented on the painting, especially its interesting texture and finish, created by various lines of poetry that the local black Zimbabwean artist, Shadreck Ndlovu, had etched into the painted work with a graphite pen.

Nick was about to return to Brenda's car to retrieve his and Rachel's suitcases from the boot. However, before he could do so, Brenda's maid, Dorothy, appeared from the kitchen. She was beaming from ear to ear and greeted Nick and Rachel warmly. She had worked for Nick's parents for about 15 years and was almost part of the family. She had first met Rachel in August 1981 when Rachel and Nick had visited Zimbabwe for a month-long holiday. She had been thrilled and excited when, a year later, Brenda told her that Nick and Rachel had gotten engaged. This excitement had bubbled over in March of the current year when Brenda informed her that Nick and Rachel were going to get married in the UK in July and would then be honeymooning in Zimbabwe. Ever since then, Dorothy had been like an excited young child as she waited for the return of *Baas*[124] Nick and his beautiful English bride.

In spite of Nick's protestations, Dorothy insisted on fetching their cases and taking them to the guest room. She sped off to complete her mission. A short time later, she reappeared to let them know that this had been done and that she had made a fresh pot of tea for them all, which she had left on the veranda. She then excused herself and disappeared into the kitchen to complete the ironing.

Brenda led the way to the veranda. Dorothy had left the tea tray and a plate of homemade cookies on the garden table. The three of them sat down, enjoying the delicious warmth of the sunshine and the relaxing view over the back garden and swimming pool.

"I apologise for Dorothy's enthusiasm," Brenda said, "but she has been so excited about seeing you both again. Her excitement is really quite endearing."

"She is so lovely," exclaimed Rachel. "I love her. I've forgotten your gardener's name. Does he still work for you?"

---

[124] Baas is a word derived from Afrikaans and means boss or master.

Brenda replied, "His name is Dennis. Unfortunately, he doesn't work for us anymore. He left about a year ago to take up a new position as a postboy. We were so pleased for him, as it means more money for him. Our new gardener is called Frank. But no more mundane stuff. I cannot wait to learn more about your trip to Himeville."

Over the next hour or so, the three of them chatted animatedly. Brenda updated them on how things were in Zimbabwe while Nick and Rachel told them about their new house in Hampshire, Rachel's job in London with Vivienne Westwood's fashion house, and Nick's upcoming position with RQI[125] in London. At about 5:30 pm, Brenda said that there were some things she needed to attend to in the kitchen. She mentioned that Matthew would be home at about 6:30 pm, and that dinner would be at about 7:00 pm. She suggested that they might like to go and unpack, and then freshen up before dinner.

---

[125] Rare Quest Imports.

Chapter 12 – Nick and Rachel relax in Harare

A few days later, Nick and Rachel were unwinding at Matthew and Brenda's house in Ballantyne Park. It was a leisurely Saturday afternoon, and after a competitive game of tennis, they were gathered around the swimming pool enjoying a braai[126].

Nick marvelled at how life in Harare appeared relatively unchanged despite the country having been independent for just over four years. Turning to his father, he said, "Dad, I can't help but wonder about your and Mum's perspectives on your futures here in Zimbabwe. At first glance, it seems not much has altered since independence. Is that really the case?"

Matthew replied, "Don't be deceived by superficial appearances, Nick. There have, in fact, been significant changes in the country, and the pace of change is only going to accelerate. Unfortunately, I fear not much of it will be positive."

"What do you mean?" inquired Nick.

---

[126] Braai is the Afrikaans word for a BBQ.

Matthew explained, "Well, politically, things have shifted dramatically. ZANU-PF[127] is firmly in control now, while ZAPU[128] seems sidelined. The Rhodesian Front, though still technically present, is fading fast and will likely vanish once the ten-year reservation period for the white seats expires. I fear Zimbabwe may well become a one-party state with Mugabe at the helm, especially as ZAPU declines and white representation in parliament comes to an end."

"And Mugabe is difficult to read. He is obviously well-educated and extremely erudite. But he is also a political animal through and through. He sees himself as the true liberator of the black Zimbabwean people. In my view, he suffers from aggrandisement and, without an effective opposition, he could very easily become a dictator, and quite a brutal one at that. I think we are beginning to see what he is capable of by what is currently occurring in Matabeleland. He is also smart enough to let the more zealous thugs in ZANU-PF and the army do his dirty work so that he can keep his hands clean. I cannot believe that the UK has not yet made any official public protestations about the atrocities taking place in Matabeleland. The British Government needs to show far stronger leadership. I would have expected a lot more from Margaret Thatcher. I simply cannot understand why she is treating him with kid gloves. I fear she is making a very big mistake."

"Mugabe is certainly a complex figure," Nick observed. "Where do you think his political allegiances lie?"

Matthew pondered, "It's hard to say. Not surprisingly, he has expressed socialist and anti-imperialist views, but his allegiances with global powers like China, the Soviet Union, or the West have been inconsistent. Publicly, he claims to be pursuing a policy of non-alignment, but I suspect he'll deal with anyone offering Zimbabwe a

---

[127] Zimbabwe African National Union – Patriotic Front. ZANU-PF is a political organisation that has been the ruling party of Zimbabwe since independence in 1980.
[128] Zimbabwe African People's Union.

good looking deal, even if that happens to be the devil himself. He does not seem to have any ideological principles, which is surprising given the fact that he was educated in Catholic mission schools."

Rachel, who had been listening quietly, interjected, "Matthew, your insights on the political landscape are most interesting, but what about the economy? How do you think ZANU-PF is managing that?"

Matthew reflected, "Initially, I think ZANU-PF managed it quite well. But one needs to remember that the new government was promised or received substantial aid from multiple countries, especially Western-aligned nations eager to ensure that Zimbabwe's fledgling democracy would thrive and survive. Also, politically, Mugabe was enjoying a honeymoon period with the electorate. However, a lot of the gloss has since been removed. Recent events in Matabeleland have significantly tarnished Mugabe's image and stirred uncertainty. Many skilled Zimbabweans, including blacks, might leave, further destabilising the economy. We're already seeing this in industries like tobacco."

Nick asked, "Given all that, do you and Mum plan to stay long-term?"

Matthew sighed and said, "Your Mum and I have debated this extensively. Leaving seems prudent, but at our age, it's daunting. We're not exactly young anymore, and our options are somewhat limited."

Rachel spoke up, "I know any decision you make is likely to be difficult. You need to make the best decision for yourselves. But when deciding on your future, please bear in mind that both you and Brenda are very dear, not only to Nick and me, but also to my parents. Before we left for our honeymoon, my parents specifically asked us to let you know that if you do decide to move from Zimbabwe, they will do anything they can to help. I am not sure how that might look, but as you know, Mum and Dad are very well-off, and I know they would be able to assist you both practically and emotionally if you were to decide to leave."

For a moment there was silence. Then Brenda, touched by the gesture, reached for Rachel's hand, saying, "That means the world to us. I'll be sure to convey our heartfelt thanks to them. But let's shift our focus from our situation to your honeymoon plans. When do you and Nick leave for the Zimbabwe Ruins, and when do you arrive at Mhuka[129] Ranch?"

---

[129] A local word meaning animals or wildlife.

Chapter 13 – Nick and Rachel travel to the Great Zimbabwe Ruins

On Monday, 23rd July 1984, Nick and Rachel left Harare at dawn to drive to the Great Zimbabwe Ruins[130], located just outside Masvingo[131], approximately 300 kilometres to the south. They travelled in a Toyota Land Cruiser that Nick's father had generously lent them.

They reached Masvingo shortly before 10:00 am and, after refuelling in town, drove the short distance to the Great Zimbabwe Hotel, conveniently located within walking distance of the ruins. Once checked in, they enjoyed a cup of coffee on the hotel's veranda before embarking on a brief stroll to the site.

Although Rachel had read up on the ruins, she wasn't entirely sure what to expect. She had initially envisioned a place of tumbled-down rocks and stones. However, she was pleasantly surprised by the scale, layout, and history revealed by the ancient site.

---

[130] The Great Zimbabwe Ruins is the name of the stone ruins of an ancient city known as Great Zimbabwe. The ruins are located just outside Fort Victoria (now called Masvingo). People lived in Great Zimbabwe from around 1100 but abandoned it in the 15th century. The city was the capital of the Kingdom of Zimbabwe, which was a Shona trading empire. Zimbabwe means "stone houses" in Shona.
[131] Masvingo was previously known as Fort Victoria. The name changed in 1982.

They entered the national park, paid the admission fees, and started their tour by leisurely strolling around the 900-year-old section of the ruins known as the Great Enclosure. The outer wall of the Great Enclosure was some 250 metres in circumference, with a maximum height just over ten metres. Next to the outer wall ran an inner wall, creating a roofless narrow parallel passage approximately 50 metres in length. This passage led to a ten-metre-high tower named the Conical Tower.

Walking along the narrow passage proved to be a profoundly spiritual experience for Rachel. With few visitors present, the site was eerily silent, punctuated only by the rustling of the wind and the soft scuffing of their shoes on the cobbled-stone pathway. Occasionally, the silence was broken by the melodious trills of vibrantly coloured sunbirds nesting in the nearby trees and shrubs.

Nick explained the remarkable construction of both the outer and inner walls of the Great Enclosure and the Conical Tower, both of which had been built entirely from roughly hewn granite blocks without mortar. He recounted how the Great Enclosure's perimeter columns were once adorned with soapstone sculptures of a silhouetted bird with human lips and five-fingered feet. Sadly, these had been plundered by frenzied European treasure seekers in the early 1900s.

He told her that the Great Enclosure had been constructed during the 11th and 12th centuries by the ancient ancestors of the Shona tribe. He also informed her that the original purpose of the Conical Tower was still unknown, but historians had surmised it might have been a symbolic grain bin or perhaps a phallic symbol.

At the mention of the possibility that the Conical Tower was a phallic symbol, Rachel raised her eyebrows and cheekily quipped, "Wow, so maybe it is true what people say about black men being well endowed!"

Nick chuckled and said, "You're wicked. But in the nicest way possible."

Following their exploration of the Great Enclosure, they embarked on the steep climb to the Acropolis[132]. Nick described the Acropolis as the spiritual and religious heart of the ancient city, covering approximately 4,500 square metres. Notable features included a massive boulder resembling the Zimbabwe Bird, from where the king would preside over important rituals such as the judgment of criminals, the appeasement of ancestors, and sacrifices to rainmaker gods. Nick told her that the sacrifices happened over a raised platform below the king's seat, where oxen were burned. If the smoke went straight up, the ancestors were appeased. If it was crooked, they were unhappy, and another sacrifice had to be made.

After touring both the Great Enclosure and the Acropolis, they visited the on-site museum. Here, they learned that Great Zimbabwe's prosperity stemmed from its strategic location on the ancient trading route between the gold-producing regions of the area and ports on the Mozambique coast. The museum showcased various trading items, including gold, ivory, copper, tin, cattle, and cowrie shells. They also discovered that Great Zimbabwe once accounted for a significant portion of the world's gold production, with over 4,000 gold and 500 copper mines found around the site. Apparently, thousands of necklaces made of gold lamé[133] had been found among the ruins, a few of which were on display in the museum.

As the afternoon sun waned, they returned to the hotel, enjoying a cold beer in the outdoor garden areas before retiring to their room for some late afternoon nookies[134], followed by a nap and then dinner.

The next morning, they set off early for Kyle National Park[135] for a safari drive followed by a picnic brunch on the northern shores of Lake Kyle[136]. Nick told her that the park had been established in 1960

---

[132] The Acropolis is now referred to as the Hill Complex.
[133] Lamé is a type of fabric woven with threads made of metallic fibre wrapped around natural or synthetic fibres like silk or nylon.
[134] Slang term for sexual intercourse.
[135] Now known as Mutirikwi National Park.
[136] Now known as Lake Mutirikwi.

upon completion of the dam wall, which was originally built as an irrigation reservoir to provide water to the farming estates in the southeast lowveld.

Nick mentioned that much of the land used for the lake had previously been farmland owned by the legendary Thomas MacDougall. He reminded her that in the 1920s and 1930s, MacDougall was responsible for the transformation of that part of the lowveld around the Triangle and Hippo Valley estates, which they had travelled through on their first trip to Zimbabwe in August 1981. He said that when Kyle Dam was completed in 1960, it was named after the Kyle District in Scotland, from where MacDougall originated.

Rachel chuckled to herself. "What's so funny?" asked Nick.

Rachel replied, "It's just so bizarre. So much of the recent history of this country is deeply embedded in its colonial origins. The new government is going to try to eradicate this colonial heritage, but that is going to be challenging."

The game drive was as spectacular as Rachel had imagined, with breathtaking views of the sunrise and abundant wildlife. They returned to the hotel after lunch, and spent the afternoon lounging by the inviting swimming pool.

After dinner, they prepared for their journey to Mhuka[137] Ranch. Despite the tumultuous events that had occurred when they were last at the ranch in August 1981, they were thoroughly looking forward to their return. The thought of reuniting with Sipho[138], the Oliver family, and reacquainting themselves with the sublime beauty of the ranch filled them both with excitement.

---

[137] A local word meaning animals or wildlife.
[138] Sipho is a Ndebele boy's name meaning Gift.

Chapter 14 – The birthing of "A Moment of Madness"

Time line – early 1984

You will recall that in August 1983, Major Tawanda Nyati was transferred as a company commander to the 2nd Battalion of ZNA's 5th Brigade, based in Lupane, Matabeleland North. His objective was to seek out and destroy any remaining armed ZIPRA[139] dissidents still operating in Matabeleland. This was a follow-up operation to complete the seek-and-destroy mission initiated by Robert Mugabe following the deployment of the 5th Brigade in January 1983.

During 1983, Robert Mugabe had also succeeded in reducing the political reach and influence of the ZAPU[140] opposition party led by Joshua Nkomo. This was achieved through a shrewd campaign initiated by Mugabe to weaken ZAPU as a political force.

Ironically, Mugabe was aided in his designs by the defence forces of the white apartheid[141] South African Government, which had adopted a far-reaching policy of destabilising black-ruled Zimbabwe. This included financial and military support to a group of ZIPRA

---

[139] Zimbabwe People's Revolutionary Army. ZIPRA was the military wing of ZAPU.
[140] Zimbabwe African People's Union.
[141] Apartheid is the Afrikaans word for apartness. It was a system of institutionalised racial segregation that existed in South Africa and South West Africa (now Namibia) from 1948 to the early 1990s.

dissidents known as "**Super-ZAPU**." These dissidents had been trained in Northern Transvaal and were now active in Zimbabwe.

The objective of Super-ZAPU and other South African operatives was to destabilise Zimbabwe by fostering suspicion between ZANU and ZAPU. They achieved this by planting incriminating evidence, including arms and explosives, in known ZAPU locations and then leaking this information to Mugabe's intelligence agencies. This led to a series of violent clashes between ZANU and ZAPU supporters and created a dangerous and volatile political climate.

In March 1983, Joshua Nkomo, fearing for his life, briefly fled Zimbabwe and went into self-imposed exile in London. This followed the arrest and imprisonment of two of his key military strategists the year before — Lookout Masuku[142] and Dumiso Dabengwa[143] — both of whom were accused of plotting against Robert Mugabe.

At the trials of both Lookout Masuku and Dumiso Dabengwa in June 1983, both men were found not guilty and acquitted. However, shortly after their acquittal, they were re-detained and imprisoned under the country's emergency power regulations.

By the end of 1983, the mission to seek out and destroy armed ZIPRA dissidents was largely complete. The 5th Brigade, with helicopter support from the Air Force of Zimbabwe, had performed remarkably well, much to the satisfaction of Prime Minister Robert Mugabe, General Solomon Mujuru[144], commander of the Zimbabwe Defence Forces, and Colonel Perrance Shiri[145], commander of ZNA's[146] 5th Brigade.

---

[142] Lookout Masuku was commander of the ZIPRA forces during the Rhodesian Bush War. After independence, he served as the deputy commander of the ZNA until his arrest in 1982 for allegedly plotting to overthrow Robert Mugabe.

[143] Dumiso Dabengwa was head of ZIPRA's intelligence service during the Rhodesian Bush War and for a time thereafter. In 1982 he was charged with treason by the Mugabe administration.

[144] Solomon Mujuru's nom de guerre during the Rhodesian Bush War was Rex Nhongo.

[145] Perrance Shiri was distantly related to Rogert Mugabe. After independence, he commanded the 5th Brigade from 1983 to 1984. In 1992 he was appointed the

Buoyed by these political and military successes and with little or no public outcry from major global powers, Mugabe and his inner circle decided to use the prevailing climate within Zimbabwe to permanently crush ZAPU as a political or military threat. This would pave the way for Mugabe to achieve his ultimate political goal of establishing a one-party state with him at the helm.

To achieve this, the inner circle expanded the scope of the existing campaign against armed ZIPRA dissidents to also target any Ndebele citizen who was, or might be, a supporter of ZAPU.

In pursuing this objective, Robert Mugabe relied on a core group of hardened senior military and political supporters known as the *'Crocodile Gang.'* This group included both Colonel Perrance Shiri and Emmerson Mnangagwa[147].

Early in 1984, Major Tawanda Nyati was summoned to the 5th Brigade's headquarters in Gweru[148] for a briefing meeting with Colonel Shiri. At this meeting, he and other senior 5th Brigade officers, received very clear orders about the wider scope of the *Gukurahundi*[149] campaign. They were informed that the expanded mission had been developed and endorsed from *"the highest levels"* and that it was now their duty to ensure its swift and effective execution. They were assured that any resources within the Zimbabwe Defence Forces would be made available to them to

---

commander of the Airforce of Zimbabwe. Shiri was influential in orchestrating the 2017 Zimbabwean coup d'état which removed Mugabe from power. On 30th November 2017, Shiri was appointed Minister of Agriculture by President Emmerson Mnangagwa.

[146] Zimbabwe National Army.

[147] Emmerson Mnangagwa was a senior member of ZANLA during the Rhodesian Bush War. Following Zimbabwe's independence in 1980, he was appointed the Minister of State Security in the President's office and oversaw the Central Intelligence Organisation. He would later become the 3rd president of Zimbabwe following the successful 2017 coup which ousted Robert Mugabe.

[148] The name of Gweru during the colonial era had been Gwelo.

[149] *Gukurahundi* is a Shona word which roughly translates as *'the early rain that washes away the chaff before the spring rain'*.

ensure mission success, and that upon completion, the nation and the Prime Minister would forever be indebted to them.

Tawanda lay on his bunk bed in his quarters at the barracks in Lupane. It was an oppressively hot day. Although his quarters had a small fan hanging from the ceiling, it was nearly useless against the relentless heat.

Despite the heat and the thin sheen of sweat on his brow, Tawanda savoured the thought of his company's upcoming mission in Matabeleland North. Although his men had performed admirably in eliminating the remnants of the armed ZIPRA dissidents in and around Matabeleland North, their operations had become increasingly difficult once the ZIPRA dissidents had abandoned their fortified positions in the former Jameson Camp Assembly Point[150] and merged with the local population, many of whom were sympathetic to their grievances.

Tawanda lasciviously licked his lips at the thought of what lay ahead now that their mission had been expanded to include any Ndebele citizen who was, or might be, a supporter of ZAPU.

---

[150] The Jameson Camp Assembly Point was one of the 16 assembly points that had been formed after the Lancaster House agreement prior to the April 1980 elections in Zimbabwe. It was designated for ZIPRA forces and was located in close proximity to Lupane in Matabeleland North Province.

Chapter 15 – Nick and Rachel travel to Mhuka Ranch

Time line – Wednesday, 25th July 1984

The drive from the Great Zimbabwe Ruins[151] to Mhuka[152] Ranch typically took about three hours. However, on this particular day, Nick and Rachel's journey was prolonged by the persistent downpour that had engulfed the area. Uncharacteristically, the typically cool and arid lowveld was now saturated with heavy rain, which compelled Nick to reduce his speed to around 90 kilometres per hour, significantly impeding their progress.

Fortunately, as they approached Buffalo Range on the A10, the weather began to improve, and the rain tapered off. By the time they passed through Buffalo Range, the sky had cleared, revealing a pristine azure expanse overhead, though a lingering chill remained in the air.

With Mhuka Ranch just 35 kilometres beyond Buffalo Range, they bypassed the central hub of Chiredzi, following the A10. After

---

[151] The Great Zimbabwe Ruins is the name of the stone ruins of an ancient city known as Great Zimbabwe. The ruins are located just outside Fort Victoria (now called Masvingo). People lived in Great Zimbabwe from around 1100 but abandoned it in the 15th century. The city was the capital of the Kingdom of Zimbabwe, which was a Shona trading empire. Zimbabwe means "stone houses" in Shona.
[152] A local word meaning animals or wildlife.

crossing a bridge that spanned the Chiredzi River, they turned right onto a dirt road and followed the signposts leading them to Mhuka Ranch.

After navigating the dirt road for another two kilometres, they arrived at the ranch just after 11:00 am. They drove through the security gates into the homestead's parking area, where they were met by Sipho[153], who greeted them with open arms and a warm smile.

"Hello, *Ishe*[154]," beamed Sipho. "It's good to see you again after our catch-up in London last month. I am so glad this lousy weather hasn't delayed you much."

Nick responded, "I understand it's pretty unusual to have such heavy rains in the lowveld in winter, but it wasn't much of a problem. By the time we got to Buffalo Range, the rain had stopped. I'm just glad we weren't travelling on dirt roads during the rain. They would have been as slippery as an eel."

Sipho chuckled at Nick's remark. However, the mention of dirt roads brought back memories of the roadblock incidents he had encountered when recently travelling to visit his parents at Inyathi Mission. He hoped Nick and Rachel had not experienced similar difficulties.

"As long as you had a safe trip," he remarked.

"Yep, the trip was pleasant and without incident, despite the rain," Nick replied.

"That's good. Well, now that you're here, let me tell you what I've arranged. I know when you were last here, you stayed at Ukuthula[155] Lodge, which you loved. So, I've arranged for you to stay there once more. I think we should go there now so you can unpack. Then we'll

---

[153] Sipho is a Ndebele boy's name meaning Gift.
[154] This is a term of respect used by RAR soldiers when referring to their officers.
[155] Ukuthula is the Zulu word for calmness or silence.

come back to the guest wing of the main homestead for lunch. Duncan, Mark, and Jenny will be joining us then."

"Sounds good," said Nick. "You lead the way, and we'll follow."

The access between the main homestead and Ukuthula Lodge was via a well-maintained dirt road, which Nick remembered. It ran in a southerly direction from the main homestead for about eight kilometres, after which they turned left onto a narrow access road that then wound back on itself, leading into the back of the lodge.

On the lodge's right-hand side stood a double carport. Nick and Rachel pulled into the carport and parked next to Sipho's vehicle.

Following Sipho along the paved pathway to the lodge's entrance, Nick and Rachel found themselves cocooned in an umbrella of familiarity and comfort. The lodge's exterior walls were built from natural stone, complemented by a beautifully thatched roof. The solid wooden entrance door opened into a generous foyer, decorated in a rustic-safari style. A few steps led down into a spacious open-plan lounge and dining area.

Though it had been over three years since their last visit, Nick and Rachel were once again enthralled by the lodge's sublime beauty. Adorned with large African soapstone carvings, comfortable sofas and chairs, a grand fireplace, and exquisite African art, the lounge radiated warmth and elegance. The polished concrete floor, dyed in soft browns and clay colours, was adorned with handwoven woollen rugs featuring bold symmetrical patterns in earthy tones.

Opening onto a generous decking area with sunbeds, umbrellas, and a firepit, the deck offered a breathtaking view of the Ingwe[156] Dam to the north, surrounded by heavily treed kopjes. The sight eclipsed their memories.

---

[156] Ingwe is a local African word meaning leopard.

Turning to Sipho, who had followed them onto the deck, Nick remarked, "This is simply stunning. It's a pity we're only here for a week. I think we could stay forever."

Sipho replied, "Yes, it is one of my favourite views on the ranch. But there are many others that are nearly as good. We have now built two other luxury lodges, which also have wonderful views. But, being your honeymoon, I thought you might want to re-experience the loveliness of Ukuthula Lodge. The entire lodge is yours for the next week."

"You are a legend," gushed Rachel. "Now, let me go and remind myself of the wonderful bedroom and bathroom wing."

Sipho led them back into the lounge area and down a light-filled passage branching off from the western wall. This was the bedroom wing, housing two luxurious bedrooms with en-suite bathrooms. Their bedroom, boasting a king-size four-poster bed and a light grey leather sofa, offered stunning views across the dam through north-facing windows. The furniture and décor exuded romance, contrasting with the safari styling of the lounge and dining areas.

The en-suite bathroom featured a free-standing bath and a large double shower. Built into the thatched roof was a glass-paned skylight directly above the bath, allowing guests to gaze up into the star-studded African night sky as they soaked in a hot bath.

"Perfect," gasped Rachel. "Nick and I have been lucky enough to stay in some pretty impressive accommodation since we first met. But Ukuthula is still my favourite."

"I have one last surprise for you," said Sipho. "Samson and Beauty are still employed by us, and when they heard that you and Nick were coming back for your honeymoon, they insisted on taking care of you during your stay. Let's go and find them."

With that, the three of them headed for the kitchen. A short time later, there were shrieks of joy and laughter as Rachel hugged the housekeeper, Beauty, and warmly shook hands with Samson, the cook and waiter.

Interrupting the re-acquaintances, Sipho said, "I will leave you to unpack. When you are ready, please drive back to the homestead. Jenny is expecting you for lunch at about 1:00 pm."

With that, he exited Ukuthula and drove back to the homestead, while Samson collected Nick and Rachel's luggage from their vehicle, and Beauty went to make them a pot of tea.

For a short period, Nick and Rachel were alone in their bedroom. Rachel turned to Nick and gave him a loving hug. "A whole week here with you. It's going to be just wonderful."

Chapter 16 – A week in heaven

The day had warmed up nicely. The early morning rain had cleared, revealing a sparkling, clean, bright blue sky. The fine weather had prompted Jenny to welcome back Nick and Rachel with a braai[157] in the garden, rather than a lunch in the guest wing's dining room. The braai had been set up next to the fenced swimming pool in the well-established front garden. The kitchen staff had arranged garden tables and chairs on the freshly mown front lawn, while the cook was in charge of the braai.

Nick and Rachel arrived at the main homestead, parked in the car park, and followed the paved path leading to the guest wing via the heavily treed eastern side of the main homestead. As they neared the guest wing, Nick's keen sense of smell picked up the unmistakable aroma of braaied steak and boerewors[158].

"Wow, that smell is making me realise how hungry I am," said Nick. "Knowing Jenny, she will have put on an amazing spread."

Jenny greeted them both in the entrance hall of the guest wing. She gave Nick and Rachel warm hugs and said how happy she was to see them again. She then led them through the lounge into the front garden, where the others were gathered.

---

[157] Braai is the Afrikaans word for a BBQ.
[158] Boerewors is a type of spicy sausage which originated in South Africa.

Nick immediately recognised Duncan, who, though now in his early seventies, still looked remarkably fit. His face was tanned but more wrinkled than Nick recalled. His eyes were still bright and clear, and he had a full head of hair, which was now heavily silvered rather than the deep brown it had once been. Despite his age, his movements were still sharp and uninhibited by arthritis or injury.

Duncan hurried over to Nick and Rachel, greeting them warmly. He kissed Rachel on both cheeks and gave Nick a firm, welcoming handshake.

"It's just great having you both back at the ranch," he enthused. "I've been so looking forward to your return, as have Jenny, Mark, and Sipho[159]. And congratulations on your wedding. You two are going to have some fine-looking children."

Rachel blushed but joined in Duncan's playful mood. "Now, don't jump the gun, Duncan. We have only just got married!"

She glanced towards the braai, where Sipho, Mark, and another young man, whom Rachel did not recognise, were engrossed in conversation. "I can see Sipho and Mark over there, but where is Hamish? Is he coming?"

Duncan replied, "No, he won't be joining us. In fact, Hamish has moved to South Africa. He's now living with his brother Tim, along with Tim's wife and their two children, in the Orange Free State. He moved about a year ago. His departure left a significant gap in the cattle ranching and big game hunting sides of the business. Fortunately, we've hired a manager to take care of those areas. His name is Mitch. He's the blond-headed bloke talking to Sipho and Mark."

Rachel and Nick both looked over to the trio by the braai. Mitch stood about six feet tall, with an athletic build. He looked to be in his mid-thirties with an unmistakable mop of blonde hair contrasting against his olive-tanned skin.

---

[159] Sipho is a Ndebele boy's name meaning Gift.

"The departure of Hamish would have been difficult," observed Nick.

"Yes, it sure has been," replied Duncan. "But Mitch has been with us now for about six months, and he is fitting in well. He's from a cattle ranch in Texas and is also passionate about sustainable big game hunting. He's hunted big game both in the States and in quite a few places in Africa. He's a bit of a wanderer. I hope he stays for a few more years. But being single and a bit of an adventurer, I think his time with us may not be as long as I would like."

"That must worry you," said Rachel.

"It sure does," said Duncan. "I'm getting too old to take on any more. In fact, I need to cut down on how much I am already doing, not increase it! And Jenny and Mark are absolutely flat out looking after our three lodges and our wildlife and photographic safaris. They certainly cannot take on any more."

Nick added, "Yes, it sounds like the classic problem of succession planning. Many family-owned and run businesses face those kinds of difficulties."

Duncan nodded thoughtfully. "Well, I'm glad Mark and Jenny are still here. Despite the difficulties we're facing in Zimbabwe, they seem pretty determined to hang in there. Mark, too, is concerned with succession planning and has finally persuaded me to take it seriously. In fact, at his insistence, we've started speaking with Sipho to see if he can be persuaded to take an equity interest in the business. Not that we are looking for any significant investment from him. What we want is a solid commitment for him to remain with us. He has done a terrific job with the rhino conservancy. If we can give him a financial interest in the business, I'm sure he will stay. I'm hopeful that we will be able to conclude our discussions with him within the next month. But that's enough of business talk. Come with me. Let's get a drink, and I'll introduce you both to Mitch."

With that, Duncan wandered across to the braai. Nick took Rachel's hand and followed Duncan. But his mind was in a whirl. Duncan's discussion about the ranch's difficulties made Nick wonder if this might be an opportunity for Rare Quest Imports. He made a mental note to discuss this with Rachel later.

Nick's contemplations were interrupted by Duncan, who introduced him to Mitch. "Mitch," he said, "I would like to introduce you to Nick and Rachel, who are visiting from the UK. It's their honeymoon, and we are absolutely delighted to be hosting them here at Ukuthula[160] Lodge. I'm sure you've heard us speak about their last visit in 1981. That is when they helped in the elimination of those three poachers who were attempting to destroy our rhino conservancy even before it had begun!"

Mitch grinned widely and drawled, "Well, howdy there, y'all! It's just downright great to finally meet ya. I heard all about your adventures back in 1981 when you were at the ranch. Mighty impressive, I must say. Now, I reckon Sipho might not have yet had a chance to fill you in on how our rhino conservancy and breeding programme has been goin' since then. But let me tell ya, it's been one heck of a ride. A real success story, if you ask me."

Nick glanced at Rachel with a raised eyebrow. Then he shook Mitch's hand vigorously and told him what a pleasure it was to meet him.

Duncan made his excuses and left Nick, Rachel, Sipho, Mark, and Mitch to continue their discussions.

Rachel smiled at Mitch, then turned to Sipho and said, "I am dying to learn more about the progress of the rhino programme. How big is the herd now?"

Sipho's face lit up, clearly passionate about the topic. "It's amazing," he said. "We now have 60 black rhinos on the ranch — 35 bulls and 25 cows. We're almost at the top end of our carrying capacity, which is 50 to 75 animals. The bulls include the Two Ronnies[161], who arrived back in August 1981 when you and Nick were here. The really exciting

---

[160] Ukuthula is the Zulu word for calmness or silence.
[161] Mhuka Ranch's first two male black rhinos had been named the Two Ronnies after the British comedic duo consisting of Ronnie Barker and Ronnie Corbett which aired on the BBC in the UK from 1971 to 1987.

news is that four of the cows are pregnant, all conceived here on the ranch. The vet thinks two are about six months into their pregnancies, while the other two are closer to twelve months. So, we're expecting the first calves to be born later this year or early next year. It's really exciting."

Rachel clapped her hands in joy. "That is so wonderful," she said. "I am so happy for you and for the Department of National Parks. I wonder who the sires were? Maybe the Two Ronnies? And did you say that the pregnancies of the four cows have been verified by a vet?"

Sipho replied, "Yes, we're lucky to have a vet from South Africa who specialises in rhinos. Her name is Vanessa van Reenan." He smiled and added, "Even though she's an expert, I doubt she can tell who the sires are, but I'm happy to assume it was the Two Ronnies! She visits the ranch every four months to check on the rhinos and stays for a couple of days before flying back. The ranch's airstrip makes it easy for her to come and go. The Department of National Parks covers the cost, and the Department of Immigration has simplified her entry requirements. Everything's running really well."

Rachel then asked, "There must be real hope that the black rhino population in Zimbabwe will now recover?"

Sipho paused for a moment, then said, "As far as the recovery of the black rhinos is concerned, I think we have definitely turned the corner. But we need to remember that the rhino breeding conservancies established by the Zimbabwean Government are well protected. Without such protection, the poachers will return. So, we need to stay alert. I am pleased to say that the anti-poaching ranger squad we have set up here at the ranch is outstanding. We are very proud of it, and I am looking forward to showing it to you."

"That will be wonderful," Rachel said. "When do you think we can do that?"

"Well," said Sipho, "If it's okay with you and Nick, I would like to take you on an early morning game drive tomorrow. After that, we can visit the rangers' barracks. They have a few pre-arranged activities starting at noon, so you can join me for those. Is that alright?"

Rachel looked at Nick, who gave her a thumbs up.

"There's your answer," she said. "I cannot wait."

"Roger," said Sipho. "Sunrise is at 5:45 am, so I will pick you up at Ukuthula at 6:15 am."

By now, lunch was ready. The cook had done a splendid job. The barbecued meat, salads, grilled tomatoes, and onions were delicious. He had also prepared a small pot of sadza[162]. Rachel accepted a spoonful and Nick showed her how to roll it into a ball before dipping it into the tomato and onion sauce. She quickly got the knack and absolutely loved it.

They spent the rest of the afternoon relaxing at the guest wing, chatting with the Olivers, Sipho, and Mitch, before driving back to Ukuthula Lodge, arriving around 5:30 pm. The sun was rapidly sinking, and it was getting decidedly chilly.

Samson had thoughtfully lit an inviting fire in the firepit on the deck, and the logs were burning brightly. Nick and Rachel collected a cashmere throw from their bedroom, made their way to the deck, and huddled close to the fire to warm themselves.

Upon their arrival, Beauty had made Nick and Rachel a cup of tea, which she now brought to them on the decking. Nick and Rachel cuddled next to each other on the bench surrounding the firepit with the cashmere throw draped over their shoulders.

Beauty asked them what they would like Samson to prepare for dinner. They had both eaten well at lunch and weren't hungry. They let Beauty know that they would not be needing dinner but requested a cold bottle of chardonnay and a plate of biltong, after which she and Samson could take the rest of the evening off.

---

[162] Sadza is a thickened porridge made with white maize meal. It is one of the staple foods in Zimbabwe.

Shortly afterward, Beauty returned carrying a silver serving tray. On it were the wine, a bucket of ice with tongs, two crystal long-stemmed wine glasses, a plate of sliced biltong, a wedge of cheddar cheese, crackers, and a jar of quince paste. Beauty placed the tray on the table near the firepit and said goodnight.

Once she had left, Nick poured a glass of wine for himself and Rachel, and they sat together in silence, taking in the beauty of the scene before them. Every now and then, they would help themselves to a slice of biltong or cut a piece of cheddar and place it on a cracker with a smudge of quince paste.

The sun quickly sank below the western shores of the dam, and darkness began to envelop the surroundings. As the darkness deepened, the lights from the lodge and the gas lamps on the decking seemed to beckon the wilderness of the bush to the safety and warmth of the haven that the Olivers had created in this little paradise.

Nick and Rachel remained on the deck, wrapped in the blanket of love they felt for each other. Very few words were spoken between them. Instead, they simply gazed into the night skies, appreciating that there was perhaps no more transcendent experience than looking up at an African night sky filled with an abundance of shining stars. The sky, though dark, was clear and pure. With no lights to detract from the stars, their view of the heavens was unobstructed and expansive.

Rachel snuggled into Nick and, with a twinkle in her blue eyes, said, "This is so lovely and romantic. But I am getting a little cold, and we are all alone. Let's go inside and have a bath to warm up."

Nick leaned into her and gave her a tender kiss on the lips. "Sounds like the perfect way to end a magical day. Why don't you go and run the bath? I will be right behind you."

Rachel slipped off the bench and went inside. Nick remained on the deck for a few minutes, soaking up the sounds and smells of the African bush at night. They quieted his mind and soothed his soul.

After a few minutes, he got up and walked through the French door leading to their bedroom and ensuite bathroom.

By now, Rachel was lying back in the bubble-filled bath. She looked gorgeous and particularly alluring, and Nick was immediately aroused. He undressed and climbed into the bath. The tub was large enough for them to lie side by side. They gazed up through the glass-paned skylight into the star-filled night skies, gently stroking each other's arms. Gradually, their passions were aroused. They climbed out of the bath, dried each other with the soft towels, and then snuggled into their enormous four-poster bed.

The warmth of their bodies against each other quickly overcame the coolness of the bed linen. It did not take long for their passions to be rekindled. The rekindling quickly grew to a hot passion, culminating in them climaxing together and then collapsing in a spent heap.

Afterward, they brushed their teeth, changed into their pyjamas, and snuggled back under the bed linen. They lay there in each other's arms, feeling safe and at peace, oblivious to the terror unfolding in nearby Matabeleland.

Chapter 17 – Nature's bounty

The following morning was bitterly cold, the air sharp with the chill of pre-dawn darkness. At 5:30 am, Nick and Rachel's alarm clock jolted them awake — a time they would normally still be fast asleep. Braving the cold, they took a steaming hot shower and followed it with a comforting cup of tea. By 6:10 am, they were bundled up and eagerly awaiting Sipho's[163] arrival.

As promised, Sipho pulled up in his Land Rover just before 6:15 am, the gentle toot of his horn marking his arrival. Nick and Rachel exited the lodge, locked the door behind them, and settled into the back seats of the vehicle. The morning air was biting cold, prompting Sipho to keep the vehicle's soft-top closed for warmth.

"Morning, all," greeted Sipho with a warm smile. "Glad to see you're dressed warmly. It'll stay cold until about 9:00 am, but I've got some rugs and gloves on the back seat for you. Once you're warmed up, we'll roll back the canvas roof so we can enjoy the sun and breeze."

"You think of everything," said Rachel. "You're a star."

Sipho chuckled modestly. "Just keeping my customers happy. But the morning should be clear and fine. Let's hope we see a lot of game."

---

[163] Sipho is a Ndebele boy's name meaning Gift.

As dawn began to paint the horizon with hues of pink and gold, Sipho expertly navigated the rugged terrain, his keen eyes scanning for wildlife. Nick and Rachel, wrapped in blankets with their hands gloved in mittens, eagerly joined in the search, though they knew Sipho would likely be the first to spot anything of note.

Rachel was particularly excited by the game drive. She still had very fond memories of the drives she had experienced with Nick back in 1981. Her eyes scoured the bush desperately seeking out any sign of wildlife. Everyone in the vehicle was quiet. The only sound was the soft murmur of the engine and the heart-warming calls of awakening birds. Their melodic songs grew steadily in number, creating a symphony of sound in the stillness of the morning.

Suddenly, a majestic silhouette emerged from the shadows — a large black rhino, its massive form illuminated by the gentle glow of sunrise. Nick and Rachel watched in awe as the magnificent creature moved gracefully through the tall grass, its horns, particularly the long front one, catching the soft light. As quickly as it had appeared, it vanished into a dense thicket of long grass and thorny bushes.

As the morning light grew stronger, the landscape came alive. Herds of impala raced gracefully across the dry bushland, blending seamlessly with the savannah's golden hues. In the distance, a family of elephants ambled leisurely towards a watering hole, led by the quiet authority of the herd's matriarch.

Then, a throaty roar echoed through the stillness of the morning — the unmistakable call of a lion, rumbling with its authoritative declaration of power. Sipho guided the vehicle towards the source of the sound, and soon they found themselves in the presence of Africa's most iconic predator. Its darkened mane shimmered in the soft light as it surveyed its domain with regal indifference. The magnificent lion remained unconcerned as the vehicle inched closer, allowing Nick and Rachel to capture the moment with their cameras.

As the sun climbed higher, casting a warm glow over the surroundings, they became fully immersed in nature's raw beauty. Buffalo grazed peacefully by the water's edge, their powerful frames silhouetted against the shimmering surface of the lake, and the casual flick of their ears chasing away the ever-present flies. Above them, various birds of prey, including a yellow-billed kite and a martial eagle, soared on unseen updrafts, hunting for prey with their sharp eyes.

They also spotted a large flock of vividly coloured southern carmine bee-eaters nesting in the clumped bushes along the banks of a small riverbed meandering across the ranch. Their bright red plumage and long tail feathers created a stunning splash of colour against the dry, brown bush.

All these sights were expertly explained by Sipho, who seemed to have developed an encyclopaedic knowledge of the flora and fauna found in this part of Zimbabwe.

Just when they thought the morning could hold no more wonders, they came upon a scene that took their breath away — a leopard, sleek and sinuous, perched gracefully in the branches of a large acacia tree. Below the leopard, the lifeless form of a small impala hung limply draped over a branch, a silent testament to the cycle of life and death in the heart of the African bush. Rachel used her camera's powerful telescopic lens to zoom in on the animal, capturing its blood-stained nose, jaws, and cheeks.

As they watched in awe, the leopard met their gaze with unblinking eyes that burned with primal intensity, offering a fleeting glimpse into the untamed soul of the wild. In that moment, amidst the beauty and magnificence of the African bush, Nick and Rachel felt a connection to nature beyond words — a bond forged in the ancient and fickle crucible of the untamed wilderness.

In this unhurried manner, the morning gradually ebbed away. Sipho took his time, allowing Nick and Rachel to absorb each special moment in this garden of paradise. At about 11:00 am, when the sun was high in the sky, having warmed up the day, they parked under the shade of a large marula tree. Sipho took out a picnic basket from the rear of the vehicle. From it, he poured them all a cup of coffee and handed them each a brown paper bag containing a ham and tomato sandwich, an orange, and a small bar of milk chocolate. The excitement of the morning had stimulated their appetites, and these unexpected treats took the edge off their hunger.

After morning tea, they slowly made their way back to Sipho's house, located on the northern side of Ingwe[164] Dam. They parked in the carport alongside his home. Sipho pointed out a long low building a short distance from the house, explaining that it was the barracks for the ten rangers employed by the ranch. Close to the barracks was a nicely lawned soccer pitch on which a squad of men were gathered.

Sipho told them that the rangers were about to begin their daily lunchtime exercises. He invited Nick and Rachel to come and witness these, and they all walked over to the soccer pitch.

The squad of rangers was assembled in front of an instructor. The instructor, a tough-looking man with a shiny bald head, was barking out orders to the men who were gathered in front of him. The squad executed his instructions with precision, like a well-choreographed machine. Nick couldn't help but draw parallels to his own military past, particularly as he observed the mutual respect between the instructor and his men.

The instructor's presence brought a pang of nostalgic sadness to Nick, reminding him of Gideon, his former platoon sergeant. Gideon had been tragically killed when Nick's platoon was ambushed by terrorists in the Chimanimani mountains, just before the end of the Rhodesian Bush War.

Sipho told them that the instructor and all the rangers were ex-RAR[165] soldiers whom he had recruited following his appointment as the ranch's anti-poaching manager. The men were a mix of Ndebele and Shona, but the instructor, Lungelo Moyo, was Ndebele. Like Sipho, Lungelo Moyo had expected to be integrated into the new ZNA[166] following the end of the Rhodesian Bush War but had

---

[164] Ingwe is a local African word meaning leopard.
[165] Rhodesian African Rifles.
[166] Zimbabwe National Army.

experienced significant tribal discrimination due to his Ndebele ethnicity. When Sipho advertised for a senior instructor to join his anti-poaching squad, Lungelo applied and was interviewed by both Sipho and Duncan. He was thrilled to subsequently learn that his application had been successful and that the position was his.

"What's with the exercise drill at noon?" asked Nick. "I would have thought these would be done early in the morning."

"The whole squad exercises at 6:00 am daily, with the exception of Sundays," replied Sipho. "Then, those men not on patrol have a second exercise drill at noon. We find a midday session helps keep the men who are in the barracks on their toes. Today, none of the men are on patrol because they're all receiving training on environmental conservation. This covers biodiversity, ecosystem management, and the role of rangers in protecting natural resources. It's crucial for our work, especially with the ranch's wildlife and photographic safaris."

"Well, I'm impressed," said Nick. "I couldn't believe how knowledgeable you were during the game drive today."

"Thanks, Nick. I need to set a good example for the men," said Sipho. "But I'm lucky. Duncan and Hamish have taught me much. And Lungelo Moyo is an absolute fundi[167] on Zimbabwean birdlife."

Nick, Rachel, and Sipho joined the rangers in the dining room at the barracks for lunch. Sipho wanted to give them both better insight into what garrison life was like for the rangers. The food served for lunch was typical African fare — sadza with relish sauce and stewed meat. Simple but nourishing. Nick was surprised by how much Rachel enjoyed eating the sadza in the traditional manner – rolling it into a ball and dipping it in the relish.

"Eating with your hands," he chuckled. "Your parents would have a fit. So much for your English public school education!"

---

[167] This is a South African slang term meaning a person who has gained a lot of knowledge about a particular subject.

"Well, you know what they say, 'When in Rome, do as the Romans do'," she replied.

Nick smiled, but Sipho looked confused.

"Don't worry," said Nick. "It's just an old English saying, which means you should follow local customs."

"I'm glad you clarified," said Sipho. "I didn't understand why we were suddenly talking about Rome!"

After lunch, the trio excused themselves from the ongoing garrison activities. Sipho then took them to tour the other two luxury lodges and to experience one of the bird hides.

Like Ukuthula[168] Lodge, the two other lodges had been built into the kopjes, harmonising with the natural landscape so well that, if Sipho had not been with them, Nick and Rachel might have easily overlooked them. Both lodges were occupied, so Sipho was unable to show Nick and Rachel their interiors. However, from the outside, it was clear that the lodges had been built, decorated, and furnished to the same exacting standards as Ukuthula Lodge. Sipho was full of praise for Jenny and Mark, who had overseen their construction and were now responsible for this side of the business. He explained how important ecotourism was to the success and profitability of the business.

From the lodges, Sipho took them to one of the six bird hides constructed on the ranch. This one had been built among the reeds and bushes on the banks of the northern shore of Ingwe Dam.

By now, it was late afternoon, and the golden hues of the sun gently bathed the dam's northern shore. The trio quietly crept into the well-concealed bird hide. Nick and Rachel had their cameras slung over their shoulders. Once they settled into the hide, the sounds of nature surrounded them — the gentle rustle of leaves, the occasional call of birds, and the rhythmic lapping of water against the shore. Suddenly,

---

[168] Ukuthula is the Zulu word for calmness or silence.

their attention was drawn to a flurry of activity nearby as a black-masked yellow weaver bird meticulously wove slender strands of grass and twigs, building its nest with remarkable precision. Mesmerised by the bird's industriousness and architectural finesse, Nick and Rachel captured the moment with their cameras. In the tranquil sanctuary of the bird hide, surrounded by the wonders of the natural world, they listened carefully as Sipho, in a quiet but knowledgeable voice, explained the breeding habits and incredible weaving skills of this iconic Zimbabwean bird.

Afterwards, they returned to the guest wing for a sundowner before heading back to Ukuthula Lodge, where Samson had prepared a delicious evening meal for them.

Over dinner, Nick and Rachel discussed the wonderful day they had just enjoyed. Both were hugely impressed by what they had seen, particularly Sipho's dedication and passion for his new role.

Their conversation led Nick to recall Duncan's earlier concerns about succession planning for Mhuka[169] Ranch. Duncan had mentioned the challenge of ensuring the ranch's long-term viability and how they were considering offering Sipho an equity interest in the business as part of their strategy.

Nick set down his knife and fork, a thoughtful expression on his face. "Do you remember Duncan mentioning how crucial it was for him and his family to finalise a succession plan for Mhuka Ranch? He also mentioned that they were considering offering Sipho an equity interest."

"Yes, I remember," Rachel responded. "I was quite impressed with their foresight in thinking about succession planning. Offering Sipho an equity stake is a smart move. He's clearly deeply invested in Mhuka Ranch and is an exceptionally intelligent young man. Securing him for the future of the ranch is a wise decision."

---

[169] Mhuka is a local word meaning animals or wildlife.

"Exactly," Nick agreed. "But I also think there might be a role for RQI[170] to play in this."

Rachel looked curious. "What do you mean?"

Nick explained, "Well, you recall your father's belief that southern Africa, including Zimbabwe, will face significant political, economic, and social challenges in the coming years. These challenges are likely to deter investors, causing a flight of capital to safer havens."

"Yes, I understand his concerns," Rachel said. "So, what are you thinking?"

"I agree that offering Sipho an equity stake is a brilliant idea," Nick said. "However, I doubt Sipho could afford to pay the full value for any shares the Olivers might offer him. But, what if the Olivers sold one-third of their business to Sipho and another third to RQI? If Sipho couldn't afford his share, RQI could cover the cost as a low-interest-bearing loan to him. This loan could be forgiven over time — say, 10% per year of service. After ten years, the loan would be fully forgiven. This way, Mhuka Ranch would receive cash upfront, and Sipho would be committed to the business long term, which would address Duncan's succession concerns."

"What about RQI's third?" Rachel asked.

"RQI would pay a fair value for its share," Nick said. "We can handle this payment from the UK, which would give Duncan access to external funds — a significant advantage for him. If this plan goes ahead, the Olivers would keep one-third, Sipho would buy one-third, and RQI would own the remaining third. This also fits with Stuart's strategy of investing in high-value tourist facilities in select parts of Africa and Asia. Mhuka Ranch is a perfect match for that strategy."

Rachel took a moment to consider. "What a fantastic idea. It aligns perfectly with Dad's philanthropic ideals. I know he has already donated to Mhuka Ranch, but your proposal is more substantial and

---

[170] Rare Quest Imports.

sustainable. It benefits everyone and ensures a long-term future for Mhuka Ranch. You're brilliant!"

Nick chuckled. "The only real risk for RQI would be if the three shareholders fell out. If that happened, the Olivers and Sipho could potentially outvote RQI. However, even in that case, RQI's financial interest would be safeguarded, as the Olivers and Sipho would need to buy us out at fair value."

Rachel clapped her hands excitedly. "It would also mean that you and I, along with Mum and Dad, would be even more motivated to visit Zimbabwe regularly. And we'd have the joy of staying here. I'm eager for you to share your ideas with Sipho, the Olivers, and my parents."

Chapter 18 – RQI looks to invest in Mhuka Ranch

Their remaining days at Mhuka[171] Ranch were as fulfilling as the first few days had been. Each morning, Sipho[172] was available to take Nick and Rachel on a game-viewing drive. The *honeymooners* looked forward to these early morning excursions. Each day, they gleaned new insights from Sipho. Not only was he extremely knowledgeable about all the game on the ranch, but he also possessed a deep understanding of birdlife, trees, wildflowers, and insects.

One morning, they were following the tracks of a herd of elephants making their way across the ranch. Sipho stopped to examine some elephant droppings to assess their freshness. The droppings had already caught the attention of dung beetles, and Sipho took the time to educate Rachel about these industrious cleaners of the bush. Three dung beetles were already atop the elephant dung, busily rolling it into balls and moving them along the ground. Rachel asked Sipho what the beetles were doing.

Sipho replied, "They're rolling the dung balls to their nests underground, where they'll store them for food and lay their eggs in them. This helps break down the dung, releasing nutrients like nitrogen, phosphorus, and potassium into the soil, which other plants

---

[171] A local word meaning animals or wildlife.
[172] Sipho is a Ndebele boy's name meaning Gift.

and trees can use. Dung beetles are important for recycling nutrients in the ecosystem. Plus, some of them eat the eggs and larvae of pests like flies that breed in dung, helping to control these pests and keep the balance in nature."

On another day, they spent nearly the entire morning in an elephant hide, located about 20 metres from one of the ranch's. They arrived mid-morning, once the day had warmed up nicely. Initially, no game of interest was at the waterhole, but after patiently waiting for about 30 minutes, they were rewarded when a large herd of elephants arrived. The herd included two adult cows with their calves. Rachel was thrilled as she watched the cows use their maternal instincts to keep the young calves safe and teach them how to lick the salt blocks that Sipho's rangers regularly placed at the waterhole. Sipho explained that the salt blocks provided elephants with essential minerals like sodium, potassium, calcium, and magnesium, crucial for their overall health, especially for young calves. That was why the breeding cows were diligent in ensuring their calves quickly learned to lick the salt blocks.

The young calves also seemed to enjoy rolling around in the mud. Rachel asked Sipho why they did this. Since it was not a hot day, she assumed the mud baths were not merely for cooling off. Sipho explained that rolling in the mud created a protective layer on the elephants' skin, helping to repel biting insects such as mosquitoes and flies. He added that, in hot weather, the mud also acted as a natural sunscreen, protecting the elephants' skin from the sun's harmful UV[173] rays.

They also spent considerable time in the various bird hides around the ranch. Sipho taught them about the wide variety of birds that frequented the ranch. One of Rachel's favourites was the lilac-breasted roller, which had stunning plumage in a vibrant mix of lilac, turquoise, blue, green, and chestnut. It was a beautiful bird to photograph. From the bird hide, both Nick and Rachel captured stunning close-up photos of this pretty bird.

---

[173] Ultraviolet.

Sipho also took the time to show Nick and Rachel the lilac-breasted rollers in flight. They were captivated as they watched these birds perform magnificent aerial manoeuvres, including twists, turns, and dives. Sipho explained that this agility made them fearsome hunters of insects, small lizards, and frogs.

On yet another day, one of the anti-poaching rangers received intelligence from a local villager that a group of three poachers had trespassed onto the ranch and were now encamped near the ranch's southern boundary. The report indicated that the poachers were only armed with low-calibre rifles, suggesting they were not targeting big game. Nick and Rachel watched as Sipho withdrew FN[174] rifles from the ranch's armoury, mobilised a team of six men plus himself, and deployed them by vehicle to the location where the poachers were encamped. The poachers were alerted by the approaching vehicle and attempted to flee. Sipho split the squad into two groups — one led by Lungelo Moyo, who pursued the poachers on foot, while Sipho and the second group attempted to outflank them in vehicles, positioning themselves a couple of kilometres beyond the poachers' line of flight, where they set up a stop group.

Fortunately, Lungelo Moyo's rangers apprehended the fleeing poachers before they reached the stop group. The captured poachers were handcuffed and handed over to the police, whom Sipho had alerted by radio at the start of the pursuit. Consequently, a small detachment from the Chiredzi police station arrived shortly after the apprehension to take the poachers into custody for detention and processing.

Overall, the operation had been very smooth. Nick asked Sipho if such encroachments by poachers were common.

Sipho replied, "These days, it's rare, but that wasn't the case two or three years ago. Fortunately, our team has always been good at catching poachers. I think word has gotten around that if you come

---

[174] This was a light automatic rifle designed in Belgium and manufactured by FN Herstal. The FN had been the standard issue rifle for the Rhodesian Security Forces.

to Mhuka Ranch with criminal intentions, you'll be caught. And if needed, we're not afraid to use lethal force. If poachers shoot at us or are about to, we respond with overwhelming force. It's the only way to stop these *isilimas*[175]. Thankfully, the Chiredzi police are now very supportive. We've spent much time explaining our tactics and methods to them, and now there's real trust and respect between us. It's been hard work, but well worth it."

*****

Nick and Rachel were due to leave the ranch on Wednesday, 1st August. On the prior Tuesday, Jenny arranged a farewell dinner for them at the main homestead, and Sipho was also invited. Nick had not yet spoken to Sipho or the Olivers about his plans for both Sipho and Rare Quest Imports (RQI) to be part of the succession plan for Mhuka Ranch. He wanted to speak to Sipho before discussing it with the Olivers. He and Rachel decided they would speak with him on the morning of Tuesday, 31st July, and, assuming he was open to Nick's suggestions, they would then raise the matter with the Olivers that night at dinner.

Accordingly, they invited Sipho to join them for coffee at Ukuthula[176] Lodge on Tuesday morning at 10:00 am. Upon his arrival, the three of them went out onto the deck into the warm sunshine. Rachel asked Beauty to bring them all coffee and biscuits, and they sat around one of the tables on the deck.

Nick explained his thoughts to Sipho, detailing how his plan would ensure the long-term future of Mhuka Ranch, give Sipho a meaningful equity interest in the business, meet the Olivers' objective of establishing a workable succession plan in which Sipho would play an important role, and improve the business's working capital. He clarified that if Sipho could not raise the necessary funds to purchase his one-third interest in the business, RQI[177] would cover

---

[175] *Isilima* is a Ndebele word meaning idiot.
[176] Ukuthula is the Zulu word for calmness or silence.
[177] Rare Quest Imports.

this as a low-interest-bearing loan, which would be forgiven at a rate of 10% per year. After ten years, Sipho would own his shares outright. He also explained the benefits RQI could offer beyond financial support, such as marketing the business to high-value customers in the UK and Europe. Nick made it clear that he would only approach the Olivers if Sipho was happy with the proposal. If Sipho agreed, he and Nick would present the proposal to the Olivers over dinner that night. Nick also stressed that everything would be contingent on Stuart Dixon's views, and that he would only discuss the proposal with Stuart if he received the green light from both Sipho and the Olivers.

Throughout Nick's explanation, Sipho remained attentive and thoughtful, occasionally asking insightful questions and seeking clarification.

After Nick finished his presentation, Sipho was quiet for a moment before his face broke into a wide grin. "Nick, that sounds like a great idea," he said. "The proposal seems very fair to me. If the Olivers agree, I'm definitely in. This deal is exactly what Mhuka and I need. I love it here, but I don't have the money to buy into the business, and I've been worried about how to respond to Duncan's offer. Now you've given me the perfect solution. Thank you, *Ishe*[178]. After all the bad news from Matabeleland, your words have brought me much happiness."

He stood up, shook Nick's hand earnestly, gave Rachel a generous hug, and said, "Here's to us all becoming partners in Mhuka."

"Our pleasure," replied Nick. "But let's not get ahead of ourselves. We still need to discuss this with the Olivers and Stuart."

"Yes, I understand," said Sipho. "But everything is going to work out. I feel it in my bones."

That night at dinner, Sipho, Nick, and Rachel presented Nick's proposal to Duncan, Mark, and Jenny. Although Nick had anticipated

---

[178] This is a term of respect used by RAR soldiers when referring to their officers.

that Duncan might eventually be persuaded of the proposal's merits, he was surprised by the enthusiasm with which not only Duncan, but also Mark and Jenny, responded to his suggestions. Duncan and Mark asked a few questions, but none were of real importance. Overall, they all seemed to have a very good grasp of the proposal and its implications for the relevant parties.

After the round-table discussion, Duncan summarised the group's views by saying, "I think we can all agree that we are very supportive of Nick's proposals. Nick will now discuss these with Stuart Dixon. If Stuart is on board, Nick will ask RQI's lawyers to draft the relevant contracts for our further consideration. Their lawyers will communicate with my lawyers in Bulawayo, whom I will brief later this week. My lawyers will ensure that copies of all draft contracts are distributed to me, Jenny, Mark, and Sipho. I know my lawyers have fax capabilities, and Nick has advised that RQI also has these capabilities. This means we will be able to communicate by fax, which will help bring this matter to a speedy conclusion."

Duncan opened a bottle of wine for a celebratory drink, and a little later, everyone made their way home for a good night's sleep.

The following morning, Wednesday, 1st August, Nick and Rachel bade farewell to the Olivers and Sipho and began their return trip to Harare. They were still elated about the potential future arrangements at Mhuka Ranch between the Olivers, Sipho, and RQI. Their Jubilation fuelled their drive back to Harare.

Sipho, Duncan, Jenny, and Mark were also bubbling with excitement about this new chapter in Mhuka Ranch's development. Their enthusiasm overshadowed any lingering concerns about the horrors still unfolding in Matabeleland. Little did they know that these horrors would soon reach Inyathi Mission[179] and have a direct and immediate impact on Sipho.

---

[179] The mission had been established by the Reverend Robert Moffat in 1859

Chapter 19 – Tightening the noose

You will recall that in August 1983, Major Tawanda Nyati had been transferred from ZNA's 3rd Brigade based in Mutare[180] to the newly formed 5th Brigade, which was rapidly gaining unfortunate notoriety. His transfer was at the request of Colonel Perrance Shiri[181], the inaugural commander of the 5th Brigade. Upon his transfer, Major Tawanda was posted to the 5th Brigade's 2nd Battalion and stationed in Lupane, Matabeleland.

Colonel Shiri had first encountered Major Nyati when they were both at the Tanzanian military training school, Morogoro, during the Rhodesian Bush War. Years later, Shiri requested Nyati's transfer to the 5th Brigade in recognition of his exemplary service with ZANLA during the war. Shiri believed that Nyati's expertise would help the 5th Brigade complete its mission to suppress perceived military and

---

[180] The name of Mutare during the colonial era had been Umtali.
[181] Perrance Shiri was distantly related to Rogert Mugabe. After independence, he commanded the 5th Brigade from 1983 to 1984. In 1992 he was appointed the commander of the Airforce of Zimbabwe. Shiri was influential in orchestrating the 2017 Zimbabwean coup d'état which removed Mugabe from power. On 30th November 2017, Shiri was appointed Minister of Agriculture by President Emmerson Mnangagwa.

political threats from ZIPRA[182] dissidents and ZAPU[183] supporters against Robert Mugabe's ruling ZANU-PF[184] Government.

Under Colonel Shiri's command, the 5th Brigade had effectively neutralised many of these threats through brutal and extreme tactics. However, this indiscriminate violence had resulted in the deaths, torture, and beatings of many innocent Ndebele citizens, leading to accusations of human rights abuses and atrocities.

Robert Mugabe was beginning to face international and internal pressures to address these allegations. While acknowledging that the actions of the 5th Brigade had, in some instances, gone too far, he also recognised their effectiveness in countering ZAPU. With the upcoming general elections in 1985, Mugabe remained resolute in his determination to neutralise any political threats from ZAPU.

In an attempt to quell criticisms of his government, it is speculated that confidential discussions between Mugabe and Shiri took place in 1984, during which Shiri agreed to step down from his command of the 5th Brigade. In return, Mugabe promised to facilitate Shiri's appointment to other prestigious positions within the Zimbabwe Defence Forces.

Additionally, it was agreed that changes were necessary to the 5th Brigade's operational tactics to minimise the possibility of further international complaints while maintaining the Brigade's proven effectiveness.

During the subsequent review of these tactics, several adjustments were identified. Significant operations would now be preceded by intensive cordoning off of the operational area to prevent unauthorised entry or exit. Telecommunications to the operational area would be cut off to control the media's access to information.

---

[182] Zimbabwe People's Revolutionary Army. ZIPRA was the military wing of ZAPU.
[183] Zimbabwe African People's Union.
[184] Zimbabwe African National Union – Patriotic Front. ZANU-PF is a political organisation that has been the ruling party of Zimbabwe since independence in 1980.

Food curfews would be imposed to regulate food supplies, allowing only those supplies sanctioned by ZANU-PF to enter the area. This *weaponisation* of food would give the 5th Brigade another blunt but effective tool to use against local civilians.

Dissenters would be detained and relocated to centralised re-education centres instead of being summarily executed. Furthermore, intelligence efforts would be enhanced to identify high-value targets perceived as threats to ZANU-PF.

Inyathi Mission School[185], approximately 75 kilometres north-north-east of Bulawayo, had already been identified as a location of interest due to its historical significance as a breeding ground for African nationalists. Notable Shona figures such as Colonel Perrance Shiri and Emmerson Mnangagwa[186] had been educated there. However, several high-profile individuals of Ndebele ethnicity had also been educated at the school, including Lookout Masuku[187] and Dumiso Dabengwa[188]. Both had been arrested in 1982 for alleged treason. According to intelligence provided by the CIO[189], there was a strong likelihood of former ZIPRA cadres and active ZAPU officials still residing in and around the Inyathi Mission area.

In early July 1984, before his transfer out of the 5th Brigade, Colonel Shiri had radioed Major Tawanda Nyati with the latest intelligence

---

[185] The mission had been established by the Reverend Robert Moffat in 1859. It is situated some 75 kilometres north-north-east of Bulawayo. Moffat was a member of the London Missionary Society, which had been established in England with the aim of spreading the knowledge of Christ among heathen and unenlightened nations.
[186] Emmerson Mnangagwa was a senior member of ZANLA during the Rhodesian Bush War. Following Zimbabwe's independence in 1980, he was appointed the Minister of State Security in the President's office and oversaw the Central Intelligence Organisation. He would later become the 3rd president of Zimbabwe following the successful 2017 coup which ousted Robert Mugabe.
[187] Lookout Masuku was the commander of ZIPRA during the Rhodesian Bush War. After independence, he served as deputy commander of the Zimbabwe National Army until his arrest in 1982 for allegedly plotting to overthrow Robert Mugabe.
[188] ZIPRA's intelligence chief during the Rhodesian Bush War and for a short time thereafter. In 1982 he was charged with treason by the Mugabe administration and arrested.
[189] Zimbabwe's Central Intelligence Organisation.

from the CIO. Shiri ordered Nyati to redeploy his company to the Inyathi Mission area and prepare for an immediate cordon and search operation. This would be a prelude to an extensive operation to cleanse the area of what he referred to as Ndebele *'filth'*.

It was elements of Major Nyati's men that Sipho encountered on 14th July 1984 at the roadblock just before Inyathi Mission School. The 5th Brigade troops manning the roadblock had allowed Sipho to proceed to the school only after he produced a letter signed by Colonel Emanuel Wushe verifying his legitimacy.

Over the next two weeks, Major Nyati strengthened the cordon around the area and began enforcing a harsh food curfew. With food now scarce, he believed it was now time to eradicate the area of the so-called Ndebele *filth*.

He wickedly licked his lips at the thought of what lay ahead.

Chapter 20 – The murder of Sipho's parents

Time line – Thursday, 2nd August 1984

The morning air was crisp, and the sky was still veiled in the soft light of dawn as the rumble of armoured vehicles echoed through the sleepy village. Three menacing vehicles, ominous harbingers of dread, rolled into the compound with an authority that sent shivers down the spines of the awakening villagers.

The arrival of the 5th Brigade had been anticipated with trepidation. Inyathi Mission[190] and the village compound had been under curfew for weeks. Rumours, having spread from other areas of northern Matabeleland, conveyed unimaginable horrors of shootings, rapes, beatings, and disappearances. The fear they instilled now gripped the villagers in a terrifying vice from which they had no power to escape.

The troops disembarked as one, bursting through the doors of the mud huts and concrete block houses. The occupants were dragged out and shoved into an open area in the middle of the village compound. Here, they were ordered to sit on their hands and remain silent.

---

[190] The mission had been established by the Reverend Robert Moffat in 1859. It is situated some 75 kilometres north-north-east of Bulawayo. Moffat was a member of the London Missionary Society, which had been established in England with the aim of spreading the knowledge of Christ among heathen and unenlightened nations.

Within minutes, the usual tranquil rhythms of rural life had transformed into a nightmare as the huddled villagers, numbering about 60 in total, dropped their eyes and stared at the ground in front of them, too afraid to look the soldiers in the face.

Among them were Sipho's parents, Mandla[191] and Nandi[192] Pukelo. They were sitting next to each other, hands beneath their legs as ordered. Mandla looked into Nandi's terrified eyes and whispered, urging her to stay calm and assuring her that everything would be okay.

Once all the huts and houses had been cleared, Major Nyati barked out his orders in Shona, instructing one of his sergeants to separate the villagers into three groups - men, women, and children. Men and women were forcibly separated from each other and from their children with callous indifference. In the process, Mandla and Nandi found themselves parted, awaiting whatever cruel fate might be unleashed by the red-bereted troops.

Overcome with fear, Nandi's cries for help pierced the air. Her desperate pleas for mercy were drowned out by the soldiers' brutality. One of them smashed the butt of his rifle into her face, splitting her top lip open and shattering two of her front teeth. Mandla, driven by a husband's instinct to protect his wife, rushed forward only to be met with a savage rifle blow across the shoulders, sending him crashing to the ground, where he was kicked repeatedly.

"Try anything like that again, and your wife will be raped, and you will be forced to watch," threatened the soldier, his words dripping with malice. Nandi whimpered in shock, pushing her fist into her bloodied mouth to stifle her shudders.

Major Nyati then addressed the three groups in Shona and English, demanding to know where the ZIPRA[193] soldiers were hiding. His demands initially fell on deaf ears as the villagers remained silent,

---

[191] Mandla is a Ndebele boy's name meaning Power and Strength.
[192] Nandi is a Ndebele girl's name meaning Sweetness.
[193] Zimbabwe People's Revolutionary Army. ZIPRA was the military wing of ZAPU.

determined to defy the tyranny before them. As the silence dragged on, Major Nyati fired his rifle perilously close above their heads to underscore his seriousness.

Still, no villager revealed the whereabouts of any ZIPRA soldier.

In anger, Major Nyati ordered one of his men to shoot a young female villager through the knee. The villagers looked on in horror as this was done with brutal coldness.

Another young woman, her courage faltering, finally spoke up. Through halting sobs, she revealed that there were no soldiers in the village but disclosed that a former RAR[194] masodja[195] had visited his parents two weeks earlier.

Mandla's heart sank as he wondered where this revelation would lead.

Major Nyati demanded that the parents of the RAR masodja identify themselves. His demands were followed by a prolonged silence. No one moved or said anything. In exasperation, Major Nyati threatened to shoot the wounded and crying female villager through the other knee.

Mandla, still winded from the kicks to his groin, painfully raised himself from the ground. In his heart, he prayed to be filled with the same courage that the Ndebele *indunas*[196] of old had displayed.

"I am the soldier's father," he said. "Yes, it is true my son was a RAR masodja during the Second Chimurenga[197]. But, after independence, he joined the 1st Brigade of the new Zimbabwe National Army. He served with it until May 1981 when he resigned. He now works as an

---

[194] Rhodesian African Rifles.
[195] Masodja is the Africanised word for soldier.
[196] In Ndebele culture, an *induna* was a title meaning a great leader, headman, or commander of a group of warriors.
[197] The Second Chimurenga, also known as the Rhodesian Bush War or the Zimbabwe Liberation War, refers to the guerilla war of 1966 to 1979 which led to the end of white-minority rule in Rhodesia.

anti-poaching manager on a ranch near Chiredzi. He came to visit me and his mother about two weeks ago."

A look of rage flashed across Major Nyati's face. In a rant, he asked Mandla why he permitted his son to join the army of the white oppressors. He accused Mandla, Nandi, and their son of being traitors and black sell-outs.

Mandla desperately denied the Major's accusations, but his denials fell on deaf ears.

The Major then asked if Mandla and his wife were members of ZANU-PF[198]. Both Mandla and Nandi had voted for ZAPU[199] in the 1980 elections. Rather than disclosing this, Mandla said they were not interested in politics but had voted for Bishop Muzorewa's UANC[200] party in the 1980 general elections.

"You are a liar and a coward," raged Major Nyati. "And Muzorewa is another black sell-out. There is only one true African liberation party, and that is ZANU-PF. I am going to teach these villagers a lesson they will never forget. From this day on, they will all vote for ZANU-PF."

With that, Major Nyati raised his rifle and shot Mandla in the head at point-blank range. He then turned his rifle on Nandi and shot her as well.

There was a gasp of horror and disbelief from the seated villagers. Some of the children began to cry in fear.

Major Nyati ordered the two lifeless bodies to be placed into one of the armoured troop carriers. He then instructed the villagers to say, if asked about the two deceased, that the soldiers had taken them away for interrogation. He warned threateningly that if any villager

---

[198] Zimbabwe African National Union – Patriotic Front. ZANU-PF is a political organisation that has been the ruling party of Zimbabwe since independence in 1980.
[199] Zimbabwe African People's Union.
[200] United African National Council.

revealed the truth, he would personally return to burn down the village compound with all the villagers locked in their huts or houses.

With callous efficiency, the soldiers loaded the lifeless bodies into one of their armoured troop carriers, while the villagers looked on in shock, disbelieving the evil they had just witnessed but too petrified to display any defiance due to the price that would be exacted for such insubordination.

And as quickly as they had come, the soldiers departed, leaving behind a village shrouded in shock and sorrow. The memory of their presence lingered in the air, a grim reminder of the fragility of peace in the new Zimbabwe and the lethal dangers faced by those who did not support ZANU-PF.

Chapter 21 – Sipho hears reports of the death of his parents

After the departure of the troops, the villagers of Inyathi Mission[201] were left in a state of shock and despair. They hurriedly gathered around Jabulile, the woman who had been shot through the knee, and carefully placed her into a donkey-drawn cart. Even though they handled her with the utmost care, her agonising cries of pain punctuated the air as they guided the cart over the bumpy track from the village compound to the mission's clinic.

Upon arrival at the clinic, the nursing staff were horrified by Jabulile's condition and injuries and demanded to know what had happened. The villagers recounted the harrowing tale of the raid by the 5th Brigade, explaining how Mandla[202] and Nandi[203] Pukelo had been taken away by the soldiers and how Jabulile had been shot through the knee for failing to answer the soldiers' questions adequately.

Realising that Jabulile's injuries required urgent attention beyond what they could provide at the clinic, the nursing staff attempted to call Mpilo Hospital in Bulawayo for an ambulance. Their efforts were

---

[201] The mission had been established by the Reverend Robert Moffat in 1859. It is situated some 75 kilometres north-north-east of Bulawayo. Moffat was a member of the London Missionary Society, which had been established in England with the aim of spreading the knowledge of Christ among heathen and unenlightened nations.
[202] Mandla is a Ndebele boy's name meaning Power and Strength.
[203] Nandi is a Ndebele girl's name meaning Sweetness.

in vain as the phone line was dead. With no other options, they turned to the school headmaster, Mr Enock Bhebhe, for help.

Frantically, one of the nurses ran to the school to locate Mr Bhebhe. After a short while, she returned with him in his Peugeot 404 station wagon. Jabulile was carefully placed in the back of the vehicle, and Mr Bhebhe wasted no time heading to Bulawayo.

But their journey was abruptly halted only five kilometres down the road when they encountered the same 5th Brigade roadblock that Sipho had faced a couple of weeks earlier. The red-beret-capped troops manning the roadblock were obstinate and unyielding, refusing to let Mr Bhebhe proceed. Despite his desperate pleas and the grievously injured Jabulile in the back of his station wagon, they insisted he return to the school, warning him that a curfew was in place and threatening him with arrest if he disobeyed their orders.

Despairingly, Mr Bhebhe obeyed their cold orders and returned to the clinic. He was racked with worry for Jabulile and concern for Mandla Pukelo, his maintenance manager, and his wife, Nandi, who was the school kitchen supervisor. Despite the villagers' accounts, he feared that a far more sinister fate had befallen both of these valued staff members.

He hurried over to his office and dictated letters detailing the events of the raid, including Jabulile's injury and his fears for his two missing staff members. He also included a few paragraphs about the recent atrocities and human rights abuses perpetrated by the 5th Brigade in northern Matabeleland.

His dictation was quickly typed by his secretary onto official school letterhead. One letter was addressed to the manager of the Bulawayo-based office of the United Congregational Church of Southern Africa (UCCSA), the current owners of Inyathi Mission. The other was directed to a black lawyer friend of his, Mr Bheki Mpofu, who had recently joined the highly regarded legal firm Webb, Low, and Barry in Bulawayo as its first black legal practitioner.

He gave these letters and a few dollars to a senior prefect from the school and instructed him to deliver them with all speed by foot to the postal agency at the general store in the Inyathi Business Centre, about five kilometres away. He told the student to purchase postage stamps at the store and to post the letters. He also stressed that the boy should only travel on dirt footpaths or through the bush and must, at all costs, avoid roads or any signs of military activity.

Over the next day, news of the raid, including the cold-blooded killing of Mandla and Nandi, spread throughout the school, creating a tense atmosphere. Basic first aid was administered to Jabulile at the school clinic, where hasty arrangements were made for her to receive 24/7 care. Meanwhile, the staff and students struggled to carry on with their daily routines amidst the trauma and uncertainty.

A few days after the violent raid, a brief but highly sanitised article appeared on page five of the local newspaper, *The Chronicle*[204]. The article reported an alleged incident that had occurred at Inyathi Mission during the 5th Brigade's attempted detention of ZIPRA[205] dissidents. It described the incident as minor, stating that one woman had sustained non-life-threatening injuries to her leg, while two staff members at the school had been arrested for failing to comply with security measures under the country's emergency regulations.

Unfortunately, no one at Mhuka[206] Ranch noticed this article, and for a brief while, life at the ranch continued undisturbed by the horrors that had occurred at Inyathi Mission.

It was only on Monday, 27th August 1984, that Sipho[207] first heard rumours about the 5th Brigade's raid on the village compound that had occurred on Thursday, 2nd August 1984, in which his parents were reportedly shot and killed.

---

[204] *The Chronicle* was published in Bulawayo and mostly reported on news affecting the Matabeleland area in the south of the country. It was first published in 1894.
[205] Zimbabwe People's Revolutionary Army. ZIPRA was the military wing of ZAPU.
[206] A local word meaning animals or wildlife.
[207] Sipho is a Ndebele boy's name meaning Gift.

This news shook Sipho to the core. His worst fears seemed to have materialised. He had an urgent meeting with Duncan and Mark, who granted him two weeks' leave to travel to Bulawayo and Inyathi Mission to confirm the details.

Still numb with shock, Sipho left for Bulawayo on Tuesday, 28th August.

Chapter 22 – Stonewalled

The two-week period beginning on Tuesday, 28th August 1984, proved to be a living torment for Sipho[208]. When he departed from Mhuka[209] Ranch that Tuesday morning, he remained in deep shock. He had always held the utmost respect for his parents, Mandla[210] and Nandi[211] Pukelo. It was beyond belief that they might now be dead, slain like defenceless lambs at the hands of the murderous 5th Brigade. He hoped against hope that the rumours he had heard might still prove false, but in his heart of hearts, he feared the worst.

Upon arrival in Bulawayo, his first stop was the offices of UCCSA[212], who currently owned Inyathi Mission[213], where he met the manager, Mr Viljoen. He had arranged this meeting prior to leaving the ranch. At the meeting, Mr Viljoen could offer little information, stating that the 5th Brigade had refused to comment on the incident. Their official position was that this was an ongoing operational matter covered by the country's Emergency Powers Act. Accordingly, no comment

---

[208] Sipho is a Ndebele boy's name meaning Gift.
[209] A local word meaning animals or wildlife.
[210] Mandla is a Ndebele boy's name meaning Power and Strength.
[211] Nandi is a Ndebele girl's name meaning Sweetness.
[212] This is the acronym for United Congregational Church of Southern Africa.
[213] The mission had been established by the Reverend Robert Moffat in 1859. It is situated some 75 kilometres north-north-east of Bulawayo. Moffat was a member of the London Missionary Society, which had been established in England with the aim of spreading the knowledge of Christ among heathen and unenlightened nations.

would be made, other than to say they had no record of any recent civilian deaths at Inyathi Mission.

Mr Viljoen also mentioned that he had been unable to make any contact with the mission as its telecommunications were still down. Furthermore, the area was still under a strict military curfew, restricting unauthorised access. However, on a more positive note, Mr Viljoen advised that he had made an appointment for Sipho to meet with a lawyer named Mr Bheki Mpofu, who worked at the Bulawayo-based law firm Webb, Low, and Barry. Mr Viljoen informed Sipho that Mr Mpofu had a keen interest in the disappearance of Sipho's parents and had begun making preliminary inquiries.

From UCCSA's offices, Sipho drove to Webb, Low, and Barry's offices and met with Mr Bheki Mpofu. Mr Mpofu's update echoed what Sipho had heard from Mr Viljoen, but he added that his firm was preparing a petition to the High Court requesting the government to disclose information about the current whereabouts of Mandla and Nandi Pukelo. However, Mr Mpofu noted that the petition's chances of success were slim, as the government would likely argue that such disclosure could compromise national security and stability.

After leaving Webb, Low, and Barry, Sipho checked into the Churchill Arms Hotel. That night, he attempted to call his friend, Colonel Emanuel Wushe, commander of ZNA's[214] 1st Brigade. Fortunately, Emanuel was at home, and they spoke earnestly for a quarter of an hour. Sipho updated Emanuel on what had befallen his parents at the mission, his fears that they may have been murdered by the 5th Brigade, and the stonewalling that had occurred in relation to all enquiries made to date.

At the mention of possible murder by elements of the 5th Brigade, Emanuel became reluctant to get involved, stating that military operations conducted by the 5th Brigade were classified and cautioning Sipho to verify his facts before making any allegations of

---

[214] Zimbabwe National Army.

murder. Sipho hung up the phone feeling dispirited. If Emanuel was unwilling to be forthcoming, he wondered who might be.

That night, his sleep was fitful and restless.

The next morning, he decided to travel to Inyathi Mission. It was only 75 kilometres north-north-east of Bulawayo, and he hoped to arrive within an hour. His plan was to go to his parents' house and speak with some of the villagers to gather information from anyone who had witnessed the 5th Brigade's raid. He expected to encounter roadblocks again. However, he still had the letter from Emanuel Wushe vouching for his credibility and hoped it would grant him access once more.

As expected, he encountered the first roadblock about 55 kilometres from Bulawayo, near the Turk Gold Mine. However, this time, the roadblock was manned by red-bereted troops from the 5th Brigade and had been significantly fortified, including a sandbagged machine gun emplacement. He was stopped and questioned at the roadblock by a very threatening soldier who warned him he was breaking the military curfew. Sipho showed the soldier the letter from Colonel Emanuel Wushe and waited while the soldier consulted his superiors via radio.

After five minutes, the soldier returned, visibly angry. He stated that the letter signed by Colonel Wushe was dated 13th July 1984 and hence no longer valid. The soldier ordered Sipho to return to his vehicle and leave immediately, or he would be arrested and detained.

In shock, Sipho complied. As he drove back to Bulawayo, he shook with outrage. He briefly considered attempting to gain access to Inyathi Mission on foot through the bush but dismissed the idea, recognising its folly and danger. He returned to his hotel, where he pondered his next move.

The next day, Thursday, 30th August 1984, Sipho drove to the central morgue to find out if any corpses were there for post-mortem examinations or temporary storage before being released to the next of kin for burial. He was fortunate that the official he spoke with was Ndebele. Sipho explained that he was trying to locate his parents, whom he feared had been killed by the 5th Brigade at the beginning of the month at Inyathi Mission. The official muttered an obscenity regarding the 5th Brigade and then checked the morgue's records. After a thorough check, he informed Sipho that, while the morgue had been incredibly busy over the last six months, there was no record of any corpses from Inyathi Mission at the morgue.

Sipho's next move was to visit all the major hospitals in Bulawayo, including both public and private facilities, to see if there was any record of either of his parents having been admitted. Once again, his inquiries were unsuccessful. However, at Mpilo Hospital[215], he was informed that a young woman from Inyathi Mission had recently been admitted with a serious gunshot wound to her leg. Sipho's heart leapt with hope. When he asked about visiting her, he was told that she was under police guard and that no visitors were allowed. When he inquired about her name, the clerk said he was not at liberty to disclose that information.

Somewhat frustrated, but armed with this information, Sipho phoned Mr Viljoen at UCCSA. Sipho told Mr Viljoen that he believed the woman from Inyathi Mission who had recently been admitted to Mpilo Hospital with a gunshot wound might have been injured during the 5th Brigade's raid and wondered if Mr Viljoen, as the owner of the Inyathi Mission, might be able to visit her to find out if she knew anything.

Mr Viljoen said that sounded like a sensible idea and told Sipho he would get back to him if he found out anything.

The following Monday, Mr Viljoen phoned Sipho at the hotel to inform him that he had contacted the hospital and learned that the patient's name was Jabulile. Furthermore, he had persuaded the

---

[215] Mpilo Hospital, is the largest public hospital in Bulawayo, and second largest in Zimbabwe after Parirenyatwa Hospital in Harare. It serves as the referral centre for the Matabeleland North, Matabeleland South and Midlands provinces of Zimbabwe. The name *Mpilo*, means *life* in the Ndebele language.

hospital manager to allow him to visit her that afternoon. Since Mr Viljoen did not speak Shona or Ndebele, he would take a staff member fluent in both. He suggested that he and Sipho meet again the following morning.

The following morning, Sipho and Mr Viljoen met at the UCCSA offices. Mr Viljoen told Sipho that he had been allowed to spend 15 minutes with Jabulile. He said Jabulile was very frightened and initially reluctant to share much information with him. But once she learned that he was from the organisation that owned the mission, she confirmed that she had been shot in the knee by a soldier from the 5th Brigade on the morning of 2nd August. This was a punishment because the 5th Brigade did not believe the villagers when they said there were no ZIPRA[216] soldiers in the village.

Mr Viljoen paused, looking at Sipho with a pained expression. In a soft and sombre voice, he told Sipho that Jabulile had also confirmed that both Mandla and Nandi had been shot and killed during the raid by the commanding soldier. They had been shot because their son had been an RAR[217] masodja[218] during the Second Chimurenga[219] and because they had not voted for ZANU-PF[220] in the 1980 general elections. She said that both bodies had been loaded into the soldiers' truck and taken away, and she had no idea where the soldiers took them.

Mr Viljoen placed his hand on Sipho's shoulder and said softly, "I am so sorry, Sipho. The news is just terrible. But please know that we will do everything possible to bring those responsible to justice. Mandla and Nandi were both highly respected staff members at the mission.

---

[216] Zimbabwe People's Revolutionary Army. ZIPRA was the military wing of ZAPU.
[217] Rhodesian African Rifles.
[218] Masodja is the Africanised word for soldier.
[219] The Second Chimurenga, also known as the Rhodesian Bush War or the Zimbabwe Liberation War, refers to the guerilla war of 1966 to 1979 which led to the end of white-minority rule in Rhodesia.
[220] Zimbabwe African National Union – Patriotic Front. ZANU-PF is a political organisation that has been the ruling party of Zimbabwe since independence in 1980.

We cannot allow their deaths to be in vain. According to Jabulile, they were both very brave throughout the ordeal."

Sipho was silent for a long time. His face was wracked with pain. He felt responsible for his parents' deaths and was distraught with the idea that their deaths had come about because he had joined the RAR.

After some minutes of silence, he stood up and thanked Mr Viljoen for organising the visit with Jabulile. He also mentioned that Mr Bheki Mpofu, a lawyer from Webb, Low, and Barry, was looking into the matter and wondered if Mr Viljoen would be prepared to meet with him and Mr Mpofu later in the week. Mr Viljoen said it would be his absolute pleasure. He looked in his diary and said that he was available any time on Wednesday or Thursday of that week.

Sipho thanked him, shook his hand, and left. His face was pained, but his shoulders were erect.

*****

Mr Viljoen, Mr Mpofu, and Sipho subsequently met at the offices of Webb, Low, and Barry on Thursday, 6th September 1984. Also present at the meeting was Mr Robert Holdman, the senior partner at Webb, Low, and Barry.

At the meeting, Mr Viljoen shared the information he had gleaned from his meeting with Jabulile at Mpilo Hospital, while Sipho shared his experiences of trying to get to the mission and what he had been told at the central morgue.

Mr Holdman then addressed the meeting, saying that he thought the deaths of Mandla and Nandi Pukelo were likely to become a touchstone event in the current political climate. As such, he said it was imperative that the case be properly investigated and that every legal means possible be used to bring those responsible for the deaths of Sipho's parents to account. To facilitate this, he said that

Webb, Low, and Barry were prepared to represent Sipho *pro bono*[221], with Mr Mpofu handling the case.

Sipho was not entirely sure what that meant, but Mr Viljoen was delighted, so Sipho assumed it must be good news.

The meeting ended with Mr Mpofu taking both Sipho's and Mr Viljoen's contact details.

The following morning, Sipho headed back to Mhuka Ranch. His heart was still heavy and wracked with guilt, though he now at least felt that there was some possibility that those responsible for his parents' deaths would be identified and brought before the courts.

---

[221] In a legal context, *pro bono* means the provision of legal services on a free or significantly reduced fee basis.

Chapter 23 – Nick and Rachel return to the UK

After five glorious days on Mhuka[222] Ranch, Nick and Rachel bid farewell to the Olivers and Sipho on Wednesday, 1st August. They then drove back to Harare, where they spent a few relaxing days at Matthew and Brenda Sinclair's home in Ballantyne Park before saying their farewells on Monday, 6th August 1984.

Thereafter, they caught a lunchtime Air Zimbabwe flight to Johannesburg. They had a few hours to pass at Johannesburg International Airport before catching their British Airways flight to London, which left at 6:30 pm.

Nick and Rachel landed at London Heathrow Airport early the following morning after a comfortable but long flight. From Heathrow, they took the London Underground's dark-blue Piccadilly Line to Earls Court, where they transferred to the green District Line and travelled to London Paddington. From there, they caught a taxi to London Waterloo station, where they took the British Rail aboveground service to Guildford. At Guildford, they phoned Lynne Dixon, who kindly picked them up and took them to her and Stuart's lovely stately home in Chantry Lane.

---

[222] A local word meaning animals or wildlife.

As they waited for Lynne, Nick reflected on their journey from London Heathrow to Guildford. He was still bemused by the hordes of people in London and the resulting difficulty in getting around. He realised that adjusting to life as a London commuter would take time.

As Nick and Rachel had not yet moved into their new bungalow in Medstead, they were staying in the guest cottage at Stuart and Lynne's house. Exhausted from their long journey, they heeded Lynne's suggestion to rest for a couple of hours before unpacking. Lynne said that if they were not up by lunch, she would come and awaken them.

*****

Nick was due to start work at RQI[223] on Monday, 27th August 1984. However, before then, he and Rachel needed to transition into their new three-bedroom bungalow located at 6 Roe Downs Road in Medstead. They had named the house **Gideon's Place** in honour of Nick's platoon sergeant, who had been killed in June 1979 when Nick's platoon had been ambushed in the Chimanimani area of Zimbabwe during the Rhodesian Bush War.

Being their first house, they were both extremely excited about settling into their own home and styling it in a way that suited their tastes. Rachel possessed a natural eye for home décor, while Nick had a strong DIY[224] bent, so between them, they hoped to make their new abode quite comfortable and presentable. Rachel's parents had kindly gifted them all the white goods they would need. They then scoured various second-hand shops for lounge, dining room, and bedroom furniture. They purchased good-quality linen, kitchenware, curtains, cushions, as well as a TV and sound system. Although the bungalow boasted new carpets, Rachel further enhanced the house's charm with carefully chosen scatter rugs. Nick applied fresh coats of paint to rooms in need, while Rachel sourced tasteful wall hangings

---

[223] Rare Quest Imports.
[224] Do it Yourself.

from local art shops. Within a few weeks, their new abode exuded warmth and comfort.

Both Nick and Rachel were thrilled with the final result. Despite its modest size, they knew it would be more than sufficient for their needs. With a spare bedroom for guests and a shared study created from the redundant third bedroom, they looked forward to creating many joyous shared memories in their new home.

*****

On Monday, 27th August, Nick arrived at the offices of RQI at 52 Cadogan Place, London, just before 9:00 am, after a 90-minute journey from his home in Medstead. He had driven to Wimbledon station, a trip of about 50 minutes, then took the green District Line north for 25 minutes to Sloane Square. From there, he walked north through Sloane Square, followed Sedding Street, and turned onto Cadogan Place, where the RQI offices were located across from a well-treed, leafy park.

Nick was initially alarmed at how long the commute was. Three hours a day seemed like an unacceptable ask. However, he quickly discovered that such a commute was considered normal in London. As Rachel often reminded him, if you want to live and work in one of Europe's greatest cities, you need to accept that traffic congestion is just one of the things you have to put up with.

Nick quickly transitioned into his new role at RQI. His rapid transition was largely due to the help and advice he received from Richard Simpson, to whom he reported. Richard had worked for Stuart Dixon for many years and hence knew the company inside out. Richard also had developed very good working relations with RQI's key customers, and he had made a point of arranging face-to-face meetings involving him, Nick, and each of these key customers in Nick's first month of employment.

After two weeks, Stuart Dixon caught up with Nick to see how things were going. He had received positive reports from Richard but wanted to check for himself on how Nick was feeling.

The meeting between Stuart and Nick was productive. Towards the end of the meeting, Stuart asked after the Olivers and Sipho[225]. This gave Nick an opportunity to discuss RQI's potential purchase of a one-third equity interest in Mhuka Ranch and to make a low-interest-bearing loan to Sipho to enable him to do likewise. Nick was careful to explain to Stuart that, from a succession planning perspective, it was important to lock Sipho into the ownership structure of Mhuka Ranch, as, in the long term, it was Sipho's expertise, along with the experience of Mark and Jenny, that would help the business navigate the challenging economic and political climate likely to face the new Zimbabwe. Stuart, of course, did not need any convincing on this matter, as it was he who had told Nick that such difficulties were likely to occur in the new Zimbabwe.

Stuart did, however, ask two searching questions of Nick. One related to Sipho's ability to repay the loan to RQI, and the other related to Sipho's political affinity with Zimbabwe's ruling party, ZANU-PF[226].

In relation to the first point, Nick informed Stuart that Sipho had little financial means himself and so had no real ability to repay any loan. Nick went on to explain that he thought RQI should be prepared to forgive 10% of the loan to Sipho per year of service, which would mean that after ten years the loan would be fully forgiven. This mechanism would mean that Sipho would be locked into Mhuka Ranch's business for at least ten years, which would be a bonus for Mhuka Ranch.

Stuart smiled and congratulated Nick on his business acumen. "Well done, Nick," he said. "I knew you were smart. That will be an extremely economical way of putting in place a succession plan for Mhuka Ranch. We may have to fine-tune things a bit, but in principle, I have no objections. However, we need to ensure that if Sipho leaves Mhuka Ranch prior to the ten-year period, some kind of penalty will

---

[225] Sipho is a Ndebele boy's name meaning Gift.
[226] Zimbabwe African National Union – Patriotic Front. ZANU-PF is a political organisation that has been the ruling party of Zimbabwe since independence in 1980.

apply. At the same time, the arrangements with Sipho must also give him the ability to repay any outstanding balance prior to ten years if he has the means to do so. If we can incentivise Sipho properly, this will enhance his value to Mhuka Ranch and hence increase the value of our investment in the business."

In relation to Sipho's likely political affinity with ZANU-PF, Nick explained that Sipho's tribal ethnicity was Ndebele and not Shona. As such, this meant that he would be more aligned with Joshua Nkomo's ZAPU[227] party as opposed to Robert Mugabe's ZANU-PF party. This disclosure brought a look of disappointment to Stuart's face, who said, "That is a pity, but certainly not a deal-breaker. I think over the coming years we are likely to see ZANU-PF's political hold over the country increase while ZAPU's influence will decrease."

Nick and Stuart then discussed how the proposed arrangements might benefit the local community around Chiredzi and what value RQI might add to Mhuka Ranch other than purely a financial one. In this respect, Stuart quickly realised that this proposed investment nicely aligned with the aims and objectives of the AHWF[228] and would be of interest to its sponsors and donors.

The meeting concluded with Stuart advising Nick that he needed to discuss the proposal with his financial director and in-house legal team and that he would then get back to Nick.

A week later, Stuart phoned Nick to let him know that RQI wished to progress discussions with Mhuka Ranch. He asked Nick to contact Duncan Oliver to let him know that this was the case and to find out the name of Duncan Oliver's lawyers so that Stuart's legal team could begin the process of finalising the arrangements.

---

[227] Zimbabwe African People's Union.
[228] Acronym for *Afro-Asian Humanity and Wildlife Foundation*.

Chapter 24 – A strange co-incidence

Time line – September 1984

Sipho's[229] return to Mhuka[230] Ranch on Friday, 7th September 1984, brought no sense of joy. Grief still hung heavily on him, his emotions oscillating between heartbreak, tormented guilt over his parents' death because of his service as a masodja[231] with the RAR[232], and extreme anger at the brutality and injustice meted out to them by the 5th Brigade. He also felt a deep sense of helplessness in the face of the seemingly untouchable power of Mugabe and his ZANU-PF[233] Government, against which even the rule of law could not prevail.

Sipho's account to the Olivers of what had transpired during his recent trip to Bulawayo, left a profound impression. While they were well aware of the unjust reign of terror being waged by the 5th Brigade against the innocent citizens of Matabeleland, the proximity of this tragedy struck them to their core. Duncan, who had lived as a young man in what was then Southern Rhodesia since 1933, had witnessed inter-tribal hostilities on numerous occasions. However, this latest violence, sanctioned by the state and carried out by its

---

[229] Sipho is a Ndebele boy's name meaning Gift.
[230] A local word meaning animals or wildlife.
[231] Masodja is the Africanised word for soldier.
[232] Rhodesian African Rifles.
[233] Zimbabwe African National Union – Patriotic Front. ZANU-PF is a political organisation that has been the ruling party of Zimbabwe since independence in 1980.

military against civilians who had done little wrong — other than not supporting the current government — felt unprecedentedly cruel. If the government was willing to treat black Zimbabweans who didn't support the ruling party this way, he hated to think what they might do to white Zimbabweans should the need arise.

For Sipho, burying himself in the relentless daily tasks of the ranch became his way of managing the intense emotions he was experiencing. He found that hard toil shifted his focus away from his dark and morose thoughts. Physically, he pushed himself harder, and he demanded more from his squad of rangers as well. For a while, he withdrew from the pleasantries of ranch life and instead focused solely on his work. His change in demeanour did not go unnoticed; however, his colleagues left him alone, respecting his need for solace as he worked through his grief.

Duncan summarised the situation best when he wisely said, "In the midst of a storm, it is often best to simply ride it out. Fretting will not quell the waves or the wind, but eventually time will do so in its own inimitable way."

*****

On Wednesday, 13th September 1984, a few days after Stuart had tasked Nick with initiating RQI's[234] proposed acquisition of shares in Mhuka Ranch, Nick phoned the ranch. He chose to phone at 5:00 pm in the UK, which was 6:00 pm in Zimbabwe. He hoped that by phoning then, Duncan, Jenny, Mark, and, with any luck, Sipho, would all be at the homestead.

Fortunately, Nick got through on his first attempt, and it was Jenny who picked up the phone. She was delighted to hear from Nick, and the two of them caught up on each other's news. Jenny wondered whether Nick was phoning in connection with the murder of Sipho's parents, but when he did not raise it, she said nothing, thinking it best that Sipho himself break the sad news to him.

---

[234] Rare Quest Imports.

Nick asked if Duncan was present. Jenny replied that he was and went off to locate him. When Duncan came on the line, Nick updated him on the positive outcome of his discussions with Stuart and advised Duncan that the next step in the process would be for Duncan's lawyers to get in touch with Stuart's lawyers. Duncan was ecstatic at this news and advised Nick that his lawyer was a person named Robert Holdman, who was the senior partner at the Bulawayo-based firm of Webb, Low, and Barry. Duncan told Nick that he had already fully briefed Robert Holdman on the proposed transaction and that Robert was now expecting a call from Stuart's lawyers.

While Nick was speaking with Duncan, Jenny had summoned Mark and Sipho, who were now gathered around the phone and listening intently to the conversation. When Nick mentioned that Stuart was keen to progress the share sale agreement, Duncan, with a broad grin, gave a thumbs-up to Jenny, Mark, and Sipho.

This news even brought a smile to Sipho's face, which was perhaps the first time he had smiled in some weeks.

Sipho was now carefully trying to follow the conversation between Nick and Duncan. When Duncan mentioned the name of his lawyer in Bulawayo, a look of disbelief flashed across Sipho's face. Robert Holdman, the senior partner from Webb, Low, and Barry, was the same person who had offered to represent Sipho, on a *pro bono*[235] basis, in identifying those murderous thugs responsible for his parents' deaths and bringing them to trial.

As this realisation sank in, Sipho's whole inner being seemed to relax. Surely, this was not simply coincidental. Definitely not. Sipho believed, without a shadow of doubt, that Mlimo[236], the ancient

---

[235] In a legal context, *pro bono* means the provision of legal services on a free or significantly reduced fee basis.
[236] Mlimo refers to the ancestral spiritual leader of the Ndebele people. Mlimo is believed to possess supernatural powers and is revered by the Ndebele community as a guardian and protector, including seeking justice and avenging wrongdoings.

ancestral spiritual leader of the Ndebele people, was looking after his parents and would ensure that they would be avenged.

Sipho was jolted out of his deep thoughts when he heard Duncan say to Nick, "Yes, Nick, luckily Sipho is here this evening. I'll let him speak to you. I know he'll be thrilled by the news you've given us, but I'm sure he'll also want to tell you about some tragic family news that you may not have heard yet."

With that, Duncan handed the phone to Sipho and ushered himself, Mark, and Jenny out of the room to give Sipho some privacy.

Nick was devastated by the news Sipho shared with him. Nick's joyous phone call quickly turned bittersweet. The situation became even more complicated when Sipho mentioned that the same firm investigating his parents' murder on a *pro bono* basis would also be handling the Mhuka Ranch share sale agreement.

At the end of the phone call, Sipho spoke with Duncan, Mark, and Jenny and shared with them that Webb, Low, and Barry was also the legal firm investigating his parents' murder on a *pro bono* basis. This revelation was met with pleasant surprise by the Olivers, who agreed it augured well.

That night at dinner, Duncan uncorked a bottle of champagne, and they all raised their glasses to the unexpected turn of events, hoping it would set the stage for a pivotal and successful chapter in their lives together.

Chapter 25 – Navigating Mugabe's dictatorial regime

Timeline – September 1984 to December 1984

Nick settled into his role at RQI[237] with a sense of purpose and determination. Under Richard Simpson's watchful eye, he ably demonstrated competence in managing RQI's contracts with its key British clients and navigating the intricate world of import and export.

Soon after joining RQI, Nick was involved in a key deal that demonstrated his resourcefulness in navigating complex geopolitical regulations. In 1977, the United Nations Security Council had unanimously adopted Resolution 418, imposing a mandatory arms embargo against South Africa. This embargo prohibited the sale of arms and military equipment to South Africa by UN[238] member states, effectively limiting the country's access to international arms markets.

However, the South African Government, in urgent need of arms to support its counter-insurgency activities against guerrilla forces in its neighbouring countries of South West Africa[239], Botswana, and

---

[237] Rare Quest Imports.
[238] United Nations.
[239] South West Africa achieved its independence from South African administration on 21st March 1990, and was renamed Namibia.

Mozambique, sought to bypass the UN arms embargo by clandestinely procuring military hardware and technology from British suppliers.

Under Nick's shrewd leadership, RQI leveraged its connections within the British arms industry to facilitate the procurement. Utilising a shelf company registered in Mauritius, RQI orchestrated the purchase of arms and other military equipment, navigating the intricate web of international regulations. The arms were discreetly logged and crated as manufacturing equipment, then shipped to Port Louis Harbour in Mauritius before being offloaded onto a cargo ship destined for Durban, effectively circumventing the UN embargo.

Nick's involvement in this deal exposed him to much of the analytical work that RQI had done regarding Russia and China's strategic interests in Africa, particularly South Africa. He learned that Russia's historical involvement in providing military support and economic assistance to various African nations was driven primarily by its aim to expand its global influence during the Cold War era. Conversely, China's strategy focused on leveraging its economic influence to gain a say in internal policies across the African continent. By strategically using trade and commerce, China sought to strengthen its foothold and shape domestic affairs in various African nations through its economic power. This included granting credit facilities to overextended African nations, thereby ensuring their financial dependence on China.

Of particular interest to Nick was the dynamic interplay between China and Russia in Zimbabwe. The research highlighted how China had adeptly outmanoeuvred Russia in vying for influence within the country. While Russia's involvement had primarily focused on military support and financial assistance to ZIPRA[240], China's multifaceted approach had proven more effective in winning over key military *and*

---

[240] Zimbabwe People's Revolutionary Army. ZIPRA was the military wing of ZAPU.

political stakeholders, particularly within ZANU[241] and its military wing, ZANLA[242].

Intrigued by these findings, Nick delved deeper into China's strategy during the Rhodesian Bush War. He discovered that China had played a key role in advising ZANLA to adopt Maoist principles, encouraging them to prioritise the indoctrination of local rural populations before engaging militarily with the Rhodesian Security Forces. This approach was part of China's broader effort to influence revolutionary movements across Africa during this period.

The insights gleaned from the research not only improved Nick's understanding of the geopolitical landscape but also highlighted how Africa's future would continue to be shaped by global powers. They also led him to realise that while Rhodesia had historically aligned itself with the West, particularly the UK and the United States of America, this alignment was rapidly shifting under Mugabe's leadership. While publicly Mugabe espoused a policy of non-alignment, in practice, the country was quickly gravitating toward the Eastern bloc. Nick wondered how this shift would affect Zimbabwe's economic, political, and social trajectory.

Alongside his daily responsibilities, Nick also acted as the intermediary between RQI's legal department in London and Webb, Low, and Barry in Bulawayo, helping finalise RQI and Sipho's share purchases in Mhuka[243] Ranch, as well as the loan agreement for Sipho's share acquisition.

The agreements progressed steadily and were finalised and signed by the end of November 1984. At this point, RQI and Sipho each acquired a one-third equity interest in Mhuka Ranch, with Sipho committing to remain at the ranch for a minimum of ten years.

---

[241] Zimbabwe African National Union.
[242] Zimbabwe African National Liberation Army. ZANLA was the military wing of ZANU.
[243] A local word meaning animals or wildlife.

During the negotiation of the agreements, Nick had many telephone conversations with Robert Holdman, the senior partner at Webb, Low, and Barry, and with Sipho. These conversations also allowed Nick to gauge how Sipho was coping with the intense grief from the murder of his parents by the 5th Brigade and the progress that Webb, Low, and Barry were making in identifying those responsible for these killings and bringing them to justice.

Progress in this regard was anything but positive. Robert Holdman advised him that the Zimbabwean Government was obfuscating the matter at every juncture. It seemed that all of the 5th Brigade's recorded references to the 2nd August raid at Inyathi Mission[244] had been destroyed, while the relevant officials at 5th Brigade were simply refusing to respond to any enquiries made by Webb, Low, and Barry. In frustration, Webb, Low, and Barry petitioned the provincial magistrate to compel the 5th Brigade to respond to the inquiries. However, these efforts were thwarted when the chief magistrate's office advised the provincial magistrate that matters involving the 5th Brigade fell exclusively within the domain of the chief magistrate.

Even inquiries made by the ZRP[245] were being ignored. Robert Holdman had a good working relationship with a police chief superintendent in Bulawayo. The chief superintendent had advised Robert, off the record, that the Bulawayo police would not be investigating the matter because he had been informed at a briefing meeting with the Matabeleland assistant commissioner of police and the 5th Brigade commander that the matter was off-limits to the police. If he continued to push for an investigation, he risked arrest for threatening national security and state stability.

---

[244] The mission had been established by the Reverend Robert Moffat in 1859. It is situated some 75 kilometres north-north-east of Bulawayo. Moffat was a member of the London Missionary Society, which had been established in England with the aim of spreading the knowledge of Christ among heathen and unenlightened nations.
[245] Zimbabwe Republic Police.

So, for all practical purposes, the 5th Brigade and its troops were regarded as being above the law unless contrary directions were first received from the Prime Minister's office.

These discouraging revelations brought both Nick and Sipho to despair. To help ease their frustrations, they began to discuss potential solutions to the current political climate in Bulawayo. Sipho's apprehensions about ZANU-PF's[246] unchecked power resonated with Nick, prompting them to contemplate ways to bring about change.

During their discussions, they identified two courses of action that they believed might be fruitful. First, Nick would attempt to contact Jonathan Khumalo, the London-based lawyer working with Amnesty International[247] who claimed to be a descendant of the royal House of Khumalo[248]. The goal would be to persuade him to return to Zimbabwe and assist in resurrecting the political fortunes of ZAPU. Second, they would consider using Mhuka Ranch as a safe house and sanctuary for ZAPU[249] members fleeing political persecution by the Mugabe regime. In doing so, Mhuka Ranch could become a beacon of hope amidst the prevailing political turmoil in parts of the country.

It was agreed that Nick would discuss the first proposed course of action with Stuart and pursue this matter subject to Stuart's views. Likewise, Sipho would discuss the second course of action with Duncan and pursue it, subject to Duncan's views.

---

[246] Zimbabwe African National Union – Patriotic Front. ZANU-PF is a political organisation that has been the ruling party of Zimbabwe since independence in 1980.

[247] Amnesty International is an international non-governmental organisation focused on human rights, with its headquarters in the UK. It was founded in 1961 with the mission of campaigning for a world in which every person enjoys all of the human rights enshrined in the Universal Declaration of Human Rights and other international human rights instruments.

[248] The House of Khumalo is the continuing royal family of the former Mthwakazi Kingdom (modern day Matabeleland). The Mthwakazi Kingdom was founded in 1823 and ended in 1894 with the First Matabele War. The House has endured to the present day.

[249] Zimbabwe African People's Union.

Sipho even proposed a more radical idea — the creation of an underground movement aimed at undermining ZANU-PF in Zimbabwe. This plan would involve Sipho working to galvanise the growing discontent with Mugabe in Matabeleland, while Nick would approach Stewart to see if he was willing to leverage his substantial political, military, and business contacts in the UK. This could help exert diplomatic pressure on Mugabe to soften his harsh policies, particularly those unfairly targeting the Ndebele nation. However, they quickly dismissed the idea due to the significant risks involved and the slim chances of achieving any meaningful change. Instead, they decided to focus their efforts on legitimate political avenues, aiming to strengthen ZAPU's political presence in Matabeleland.

Chapter 26 – Nick meets with Joshua Nkomo

Time line – January 1985

Christmas 1984 swiftly approached for Nick and Rachel, marking five months since their return from their mesmerising honeymoon to the Drakensberg, the Great Zimbabwe Ruins[250], and Mhuka[251] Ranch. In this brief period, they had settled comfortably into their charming cottage in Medstead, Hampshire.

On the professional front, Nick was flourishing in his new role at RQI[252]. He had played a crucial role in orchestrating an arms deal between the South African Government and the British arms industry. He also played a key role in finalising RQI's acquisition of shares in Mhuka Ranch. Meanwhile, Rachel had achieved success in her career, completing her management trainee programme with

---

[250] The Great Zimbabwe Ruins is the name of the stone ruins of an ancient city known as Great Zimbabwe. The ruins are located just outside Fort Victoria (now called Masvingo). People lived in Great Zimbabwe from around 1100 but abandoned it in the 15th century. The city was the capital of the Kingdom of Zimbabwe, which was a Shona trading empire. Zimbabwe means "stone houses" in Shona.
[251] A local word meaning animals or wildlife.
[252] Rare Quest Imports.

Vivienne Westwood[253] and assuming the role of brand manager for a new line of fashionwear.

Shortly after the Christmas holidays, Stuart invited Nick and Rachel to lunch at the newly opened and highly popular Santini restaurant in Belgravia, which specialised in fine Italian dining. The purpose of the meeting was for Stuart to discuss Nick and Rachel's proposed fundraising roles with AHWF[254]. The timing seemed opportune, given the favourable tax advantages introduced by the Charities Act of 1980. Stuart therefore felt it was now time for Nick and Rachel to commence their AHWF fundraising efforts, particularly focusing on activities aimed at supporting endangered animals in southern Africa.

Nick and Rachel were still eager to be involved in these activities. Over lunch with Stuart, they brainstormed ideas for the year ahead, including specific fundraising efforts to support endangered animals in southern Africa. Stuart had recently met a BBC[255] film-maker named Terry Ashborough, who was ambitiously creating a body of work, exemplifying quality in wildlife films. In principle, Terry had agreed to be the guest speaker at a donors' luncheon in London, and Stuart was keen to bring this project to a successful conclusion. The project was being managed by AHWF's fundraising director, who needed assistance in getting it up and running. Stuart wanted to know if Nick and Rachel were interested in being involved, and if so, he would make the necessary introductions.

Nick and Rachel responded enthusiastically to Stuart's suggestions and expressed their eagerness to meet with the fundraising director.

During lunch, Nick also took the opportunity to update Stuart and Rachel on his recent discussions with Sipho, specifically regarding

---

[253] Vivienne Westwood was one of London's leading fashion designers and businesswomen.
[254] Acronym for Afro-Asian Humanity and Wildlife Foundation.
[255] British Broadcasting Corporation.

Nick's plans to make contact in London with Jonathon Khumalo, who claimed to be a descendant of the royal House of Khumalo[256].

Nick provided details of Jonathon's background. He explained that Jonathon had been educated at Inyathi Mission[257] in Zimbabwe during the 1960s. The headmaster, sympathetic to black nationalist aspirations, had recognised Jonathon's potential as a future leader of the country once it broke free from colonial rule and had arranged for him to be smuggled out of Zimbabwe to the UK at the age of 13. Once in the UK, Jonathon received support from donors and excelled in the British educational system. After achieving straight A's in his A-Level exams[258], he won a scholarship to Oxford University to study law. Although he had planned to return to Zimbabwe after independence in 1980 to join Joshua Nkomo's ZAPU party, he had remained in the UK due to concerns about Robert Mugabe's future intentions, particularly regarding the Ndebele nation. Jonathon was still living in London and was now working as a human rights lawyer with Amnesty International[259].

Nick explained that he wanted to meet with Jonathon to gauge his perspective on the current political situation in Zimbabwe and to explore the possibility of Jonathon's return to the country to re-establish the royal House of Khumalo and revive the political fortunes of ZAPU.

---

[256] The House of Khumalo is the continuing royal family of the former Mthwakazi Kingdom (modern day Matabeleland). The Mthwakazi Kingdom was founded in 1823 and ended in 1894 with the First Matabele War. The House has endured to the present day.

[257] The mission had been established by the Reverend Robert Moffat in 1859. It is situated some 75 kilometres north-north-east of Bulawayo. Moffat was a member of the London Missionary Society, which had been established in England with the aim of spreading the knowledge of Christ among heathen and unenlightened nations.

[258] A-Levels were the Advanced Level of school examinations. It was conferred as a school leaving qualification to senior school pupils as part of the Cambridge International General Certificate of Education.

[259] Amnesty International is an international non-governmental organisation focused on human rights, with its headquarters in the UK. It was founded in 1961 with the mission of campaigning for a world in which every person enjoys all of the human rights enshrined in the Universal Declaration of Human Rights and other international human rights instruments.

Stuart and Rachel were surprised by these revelations but remained supportive of Nick's plans, albeit with a word of caution due to the delicate relationship between ZANU-PF[260] and ZAPU.

A week later, Nick phoned Jonathon using the contact number Sipho had provided. Nick introduced himself as a friend of Sipho Pukelo. Jonathon responded favourably, and they had a friendly and open discussion over the phone. Nick was initially surprised by how *'British'* Jonathon's accent was but realised that, having lived and worked in the UK for around 15 years, his accent was not so remarkable after all!

Jonathon showed interest in the matters Nick was raising and suggested they meet for coffee and an informal chat. He proposed meeting at 10:00 am on Monday, 14th January 1985, at the *Hideaway Coffee House* near Piccadilly Circus, roughly equidistant between RQI's offices in Belgravia and Amnesty International's offices in Easton Street, Islington. Nick noted the coffee house's address, 7 Farriers Passage, Soho, and then hung up.

Nick arrived at the *Hideaway Coffee House* just before 10:00 am on Monday. The café lived up to its name, being discreet and charming with an old-world feel. Given its name and address, Nick's imagination turned to thoughts of smuggling and piracy! A few minutes after Nick arrived, a tall, imposing young man entered the café. He had an open face, dark brown skin, short black wiry hair, and was well-dressed in a royal blue suit, white shirt, and red and gold striped tie. He was scanning the café, obviously searching for someone. Nick caught his eye, stood up, and said, "Are you looking for me by any chance? My name is Nick Sinclair."

Jonathon greeted him with a broad smile, the whites of his teeth and the pink of his gums standing out vividly against his dark brown skin. "So nice to meet you, Nick. Thanks for coming."

---

[260] Zimbabwe African National Union – Patriotic Front. ZANU-PF is a political organisation that has been the ruling party of Zimbabwe since independence in 1980.

"Not at all," said Nick. "Please take a seat. Here is the menu. I am having coffee and a croissant. What would you like?"

Jonathon said he would have a cup of tea and a toasted cheese sandwich, and Nick went to the counter to order. They then sat at the table Nick had reserved.

After some small talk, Nick began to ask Jonathon about his links to the House of Khumalo and his seriousness about returning to Zimbabwe to revive the royal lineage. Jonathon's responses were thoughtful, expressive, and convincing. Despite his years in the UK, it was clear he had a deep longing to return to Zimbabwe. Surprisingly, his interest was not so much in politics but more about resurrecting the Khumalo line and seeking justice for the Ndebele nation. However, he was concerned about the potential risks to him of returning to Zimbabwe given the current political situation.

Jonathon also revealed that he had developed a personal friendship with Joshua Nkomo following Nkomo's arrival in London after fleeing Zimbabwe in March 1983. Although Nkomo had returned to Zimbabwe six months later, he still occasionally visited the UK for high-level discussions with British officials and others about Zimbabwe's political future. During a recent visit, Nkomo had met with Jonathon and they had mooted the idea of Jonathon returning to Zimbabwe to re-establish the royal House of Khumalo. While Nkomo supported the idea, he felt that the time was not yet right.

At the mention of Joshua Nkomo, Nick tentatively proposed a second meeting, suggesting that Nkomo join by phone from Zimbabwe. Jonathon was non-committal but revealed that Nkomo was currently in London, discussing various national matters, including Zimbabwe's upcoming general elections, with British advisers. Jonathon said he would check if Nkomo was interested in meeting and would get back to Nick.

To Nick's surprise and delight, not long after, Jonathon called to inform him that Nkomo was prepared to meet with both of them.

Jonathon added that Nkomo was still fearful for his life, believing that operatives from either the South African NIS[261] or the Zimbabwean CIO[262] might attempt to locate and harm him. Nick assured Jonathon that he understood Nkomo's concerns and was willing to meet at a time and place of Nkomo's choice. Jonathon said he would get back to him once he had spoken with Nkomo.

A few days later, Jonathon called to confirm that the meeting was arranged for Friday, 1st February 1985, at 1:00 pm. He advised Nick to return to the *Hideaway Coffee House* at 12:00 noon that day. Jonathon would meet Nick there and accompany him to the meeting. Nick was surprised by the subterfuge but agreed to the arrangements.

Later that night, Nick shared the significant developments with Rachel. He expressed his uncertainty about how he might react to meeting with Nkomo in person due to his vivid and distasteful memories of a BBC interview with Nkomo shortly after the downing of Air Rhodesia flight 825 on 3rd September 1978 by ZIPRA guerrillas. In that interview, Nkomo had laughed about the incident and had claimed the civilian aircraft was a legitimate target as it might have been carrying Rhodesian Government or military officials.

On Friday, 1st February 1985, an apprehensive Nick Sinclair arrived at the *Hideaway Coffee House* just before noon. Jonathon, accompanied by two burly-looking men, was already there, having arrived in a smart black Mercedes Benz at 11:45 am.

As Nick entered the café, Jonathon stood up and shook his hand. He explained that the two burly men were Joshua Nkomo's security personnel, who would be driving Nick and Jonathon to the meeting.

---

[261] National Intelligence Service. The NIS was established in 1980, succeeding the Bureau of State Security (BOSS). Its primary role was to gather intelligence, conduct covert operations, and support the South African Government's counter-intelligence efforts.
[262] Zimbabwe's Central Intelligence Organisation.

Jonathon, Nick, and the two security officers left the café and climbed into the Mercedes, which was parked immediately in front of the coffee house. One of the security officers took the driver's seat, while Jonathon sat in the passenger seat. Nick and the other security officer sat in the back seat. The security officer next to Nick apologised but explained that, for security reasons, Nick would need to wear a special pair of wrap-around sunglasses that were blacked out to prevent him from seeing where they were going. Feeling somewhat alarmed, Nick had little choice but to comply.

Their car then sped off. After about 40 minutes, during which there was little conversation among the occupants, the vehicle came to a halt. Nick was instructed to remove the sunglasses and exit the car. Following these instructions, Nick discovered they were somewhere in the English countryside, parked in the driveway of an attractive double-storey house.

The security officer who had been sitting next to Nick led him and Jonathon to the front door of the house. Before entering, he conducted a quick search of Nick, apologising once again for the intrusion.

Once inside, the security officer directed Nick and Jonathon to a comfortable lounge area and asked them to take a seat, mentioning that Joshua Nkomo would join them shortly.

While waiting, Nick asked Jonathon about the need for such stringent security measures. Jonathon explained that, without these precautions, Nkomo would not have agreed to the meeting. He added that Nkomo had legitimate reasons to believe he might be targeted, even in London.

Shortly after, Nkomo entered the room. Nick, feeling somewhat uncomfortable, stood up and shook his hand, saying, "Mr Nkomo, I am pleased to meet you."

Joshua Nkomo's appearance was much as Nick had imagined. He wore smart but casual clothes, was clean-shaven, and his greying crinkly hair was neatly brushed back. Although he appeared healthy, he was somewhat overweight.

Nkomo started the conversation, "It's a pleasure to meet you, Nick. Jonathon has spoken highly of you and your efforts to persuade him to return to Zimbabwe to revive the royal House of Khumalo. Before we continue, I must apologise for the security measures. But I have to be careful. As you may know, I had to flee Zimbabwe in March 1983. It wasn't my choice, and I was very sad to leave my country so soon after independence. It's tragic that the first democratically elected government in Zimbabwe made me fear for my life. Just before I left, Mugabe publicly compared me and my party, ZAPU, to a cobra in the house, saying the only way to deal with a snake is to strike its head. My security team had strong evidence showing that if I stayed, I would be arrested and imprisoned on false charges of treason."

Nkomo continued, explaining that he initially sought refuge in Botswana but later flew to Britain. In London, he collaborated with other Ndebele exiles and senior British officials regarding his potential return to Zimbabwe. After various assurances from ZANU-PF, he had returned to Zimbabwe in August 1983.

Nkomo disclosed that the British Government was keen to broker a peace deal between ZANU-PF and ZAPU and to ensure the formation of a government of national unity in Zimbabwe. He had returned to the UK several times since August 1983 to progress these discussions. However, ZANU-PF had shown little inclination to negotiate directly with ZAPU. On this basis, Nkomo indicated that it might be premature for Jonathon to consider returning to Zimbabwe but noted that if peace discussions advanced, Jonathon's return could be appropriate.

Nick was stunned by these revelations. He hadn't realised that Britain had been involved in behind-the-scenes efforts to broker peace between ZANU-PF and ZAPU. He speculated that UK power brokers, after refusing to recognise the election of Bishop Muzorewa's[263] government in April 1979 due to both ZANU[264] and ZAPU boycotting the general elections, were now left with blood on their hands following the outbreak of tribal violence in Zimbabwe. They were now doing their best to try and ease the tribal tensions and restore stability to the country.

That night, Nick went home and recounted the day's incredible events to Rachel.

*****

Unbeknown to Jonathon and Nkomo's security guards, the black Mercedes-Benz they had arrived in at the *Hideaway Coffee House* had been followed by a Ford Escort driven by a young white man. The Ford Escort had been parked some distance behind the Mercedes, but a short time later, it pulled away from the kerb and sped off.

The Ford Escort was driven by a young white South African named Pieter Hendrik. Pieter was a student at the London School of Economics and Political Science. He had arrived in London from Pretoria a couple of years earlier to commence his tertiary education. His parents were ardent supporters of the South African Nationalist Party and its leader, South Africa's State President PW Botha[265].

Shortly after arriving in London, Pieter was recruited by a British-based intelligence officer working for South Africa's National Intelligence Service (NIS). One of Pieter's responsibilities was to keep specified buildings of interest under surveillance. In January 1985, he was tasked with monitoring the Amnesty International offices on Easton Street during specified business hours.

---

[263] Bishop Abel Muzorewa served as the first and only Prime Minister of Zimbabwe Rhodesia. His election in April 1979 followed the Internal Settlement which had been concluded in March 1978 between the RF Government and other non-exiled black nationalist leaders. He held office for less than a year.

[264] Zimbabwe African National Union.

[265] Pieter Willem Botha was a South African politician who was the last Prime Minister of South Africa from 1978 to 1984 and its first executive state president from 1984 to 1989.

On Friday, 1st February 1985, Pieter was parked outside Amnesty International's offices when the black Mercedes arrived at 11:00 am. Inside the vehicle were two burly-looking black men. One of these men emerged from the passenger seat and entered the Amnesty International offices. He reappeared a short time later with a distinguished black man in a suit. The suited man was not known to Pieter but was, in fact, Jonathon Khumalo.

Acting on a gut feeling, Pieter photographed Jonathon getting into the Mercedes and then followed the car to the *Hideaway Coffee House* in Soho. There, he maintained surveillance on the Mercedes. He photographed the three occupants getting out of the car and entering the *Hideaway Coffee House*. About fifteen minutes later, they reappeared with another man, this time a young white man. Pieter photographed the fourth man and the departing vehicle before driving away and returning to his student digs. He subsequently developed the photographs in the darkroom he had set up in the basement of his digs.

That Sunday, as was his custom, Pieter discreetly met his '*handler*' at Trafalgar Square. There, he surreptitiously handed over a manila envelope containing the photographs he had taken and developed.

Chapter 27 – SA intelligence services muddy the waters

Time line – early 1985

Pieter Hendrik's *handler*, a man named Charlie Montgomery, had formerly been a senior officer with the BSAP[266] Special Branch. Charlie, an Englishman, was recruited by the BSAP in the early 1950s, enticed by clever advertisements in leading British newspapers. These targeted adventurous young men seeking opportunities in the British self-governing colony of Southern Rhodesia. At that time, Southern Rhodesia was touted as one of Britain's colonial success stories, offering a comfortable lifestyle, good pay, a wonderful climate, and fulfilling work.

In March 1951, Charlie received a telegram from the London Office of the High Commissioner for Southern Africa, notifying him that his application for a police appointment in the BSAP had been approved. A month later, Charlie boarded the Union Castle mail ship, the *Stirling Castle*, in Southampton en route to Cape Town. After a day of sightseeing in Cape Town, including a cable car trip up to the peak of Table Mountain, he travelled by train from Cape Town to Salisbury, a journey that, in those days, took four days.

---

[266] British South Africa Police.

Charlie successfully completed the initial six-month training period at the Morris Training Depot in Salisbury[267], after which he graduated as a patrol officer.

Charlie's policing career took him through various roles within the police force, with postings in Salisbury and Bulawayo. However, the work he found most enjoyable and rewarding was as an intelligence officer with Special Branch. This role aligned perfectly with his interest in global affairs, and he quickly rose through the ranks, eventually becoming Chief Superintendent in charge of the country's counter-insurgency work before retiring in 1975. During his tenure, he built a network of contacts in intelligence circles, particularly in South Africa, the UK, Mozambique, and Portugal.

Upon returning to the UK in 1975, Charlie was uncertain about his future. Leveraging his network of contacts within the South African Bureau for State Security (BOSS), he reconnected with an old acquaintance to explore potential roles that might make use of his in-depth knowledge of Rhodesian COIN[268] operations. After various discussions with high-ranking officials in BOSS[269], he agreed to become an undercover BOSS agent based in the UK, tasked with keeping BOSS informed about matters of interest to the South African Government, particularly concerning the policies of the UK Government, the OAU[270], the ANC[271] of South Africa, Amnesty International, and the South African Communist Party.

As part of Charlie's intelligence-gathering responsibilities, he became well-versed in Amnesty International's various campaigns directed against the South African apartheid regime. He also learned about a

---

[267] Salisbury was renamed Harare in 1982.

[268] Counter-insurgency.

[269] Bureau of State Security. This was the main South African intelligence agency from 1969 to 1980. In 1980 BOSS was significantly restructured and transformed to become the National Intelligence Service (NIS). The NIS is now, however, defunct.

[270] The Organisation of African Unity (1963 to 2002). In 2002 the OAU was superseded by the African Union (AU).

[271] This is the acronym for the African National Congress. The ANC is one of the oldest and most well-known liberation movements in South Africa. It was founded in 1921 and played a central role in the fight against apartheid.

young black lawyer named Jonathon Khumalo, who had joined Amnesty International in 1981 and who was making a significant impact. Through his investigations, Charlie discovered that Jonathon had arrived in the UK in the late 1960s at the age of 12 or 13. He had received his secondary and tertiary education in England, graduating from the University of Oxford in 1980 with a degree in law. Interestingly, Jonathon claimed to be a descendant of the royal house of Khumalo[272], although this claim had never been definitively substantiated.

Consequently, when Charlie, who was now residing in Wimbledon, received the latest intelligence supplied by Pieter Hendrik, the photographs of Jonathon Khumalo did not come as a surprise. However, the identities of the two burly black men who had picked up Jonathon from Amnesty International offices in Islington remained unknown to Charlie, as did the identity of the young white man Jonathon had met at the *Hideaway Coffee House*. These unanswered questions piqued Charlie's curiosity, prompting him to seek answers.

Initially, Charlie set out to update himself on Amnesty International's projects concerning South Africa. He soon found that Amnesty was focused on several key areas including — campaigning against the widespread torture and mistreatment of political prisoners by South African security forces; providing legal support for those facing arbitrary detention or unfair trials; and advocating for legal reforms to dismantle apartheid[273] laws and protect freedoms of expression and assembly.

Next, Charlie focused his efforts on identifying the three unknown individuals photographed by Pieter Hendrik. By utilising his contacts within the British and Zimbabwean intelligence communities, Charlie

---

[272] The House of Khumalo is the continuing royal family of the former Mthwakazi Kingdom (modern day Matabeleland). The Mthwakazi Kingdom was founded in 1823 and ended in 1894 with the First Matabele War. The House has endured to the present day.
[273] Apartheid is the Afrikaans word for apartness. It was a system of institutionalised racial segregation that existed in South Africa and South West Africa (now Namibia) from 1948 to the early 1990s.

quickly established that the two burly black men who had picked up Jonathon from the Amnesty's offices were personal security details for Joshua Nkomo. He learned that Joshua Nkomo had arrived in the UK with them on a British Airways flight from Johannesburg on 28th January. The two security details, along with Joshua Nkomo, had flown back to Johannesburg two weeks later on a British Airways flight that departed from London Heathrow on 11th February.

Regarding the identity of the third man photographed by Pieter Hendrik — a white man in his mid-twenties — Charlie had little success beyond determining that he had not been on the same flight as Joshua Nkomo and his two security details.

Charlie reasonably assumed that Jonathon Khumalo and Joshua Nkomo had likely met somewhere in London to discuss matters of mutual interest. Considering Jonathon's claimed ancestry to the royal house of Khumalo and the political difficulties in Zimbabwe, Charlie wondered if they were discussing Jonathon's potential return to the country. Regardless of the truth behind these speculations, he instinctively knew that if ZANU-PF[274] learned of a meeting between Jonathon Khumalo and Joshua Nkomo, they would suspect the worst. Given the existing hostilities between ZANU-PF and ZAPU[275], Charlie was confident that any such suggestion would further inflame tribal tensions in Zimbabwe and exacerbate regional destabilisation, which would work to South Africa's advantage.

After replaying this scenario in his mind numerous times, Charlie compiled a secret report for his NIS/BOSS[276] contact in Pretoria. The report detailed the relevant intelligence he had gathered, suggesting that Joshua Nkomo had secretly travelled to the UK to meet with

---

[274] Zimbabwe African National Union – Patriotic Front. ZANU-PF is a political organisation that has been the ruling party of Zimbabwe since independence in 1980.

[275] Zimbabwe African People's Union.

[276] National Intelligence Service. The NIS was established in 1980, succeeding the Bureau of State Security (BOSS). Its primary role was to gather intelligence, conduct covert operations, and support the South African Government's counter-intelligence efforts.

Jonathon Khumalo, who claimed descent from the royal house of Khumalo, to plan Jonathon's return to Zimbabwe. Charlie suggested that NIS/BOSS leak this information to agents in the Zimbabwean CIO[277], which would likely prompt the Zimbabwean Government to take hostile measures against ZAPU. Such actions would work to South Africa's advantage by further destabilising its northern neighbour, Zimbabwe.

Charlie meticulously typed his report onto waxed paper on the reverse side of an innocuous letter and posted it to a cover address in Pretoria. To ensure secrecy, the intended NIS/BOSS recipient of the letter could decipher its contents by dusting the reverse side with graphite powder. His report was sent via first-class airmail in late March 1985.

In early April 1985, Charlie Montgomery's secret report was decoded and provided to Max Geldenhuys, the NIS/BOSS Divisional Director, in Pretoria. It took Max a few days to read and assimilate the report's contents. At that time, NIS/BOSS activities were primarily focused on direct threats to South African security, so Charlie's recommendations were not considered a high priority. However, they were intriguing enough for Max to send a fax to the intelligence officer overseeing the Zimbabwean desk at NIS/BOSS. He recommended that fabricated intelligence be covertly leaked to the Zimbabwean CIO. The fabricated intelligence would state that Joshua Nkomo had recently travelled to the UK to persuade Jonathon Khumalo, a Zimbabwean citizen residing in the UK and claiming descent from the royal house of Khumalo, to return to Zimbabwe to re-establish the Khumalo royal line, thereby strengthening the Ndebele nation.

---

[277] Zimbabwe's Central Intelligence Organisation.

Chapter 28 – The lead up to the 1985 general elections

"A wise man may change his mind; a fool never will." — Seneca the Younger.

Sipho often found he did his best thinking when alone, gazing out over the beauty of the African bush from the decking of his house on the banks of Ingwe[278] Dam.

When Sipho had agreed, in late 1984, that he would discuss with Duncan the idea of using Mhuka[279] Ranch as a safe house and sanctuary for ZAPU[280] supporters fleeing political persecution by the Mugabe regime, he secretly hoped to persuade Duncan to expand this idea further. In particular, he wished to use Mhuka Ranch more proactively to undermine ZANU-PF's[281] position in Zimbabwe. Initially, his primary motivation was to avenge the cruel and unjust murder of his parents by striking out at ZANU-PF whenever possible. However, if suitable opportunities for this to occur did not arise naturally, he was prepared to orchestrate and engineer such moments.

---

[278] Ingwe is a local word meaning leopard.
[279] A local word meaning animals or wildlife.
[280] Zimbabwe African People's Union.
[281] Zimbabwe African National Union – Patriotic Front. ZANU-PF is a political organisation that has been the ruling party of Zimbabwe since independence in 1980.

Sipho had shared his thoughts on these matters with Duncan several times. During these discussions, Duncan quickly realised that Sipho was driven more by a desire for revenge than by a genuine interest in promoting ZAPU politically. Although Duncan empathised with Sipho's grief and anger, he knew that letting Sipho be consumed by his rage could lead to negative outcomes and pose significant risks for Mhuka Ranch and its business.

Accordingly, Duncan adopted a fatherly role. He quietly listened as Sipho poured out his thoughts. Whenever these thoughts turned to musings involving vengeance, or the injustice of what had happened, Duncan acknowledged Sipho's feelings while suggesting there might be better ways to seek justice other than lashing out indiscriminately at ZANU-PF.

Rather than dismissing Duncan's opinions, Sipho let his subconscious mull over Duncan's views, especially during solitary moments amidst the ranch's incomparable beauty. As he reflected, he sensed a definite shift in his thinking. He was now prepared to play the long game, acknowledging that ZANU-PF was both militarily and politically formidable and likely to remain so. Major political or military victories against ZANU-PF seemed improbable and could backfire, causing significant harm to Mhuka Ranch and its business. Instead, Sipho now sought moral victories to temper his anger.

In this context, Sipho and Duncan had developed a well-thought-out plan of action to be implemented in the six-month period leading up to the 1985 general elections which were scheduled for mid-year.

Their plans were comprehensive and multifaceted. First, they intended to play an active role in the upcoming elections, focusing particularly on Masvingo province, which was a political stronghold for ZANU-PF. Although they understood that ZAPU's chances of making significant political inroads were slim, they nonetheless aimed to build strong relationships with ZAPU's candidates in the Chiredzi constituencies. This included offering Mhuka Ranch's resources to assist with campaigning, if needed.

Another key objective was to minimise political intimidation. They aimed to prevent ZANU-PF from coercing or intimidating ZAPU candidates and their supporters. With the ranch's strong relationship with the Chiredzi police, they planned to further reinforce these ties. As the elections approached, they resolved to immediately report any instances of intimidation to the police and press for swift action to stop such behaviour.

They also made contingency plans to mitigate the impact of any election-related violence in Chiredzi and at Mhuka Ranch. Security measures would be enhanced around the homestead, the three luxury lodges, the village compound, the airstrip, and Ingwe Dam. Additionally, ranger training would be adjusted to ensure they could effectively manage any politically motivated violence.

To protect their supply chains, they decided to develop relationships with alternative suppliers in Northern Transvaal, particularly for critical supplies like food and fuel. In establishing these connections, they relied heavily on the advice of Duncan's two sons, Tim and Hamish, who were now living in the Orange Free State.

They also planned to install additional generators and build diesel storage tanks strategically around the ranch as a backup in case of power disruptions.

Lastly, they intended to use RQI's[282] offices in London to develop a robust public relations campaign. This campaign would advocate for Mhuka Ranch's role as a government-sanctioned rhino conservation site, positioning the ranch as a key player in wildlife preservation.

Once the plans were agreed upon, Sipho, alongside Duncan and Mark, diligently set out to complete all the agreed tasks. As circumstances would soon demonstrate, it was wise that the ranch invested time and resources in executing these plans.

****

---

[282] Rare Quest Imports.

Sipho and Mark quickly established a strong working relationship with the two ZAPU candidates for the constituencies of Chiredzi North and Chiredzi South, Stephen Maseko and Titos Chauke. In support of these candidates, about a week before polling day, Joshua Nkomo and his deputy, Josiah Chinamano, organised a rally at the local soccer ground in Chiredzi. Through his local contacts, Sipho received intelligence that the ZANU-PF Youth League was planning to disrupt the event.

Acting swiftly, Sipho informed both the ZAPU campaign organisers and the Chiredzi police of the potential threat. He also offered the services of Mhuka Ranch's anti-poaching squad to strengthen security at the rally. ZAPU gratefully accepted the offer, but the Chiredzi police declined, assuring him that they had enough manpower to manage any trouble the ZANU-PF Youth League might create.

The rally was scheduled for Saturday, 22nd June 1985 at 2:00 pm. As agreed between ZAPU and Mhuka Ranch, their respective security personnel were inconspicuously deployed at strategic points around the soccer field by 11:00 am. At that time, there was no evidence of any Chiredzi police presence.

At 1:15 pm, approximately 45 minutes before Nkomo and Chinamano were due to arrive, three busloads of ZANU-PF Youth League supporters arrived and debussed. They waved ZANU-PF slogans, sang anti-ZAPU songs, and were demonstrative and threatening in their actions.

ZAPU and Mhuka Ranch security personnel remained at their postings, not revealing themselves as security personnel. Just before 2:00 pm, the head of ZAPU security received a radio message that Nkomo and Chinamano's vehicle was about five minutes away. The head of security advised Sipho accordingly.

At this point, the ZAPU and Mhuka Ranch personnel revealed themselves and moved into the centre of the soccer field, where a podium had been set up for Nkomo and Chinamano to address the gathered supporters. In total, about 30 armed security personnel were present.

Shortly afterward, the vehicle carrying Nkomo and Chinamano arrived at the scene, accompanied by two additional vehicles, each transporting more armed security personnel. This brought the total number of armed guards to 40.

Upon seeing the significant deployment of armed security personnel, the ZANU-PF Youth League wisely ceased their anti-ZAPU chants and put away their ZANU-PF slogans. This allowed Joshua Nkomo and Josiah Chinamano to address the gathered supporters without interruption.

The general elections were subsequently held in June 1985, and while some regions faced widespread issues such as intimidation, restrictions on opposition campaigning, and a biased electoral process — leading to criticism that the elections were not entirely free and fair — Chiredzi remained largely unaffected by such practices.

Unsurprisingly, ZANU-PF performed strongly in the elections and even increased their number of seats. The final results were as follows:-

PARTY	Seats won in 1980 elections	Seats won in 1985 elections
ZANU-PF	57	65[283]
PF-ZAPU[284]	20	15
UANC[285]	3	0
RF[286]	20	N/A

---

[283] This includes the results in the Kariba constituency. Elections were postponed due to the death of one of the candidates. The ZANU-PF candidate eventually won the seat.

[284] ZAPU's use of 'PF' in front of its name was a bid to differentiate itself from ZANU-PF while still recognising the significant role it had played in the Patriotic Front coalition between ZANU and ZAPU during the negotiations that led to Zimbabwe's independence.

[285] The United African National Council.

PARTY	Seats won in 1980 elections	Seats won in 1985 elections
CAZ[287]	N/A	15
IZG[288]	N/A	4
Independents[289]	0	1
TOTAL	**100**	**100**

The primary concern after the elections was whether ZANU-PF could secure enough support from other parties to amend the Constitution established under the Lancaster House Agreement. If successful, this would enable ZANU-PF to rapidly transition to its preferred one-party system, eliminating the special privileges reserved for whites before the ten-year period stipulated in the Constitution had expired.

The contingency plans developed by Duncan, Mark, and Sipho also ensured that Mhuka Ranch experienced no supply chain issues either before or immediately after the elections. As a result, for Mhuka Ranch's paying clientele, the general elections were largely a non-event, passing without incident and leaving operations at the ranch unaffected.

---

[286] The Rhodesian Front.

[287] Conservative Alliance of Zimbabwe, formerly known as The Republican Front. The CAZ was led by Ian Smith. These House of Assembly members were elected by voters on the White Roll.

[288] Independent Zimbabwe Group. These House of Assembly members were elected by voters on the White Roll.

[289] Jonas Andersen, who stood as an Independent, was successful in the Mount Pleasant constituency.

Chapter 29 – Zimbabwe's intelligence agency is fooled

Time line – July 1985

In accordance with Max Geldenhuys' instructions, Charlie Montgomery's fabricated intelligence was clandestinely leaked to Zimbabwe's CIO[290]. This was accomplished through double agents within Zimbabwe's CIO who were also secretly on the payroll of South Africa's National Intelligence Service.

The false intelligence contained enough verifiable details to make the overall report convincing. It claimed that Joshua Nkomo, along with two of his security personnel, had recently made a secret trip to the UK to discuss the upcoming Zimbabwean general elections with senior British officials and with ZAPU[291] supporters, who had fled to the UK fearing for their lives following the 5th Brigade's campaign of violence against the Ndebele nation.

According to the intelligence, while in the UK, Nkomo had met with an unnamed white businessman and a well-educated black man named Jonathon Khumalo. Jonathon, a Zimbabwean citizen and alleged descendant of the royal House of Khumalo[292], had been

---

[290] Zimbabwe's Central Intelligence Organisation.
[291] Zimbabwe African People's Union.
[292] The House of Khumalo is the continuing royal family of the former Mthwakazi Kingdom (modern day Matabeleland). The Mthwakazi Kingdom was founded in 1823

educated at Inyathi[293] Mission School near Bulawayo in the 1960s, where he was influenced by African nationalist ideas.

The school headmaster, who opposed the white-minority Rhodesian Government, had identified Jonathon as a talented student destined for leadership in post-colonial Zimbabwe. In the late 1960s, the headmaster collaborated with the Council for World Mission[294] to secretly send Jonathon to the UK. There, Jonathon completed his secondary and tertiary education, eventually graduating from the University of Oxford in June 1980 with a law degree. After graduating, he had intended to return to Zimbabwe to join Nkomo's ZAPU party. However, on the advice of his minders, Jonathon delayed his return due to political uncertainties following independence. Instead, he joined Amnesty International[295] in 1981 as a human rights lawyer.

The intelligence claimed that Nkomo had met with Jonathon to persuade him to immediately return to Zimbabwe to re-establish the Khumalo royal line, thereby helping to bolster morale among the Ndebele nation and improve ZAPU's political prospects in the upcoming general elections.

The deceptive intelligence stated that it was unclear whether Jonathon Khumalo had yet returned to Zimbabwe, but that such a

---

and ended in 1894 with the First Matabele War. The House has endured to the present day.

[293] The mission had been established by the Reverend Robert Moffat in 1859. It is situated some 75 kilometres north-north-east of Bulawayo. Moffat was a member of the London Missionary Society, which had been established in England with the aim of spreading the knowledge of Christ among heathen and unenlightened nations.

[294] The Council is a worldwide community of mainly Protestant Christian churches. The organisation works to spread the knowledge of Christ throughout the world and to strengthen their members in their mission work by sharing their resources of money, people, skills, and insights. It was formerly named the London Missionary Society.

[295] Amnesty International is an international non-governmental organisation focused on human rights, with its headquarters in the UK. It was founded in 1961 with the mission of campaigning for a world in which every person enjoys all of the human rights enshrined in the Universal Declaration of Human Rights and other international human rights instruments.

return was considered highly probable. The intelligence included photographs of Jonathon, the unnamed white businessman, the two black security officers, and photos of Nkomo arriving at and departing from London Heathrow with his two security details.

This intelligence eventually reached the Harare offices of Zimbabwe's CIO in late June 1985, just before the 1985 general elections. However, due to the CIO's focus on election-related matters, it was not analysed until late July 1985.

By the time the intelligence was reviewed, the election results had revealed a strong performance by ZANU-PF[296] and a disappointing outcome for ZAPU. As a result, the CIO analyst examining the intelligence report intended to disregard it.

However, by chance, a second analyst had just completed his analysis of the recent election results by constituency. His analysis showed that while ZAPU had not won any seats in the province of Masvingo[297], it had performed reasonably well in the seats of Chiredzi North and Chiredzi South. The analyst wondered why this was the case and had undertaken further research to understand if there were any local dynamics explaining ZAPU's relatively good performance in these two constituencies.

This subsequent investigation uncovered a report lodged by ZANU-PF's Youth League shortly before the elections. The report revealed that several busloads of Youth League members had been dispatched to Chiredzi on Saturday, 22nd June, with the intent of disrupting a ZAPU rally where Joshua Nkomo and his deputy, Josiah Chinamano, were scheduled to address local supporters. However, their efforts to disrupt the rally were thwarted by the effective security measures provided by ZAPU personnel, as well as by the owner of a nearby cattle ranch and rhino conservancy named Mhuka Ranch.

---

[296] Zimbabwe African National Union – Patriotic Front. ZANU-PF is a political organisation that has been the ruling party of Zimbabwe since independence in 1980.
[297] Masvingo was previously known as Fort Victoria. The name changed in 1982.

The analyst subsequently met with the Registrar of Companies to shed some light on Mhuka[298] Ranch. Through this meeting, the analyst established that, until recently, the ranch had been 100% owned by a local businessman and rancher named Duncan Oliver. However, at the end of 1984, Duncan Oliver sold one-third of the shares of Mhuka Ranch to one of his employees, Sipho[299] Pukelo, who managed the rhino conservancy, and another one-third to a British-registered company named Rare Quest Imports Pty Ltd.

The analyst then reached out to the Chiredzi police station to inquire if they had any information regarding Mhuka Ranch. He spoke with Chief Inspector Gwata, who was familiar with the ranch. Chief Inspector Gwata stated that he had led the investigation into the shooting deaths of three white poachers on the ranch in 1981. These deceased poachers, all former members of the Rhodesian Security Forces, had been killed in a firefight with an anti-poaching security team from the ranch that had been deployed to investigate illegal poaching activities.

The anti-poaching security party comprised two of Duncan Oliver's sons, Hamish and Mark, Sipho Pukelo, the ranch's anti-poaching manager, and a man named Nick Sinclair. Nick was a white Zimbabwean who was, at the time of the incident, studying in Edinburgh. He had returned to Zimbabwe for a holiday with his girlfriend. Interestingly, both Sipho Pukelo and Nick Sinclair had served with 3RAR[300] during the Rhodesian Bush War.

The three poachers had been shot and killed without any injuries reported among the anti-poaching security team. Police investigations determined that the anti-poaching personnel acted in self-defence when the poachers opened fire on them. Consequently, no charges were filed, and the case was closed. The Chief Inspector also provided photographs of the four members of the anti-poaching security team, as well as images of the three deceased poachers.

---

[298] A local word meaning animals or wildlife.
[299] Sipho is a Ndebele boy's name meaning Gift.
[300] 3rd Battalion of the Rhodesian African Rifles.

Both analysts were part of the internal security branch of the CIO. Their reports were fortuitously reviewed by the assistant director of the branch, who noted commonalities between the two documents. Recognising their significance, he decided to upgrade the security classification and escalated the matter to the most senior analyst within the internal security branch. He instructed that both reports be examined for connections and that a top-secret consolidated report be finalised promptly.

The assistant director received the report within three weeks. The senior analyst's findings confirmed that Sipho Pukelo, a member of the anti-poaching security team and owner of one-third of Mhuka Ranch's shares, was the same individual who had thwarted ZANU-PF's Youth League's plans to disrupt the ZAPU rally featuring Joshua Nkomo and Josiah Chinamano on 22nd June in Chiredzi. More concerning, the report indicated that Sipho was currently pursuing allegations against the ZNA's[301] 5th Brigade regarding the alleged murder of his parents, Mandla[302] and Nandi[303] Pukelo, at Inyathi Mission on 2nd August 1984. He was being assisted in this effort, on a *pro bono*[304] basis, by a prominent Bulawayo-based legal firm, Webb, Low, and Barry. Additionally, the United Congregational Church of Southern Africa, the current owners of Inyathi Mission School and employers of the late Mandla and Nandi Pukelo, were also pursuing the matter.

Regarding Nick Sinclair, a member of the anti-poaching squad involved in the shooting incident at Mhuka Ranch, a search of the Ministry of Home Affairs' records revealed that he had last entered Zimbabwe on 18th July 1984 and left on 6th August 1984 on a plane bound for Johannesburg. The report indicated that Nick Sinclair was the same unidentified white businessman photographed leaving a coffee house in Soho, London, in February 1985, accompanied by

---

[301] Zimbabwe National Army.
[302] Mandla is a Ndebele boy's name meaning Power and Strength.
[303] Nandi is a Ndebele girl's name meaning Sweetness.
[304] In a legal context, *pro bono* means the provision of legal services on a free or significantly reduced fee basis.

Jonathon Khumalo and two members of his security detail. While Nick Sinclair's current whereabouts were unknown, it was confirmed that his parents, Matthew and Brenda Sinclair, lived in Ballantyne Park, Harare, where Matthew held a senior position within Zimbabwe's Tobacco Marketing Board.

The senior analyst's report also indicated that there was no record of any individual named Jonathon Khumalo entering Zimbabwe by plane, rail, or road in the past twelve months. Consequently, it was presumed he was still living in London.

Finally, the report stated that investigations were still ongoing to ascertain the corporate identity of Rare Quest Import Pty Ltd and why it held a shareholding in Mhuka Ranch.

Upon reading and digesting the contents of the senior analyst's report, the assistant director telephoned the executive assistant of the Head of CIO, Emmerson Mnangagwa, who was also the Minister of State Security, requesting an urgent and top-secret meeting with him. This was to be held on Thursday, 1st August 1985.

Chapter 30 – The madness continues

Time line – August 1985

"The danger of having a strong opinion is that you might mistake it for the truth!" — Daniel Kahneman

The assistant director of the CIO's[305] internal security branch left Emmerson Mnangagwa's office feeling concerned. The Minister had given him a good hearing and allowed him sufficient time to summarise the top-secret report prepared by the assistant director's senior analyst. However, the Minister had asked no probing questions. With a scowl, Mnangagwa had merely instructed the assistant director to leave behind a copy of the report and advised that he would get back to him shortly. He then politely ushered him out of the office.

Immediately afterwards, Mnangagwa phoned the Prime Minister's office, requesting an urgent meeting with Prime Minister Robert Mugabe and his inner cabinet circle.

At that meeting, two unequivocal decisions were made. *Firstly*, Robert Mugabe was thrilled with ZANU-PF's[306] excellent performance in the recent general elections. Buoyed by these results, he believed

---

[305] Zimbabwe's Central Intelligence Organisation.
[306] Zimbabwe African National Union – Patriotic Front. ZANU-PF is a political organisation that has been the ruling party of Zimbabwe since independence in 1980.

his long-term aim of transforming Zimbabwe's fledgling democracy into a one-party state with him at the helm was within reach. He was certainly not willing to risk this progress by allowing the political fortunes of ZAPU[307] to improve due to the influence of someone residing in the UK who claimed to be a direct descendant of King Lobengula Khumalo[308] and who intended to return to Zimbabwe to re-establish this defunct royal house.

Secondly, Mugabe had already acted to insulate himself from the global political fallout arising from the worst excesses of the 5th Brigade's violent implementation of the *Gukurahundi*[309] campaign against the Ndebele nation by throwing his colleague, Colonel Perrance Shiri[310], under the bus. Having taken these steps, Mugabe was unwilling to allow the same political heat to reignite due to legal manoeuvres by a former black RAR[311] soldier whom he perceived as a sell-out of Zimbabwe's black citizenry.

Accordingly, Mugabe's inner cabinet verbally agreed that necessary measures should be undertaken by the appropriate government agencies to ensure that Jonathon Khumalo would never be allowed to re-enter Zimbabwe and that Sipho Pukelo should be permanently silenced.

A few days after this unminuted cabinet meeting, Minister Mnangagwa phoned the assistant director of the CIO's internal security branch to thank him for his report and inform him that it was being given due consideration by the government.

---

[307] Zimbabwe African People's Union.

[308] King Lobengula Khumalo (1845 to circa 1894) was the second and last official King of the northern Ndebele people.

[309] *Gukurahundi* is a Shona word which roughly translates as *'the early rain that washes away the chaff before the spring rain'*.

[310] Perrance Shiri was distantly related to Rogert Mugabe. After independence, he commanded the 5th Brigade from 1983 to 1984. In 1992 he was appointed the commander of the Airforce of Zimbabwe. Shiri was influential in orchestrating the 2017 Zimbabwean coup d'état which removed Mugabe from power. On 30th November 2017, Shiri was appointed Minister of Agriculture by President Emmerson Mnangagwa.

[311] Rhodesian African Rifles.

Chapter 31 – Nick befriends Jonathon Khumalo

Time line – February 1985 to August 1985

Nick's initial meetings with Jonathon Khumalo in London in January and February 1985 had a profound impact on him. Jonathon was a bright, intelligent man with undeniable charisma. Nick was certain that, if he could persuade Jonathon to return to Zimbabwe, Jonathon could play a significant role in the country's future. However, Nick wasn't convinced that Jonathon was necessarily seeking a political role in Zimbabwe. This had been hinted at during their first meeting at the *Hideaway Coffee House*, where it became clear that Jonathon's motivations to return to Zimbabwe centred around a desire to resurrect the royal House of Khumalo[312] and seek justice for the wrongs inflicted upon the Ndebele nation during the *Gukurahundi*[313] campaign.

---

[312] The House of Khumalo is the continuing royal family of the former Mthwakazi Kingdom (modern day Matabeleland). The Mthwakazi Kingdom was founded in 1823 and ended in 1894 with the First Matabele War. The House has endured to the present day.

[313] *Gukurahundi* is a Shona word which roughly translates as '*the early rain that washes away the chaff before the spring rain*'.

Nick was fully aware that Jonathon was a human rights lawyer for Amnesty International[314] and hence understood Jonathon's motive to expose the violent excesses and injustices of the *Gukurahundi* campaign. Although Jonathon was unaware of the tragic deaths of Sipho's parents at the hands of the 5th Brigade in August 1984, Nick believed that once informed, Jonathon could become a powerful advocate in the effort to hold the perpetrators accountable. Given Jonathon's background, Nick was also confident he would relate to the *pro bono*[315] work being undertaken by the Bulawayo-based law firm of Webb, Low, and Barry.

Nick had a broader agenda as well. Considering Jonathon's ancestral links to the country, he thought that Jonathon might help galvanise support for AHWF's[316] work in supporting endangered animals in southern Africa.

Before pursuing these ideas further, Nick decided to discuss them with Rachel.

A couple of days later, they were relaxing at home after dinner. Rachel was snuggled into Nick's lap, and their recently acquired golden Labrador, Calico, was asleep next to her on the sofa.

Luke Worthington, the fundraising director of AHWF, had recently met with Rachel to debrief her on the successful donors' luncheon hosted by AHWF in London a few weeks earlier. Terry Ashborough's address on the precarious state of southern Africa's wildlife had resonated with attendees, leading to significant funding pledges. After the luncheon, Luke Worthington and Terry Ashborough discussed RQI's recent investment in Mhuka[317] Ranch in Zimbabwe,

---

[314] Amnesty International is an international non-governmental organisation focused on human rights, with its headquarters in the UK. It was founded in 1961 with the mission of campaigning for a world in which every person enjoys all of the human rights enshrined in the Universal Declaration of Human Rights and other international human rights instruments.

[315] In a legal context, *pro bono* means the provision of legal services on a free or significantly reduced fee basis.

[316] Acronym for Afro-Asian Humanity and Wildlife Foundation.

[317] A local word meaning animals or wildlife.

particularly the rhino conservancy established there. This aroused Ashborough's interest, and he expressed a desire to feature the ranch in a BBC[318] documentary about the threats to rhinos and efforts to ensure their survival in southern Africa.

Rachel serendipitously shared this discussion with Nick, seeking his thoughts on whether Duncan and Sipho would agree to feature Mhuka Ranch in a collaboration between AHWF, Mhuka Ranch, and the BBC.

Nick was immediately enthusiastic, and he and Rachel eagerly discussed how to bring such a project to fruition. During their conversation, Nick shared his thoughts on trying to persuade Jonathon to allow the Khumalo royal house name to be used to help promote wildlife conservation efforts in Matabeleland. Initially hesitant, Rachel warmed to the idea once Nick explained the significant influence of the Khumalo name in the region. However, she remained cautious about potentially ruffling feathers by venturing too deeply into Zimbabwe's tribal complexities.

Before retiring to bed, they agreed to discuss both ideas with Stuart before proceeding further.

A week later, during their regular catch-up meeting with Stuart, they presented both ideas. Stuart supported both but agreed with Rachel that they needed to be cautious about political and tribal sensitivities in Zimbabwe. He emphasised the need to avoid political controversies involving ZANU-PF[319] and ZAPU[320], given Zimbabwe's fragile democracy and recent violent history.

Accordingly, it was agreed that before discussions with the BBC or Terry Ashborough progressed further, Nick should first meet with Jonathon to gauge his views on using the Khumalo royal name to

---

[318] British Broadcasting Corporation.
[319] Zimbabwe African National Union – Patriotic Front. ZANU-PF is a political organisation that has been the ruling party of Zimbabwe since independence in 1980.
[320] Zimbabwe African People's Union.

promote wildlife conservation projects in Matabeleland, and with Duncan and Sipho to discuss their thoughts on allowing Mhuka Ranch to be featured in a BBC documentary.

Subsequently, Nick met with Jonathon a couple of times, and these meetings further deepened Nick's respect for him. Although Jonathon was open to using the Khumalo royal name for public relations purposes in Matabeleland, he was opposed to its use in marketing wildlife conservation. He believed that while conservation projects were commendable, leveraging the Khumalo name in this context might be seen as opportunistic and tokenistic, adding little value to the family's reputation or to the conservation efforts themselves.

Nonetheless, Jonathon did reconfirm his intention to return to Zimbabwe in October 1985, a couple of months after the results of the 1985 Zimbabwean general elections were known. In the meantime, he and Nick agreed to stay in touch.

While Jonathon was lukewarm about using the Khumalo royal name to promote conservation efforts, Duncan and Sipho were ecstatic about the proposal to feature Mhuka Ranch in a BBC documentary on rhino conservation. They believed the documentary would educate a global audience on the perils facing rhinos in Africa and showcase the work being done at Mhuka Ranch in its conservation and breeding programmes. They urged Nick to do whatever he could to bring the project to fruition.

After these meetings, Nick updated Stewart, Rachel, and Luke on the outcomes. They were delighted that Duncan and Sipho had fully endorsed the idea of featuring Mhuka Ranch in the BBC documentary. Luke was authorised to return to the BBC/Terry Ashborough to work out a project implementation plan and timetable.

Regarding Jonathon's views, Rachel was relieved that he was opposed to the suggestion of using the Khumalo royal name to promote wildlife conservation efforts. She had a nagging concern that the use of the name might result in political difficulties for Mhuka Ranch and RQI.

Little did Nick know that Zimbabwe's political tentacles would soon entangle him, Jonathon, and Sipho ever deeper into the perilous web of Zimbabwean politics.

Chapter 32 – ZANU-PF's approach to the Khumalo problem

"The most dangerous thing for a country is when its government has no fear of the people." — Anonymous

Jonathon Khumalo, a 13-year-old schoolboy, had been whisked out of Rhodesia in 1969, bound for the UK. His departure, orchestrated by the headmaster of Inyathi Mission School[321] in collaboration with the Council for World Mission[322], faced numerous administrative hurdles. As a black child with only his mother alive — his father having perished in a mining accident at Wankie Colliery[323] when Jonathon was an infant — obtaining a passport proved challenging. However, the school's persistence paid off, resulting in Jonathon being issued a Rhodesian passport valid for five years due to his status as a minor.

---

[321] The mission had been established by the Reverend Robert Moffat in 1859. It is situated some 75 kilometres north-north-east of Bulawayo. Moffat was a member of the London Missionary Society, which had been established in England with the aim of spreading the knowledge of Christ among heathen and unenlightened nations.
[322] The Council is a worldwide community of mainly Protestant Christian churches. The organisation works to spread the knowledge of Christ throughout the world and to strengthen their members in their mission work by sharing their resources of money, people, skills, and insights. It was formerly named the London Missionary Society.
[323] Wankie Colliery, which is now known as Hwange Colliery, was established in 1899 and is one of Zimbabwe's oldest and largest coal mines.

Despite securing the passport, its international value was limited due to widespread sanctions imposed by the United Nations following Rhodesia's 1965 illegal unilateral declaration of independence. Under these sanctions, the Rhodesian passport was not recognised by most countries, including the UK. To facilitate Jonathon's entry into the UK, the headmaster successfully pressured the Council for World Mission to lobby the UK Passport Office for a special dispensation. In response, the Passport Office provided the school with a letter acknowledging Jonathon's unique circumstances and confirming that British immigration officials would permit his entry and issue a student visa valid for up to five years, despite the British Government's non-recognition of Rhodesian passports.

Thus, when Jonathon left Rhodesia in 1969, he carried his Rhodesian passport along with several important documents, including a consent letter from his mother permitting his travel to the UK, a copy of his father's death certificate, a letter from the Council for World Mission agreeing to act as his guardian and support his financial, medical, educational, and living needs while in the UK, and a letter from the UK Passport Office endorsing their acceptance of his Rhodesian passport.

When Jonathon's passport expired in 1974, the Council for World Mission lobbied the British Secretary of State for Foreign and Commonwealth Affairs to grant Jonathon British citizenship using its discretionary Royal Prerogative powers. After intense lobbying, citizenship was granted.

In early 1980, just before the general elections in Zimbabwe, Jonathon applied for a British passport to facilitate his proposed return to Zimbabwe to take up a leadership position with ZAPU. He was subsequently granted a British passport valid for ten years.

*****

In early August 1985, following an urgent meeting of Mugabe's inner circle, convened to consider a top-secret report from the assistant director of the CIO's[324] internal security branch, two task teams were formed — one to manage the Khumalo matter and the other the Pukelo matter.

The team responsible for the Khumalo matter comprised two Harare-based lawyers, both high-profile ZANU-PF[325]members. It was hoped that this small legal team could resolve the Khumalo matter via administrative decree. However, if this proved difficult, the matter would be referred to an active CIO intelligence cell based in London.

The lawyers inquired via the Registrar General's Harare-based office in the Ministry of Home Affairs and verified that in 1969, the former Rhodesian Government had issued a Rhodesian passport, valid for five years, to Jonathon Khumalo. They established that this passport had never been renewed.

This meant that if Jonathon intended to return to Zimbabwe, he would first have to apply for a new Zimbabwean passport. Alternatively, if he was now travelling on a British passport or one issued by another country, he would need to apply for a visa before re-entering Zimbabwe.

Based on the lawyers' advice, the Zimbabwean Government, by Executive Order, declared Jonathon Khumalo an undesirable person and stipulated that he was not to be issued a Zimbabwean passport or granted a visa to enter Zimbabwe. These orders were issued despite their likely illegality and contravention of various provisions of Zimbabwe's constitution and other relevant legislation.

Copies of these orders were faxed to all of Zimbabwe's consular offices in South Africa, the UK, and Europe.

The possibility that this Executive Order could be legally challenged did not particularly concern Mugabe. By then, he had not only

---

[324] Zimbabwe's Central Intelligence Organisation.
[325] Zimbabwe African National Union – Patriotic Front. ZANU-PF is a political organisation that has been the ruling party of Zimbabwe since independence in 1980.

politicised the ZNA[326] but had also begun the politicisation of the judiciary and police force. Accordingly, he was confident that if the Executive Order was legally challenged, he could exert enough pressure on the judiciary to ensure a favourable judgment for the Zimbabwean Government.

However, Mugabe's confidence was shaken when he was reminded that Jonathon Khumalo was a human rights lawyer with Amnesty International[327], well-versed in challenging authoritarian governments attempting to bypass the rule of law.

Opting to be cautious, Mugabe directed that the CIO intelligence cell in London to be immediately activated to conduct 24/7 surveillance on Jonathon Khumalo and to make the necessary arrangements to ensure the absolute resolution of the Khumalo matter.

*****

On Wednesday, 11th September 1985, Nick thought it was opportune to meet with Jonathon again for coffee and a chat. He enjoyed Jonathon's company and listening to his views on various topics, but on this occasion, he was particularly interested in finding out if Jonathon still intended to return to Zimbabwe in October.

He phoned Jonathon's office at Amnesty International and asked to be put through to Mr Jonathon Khumalo. There was an awkward silence on the other end for a few seconds before the receptionist informed him that Mr Khumalo had recently been killed in a hit-and-run incident in London, which the police were still investigating.

Nick was stunned. After ending the call, he scanned back copies of local London newspapers from the past fortnight and verified what the receptionist had told him. According to press articles, Jonathon

---

[326] Zimbabwe National Army.
[327] Amnesty International is an international non-governmental organisation focused on human rights, with its headquarters in the UK. It was founded in 1961 with the mission of campaigning for a world in which every person enjoys all of the human rights enshrined in the Universal Declaration of Human Rights and other international human rights instruments.

had been killed in a hit-and-run incident on the evening of Wednesday, 4th September 1985. Apparently, as was his custom, Jonathon had taken the Tube from Amnesty International's offices in Islington to his home in Croydon, south London. He had disembarked at West Croydon and was walking the remaining mile to his home. According to two witnesses, a white delivery van travelling at about 30 mph had suddenly veered off the road onto the pavement where Jonathon was walking. The van hit Jonathon in the back, then slammed on its brakes and came to a halt. To the surprise of the witnesses, the van then reversed at speed over the body before speeding off. Neither witness saw the vehicle's number plate, but both were certain that the driver and passenger were black men. Police investigations were ongoing.

That night at home, Nick and Rachel discussed the tragedy. Given what Nick knew about the ongoing tribal jealousies in Zimbabwe, along with Jonathon's claim of being an ancestral descendant of King Lobengula Khumalo[328] and his plans to resurrect the royal House of Khumalo[329], Nick was convinced that the hit-and-run incident was politically motivated. Rachel agreed and wondered whether the police were aware of these possibilities. Nick doubted it and decided to contact the police the next day to share his suspicions.

Later that night, just before they drifted off to sleep, Rachel nudged Nick and said, "You know, Nick, I'm absolutely convinced that poor Jonathon was murdered, probably by Mugabe's thugs. I am sure the Zimbabwe Government would not want to see Jonathon return to Zimbabwe. So, they had a definite motive. Mugabe's Government is so wicked and ruthless. We need to be very careful about how we interact with Zimbabwean officials, especially at Mhuka[330] Ranch."

---

[328] King Lobengula Khumalo (1845 to circa 1894) was the second and last official King of the northern Ndebele people.

[329] The House of Khumalo is the continuing royal family of the former Mthwakazi Kingdom (modern day Matabeleland). The Mthwakazi Kingdom was founded in 1823 and ended in 1894 with the First Matabele War. The House has endured to the present day.

[330] A local word meaning animals or wildlife.

"I totally agree," said Nick. "We need to be cautious. Regrettably, Mugabe's rule seems to be getting even more irrational and paranoid. If it's true that Jonathon's death was ordered by Mugabe, then the country has lost a wonderful person. It is just so pointless and sad. But let's try to get some sleep. It has been a difficult and harrowing day."

Chapter 33 – Nick meets with Scotland Yard

The following day at work was hectic for Nick, but he made a special effort to phone Scotland Yard to report his suspicions regarding the death of Jonathon Khumalo. The person he spoke to, Constable Doncaster, proved most helpful, particularly when Nick mentioned it concerned the reported death of Jonathon Khumalo in a hit-and-run incident.

However, Constable Doncaster was reluctant to take detailed information over the phone and suggested that it might be better for Nick to visit Scotland Yard and meet with Inspector Sleigh, one of the investigating officers. Nick agreed, and an appointment was set for 1:30 pm the following day at Scotland Yard's offices in Whitehall Place.

On Friday, Nick took the Tube from his office to Charing Cross and then walked the rest of the way, arriving at Scotland Yard's office complex by 1:00 pm. He was glad he had allowed himself plenty of time, as navigating the complex proved quite daunting.

His meeting with Inspector Sleigh was enlightening. According to the Inspector, the police had very few leads. When Nick informed Inspector Sleigh about Jonathon's supposed ancestral links to Zimbabwe and his intention to return to Zimbabwe to re-establish the royal House of Khumalo[331] — a move likely to be viewed with hostility by the current Zimbabwean Government — the Inspector became highly interested and took copious notes. His interest peaked further when Nick mentioned that, as a human rights lawyer, one of Jonathon's goals upon returning to Zimbabwe was to hold the Zimbabwean Government accountable for the atrocities committed by the 5th Brigade against the Ndebele nation. The Inspector was unaware of who the 5th Brigade was and what they were alleged to have done against the Ndebele nation, so Nick provided relevant information. Armed with this information, it appeared to Nick that the Inspector was now able to establish a possible motive for Jonathon's killing and was confident this would aid the police in their inquiries.

At the conclusion of their meeting, Inspector Sleigh gave Nick his card and asked him to reach out if he came across any further information that might help identify the two black men who had been driving the van that struck and killed Jonathon.

That evening, Nick phoned Mhuka[332] Ranch in Zimbabwe and spoke with Sipho[333], informing him of Jonathon's death and his suspicions that Jonathon had possibly been murdered in London by Zimbabwean secret agents. Sipho was shocked by the news. Though not a personal friend of Jonathon's, Sipho had gotten to know him quite well during Sipho's visit to the UK for Nick and Rachel's wedding in July 1984. Like Nick, Sipho was greatly impressed by Jonathon's personality and demeanour during their few meetings. Sipho had no doubt that if Jonathon had returned to Zimbabwe, he would have been a great asset to the country, though undoubtedly he would have been regarded as a significant threat by Robert Mugabe's government. Consequently, Sipho found it easy to believe Nick's

---

[331] The House of Khumalo is the continuing royal family of the former Mthwakazi Kingdom (modern day Matabeleland). The Mthwakazi Kingdom was founded in 1823 and ended in 1894 with the First Matabele War. The House has endured to the present day.
[332] A local word meaning animals or wildlife.
[333] Sipho is a Ndebele boy's name meaning Gift.

suspicions that Jonathon had been assassinated by Zimbabwean secret agents in London.

Nick's suspicions further deepened Sipho's disdain for Mugabe's government. In his view, Mugabe and the entire leadership of ZANU-PF[334], along with their various instruments of power, had quickly descended into a contemptible mob, doing irreparable damage to the fabric of the country.

---

[334] Zimbabwe African National Union – Patriotic Front. ZANU-PF is a political organisation that has been the ruling party of Zimbabwe since independence in 1980.

Chapter 34 – ZANU-PF's approach to the Pukelo problem

"All power tends to corrupt, but absolute power corrupts absolutely."
— Lord Acton

While Mugabe's inner cabinet initially had hoped — in vain, as it later turned out — that the Khumalo issue could be resolved by administrative decree, they recognised from the start that the Pukelo matter would demand a military solution, likely involving the ZNA's[335] 5th Brigade. Consequently, the team assigned to handle the Pukelo case was led by one of the CIO's[336] most senior and distinguished intelligence officers, Farai Mutasa, who also had a strong military background.

Farai was of Shona ethnicity. During the Rhodesian Bush War, he had served with ZANLA[337], earning distinction for his actions, including the killing of several members of the Rhodesian Security Forces and white farmers in northern Mashonaland. After Zimbabwe became independent, he was recruited by the CIO as an intelligence officer, quickly rising to prominence due to his analytical skills, critical thinking, and attention to detail. He was also fluent in Shona,

---

[335] Zimbabwe National Army.
[336] Zimbabwe's Central Intelligence Organisation.
[337] Zimbabwe African National Liberation Army. ZANLA was the military wing of ZANU.

Ndebele, and English, which enabled him to competently navigate Zimbabwe's diverse racial and tribal landscape.

Upon being tasked with leading the Pukelo matter, Farai's initial priority was to gain a comprehensive understanding of Sipho[338] Pukelo before formulating a plan to silence him permanently. Unlike Mugabe's inner circle, he didn't preconceive a 5th Brigade-style attack as the solution.

Farai quickly dismissed the possibility that Sipho was a dissident. His investigation into Sipho's background revealed no links to ZIPRA[339] or any official role within ZAPU[340]. However, based on Sipho's involvement in legal proceedings against the government, Farai rightly assumed he was not a ZANU-PF[341] supporter. These proceedings sought answers to questions about the 5th Brigade's assault on Inyathi Mission School[342] in August 1984, during which his parents had been killed. Farai was certain that if Sipho also met his death at the hands of the 5th Brigade, it would provoke an outcry both within and outside Zimbabwe, which would be politically damaging to Prime Minister Robert Mugabe and his government.

Through the work already conducted by the CIO, Farai learned that Sipho was both an employee and a shareholder at the prestigious Mhuka[343] Ranch, which was widely regarded as the country's leading rhino conservancy with a global reputation in environmental circles. One of Sipho's most notable achievements was his involvement in eliminating three white poachers — former members of the Rhodesian Security Forces — who had trespassed onto the ranch to

---

[338] Sipho is a Ndebele boy's name meaning Gift.
[339] Zimbabwe People's Revolutionary Army. ZIPRA was the military wing of ZAPU.
[340] Zimbabwe African People's Union.
[341] Zimbabwe African National Union – Patriotic Front. ZANU-PF is a political organisation that has been the ruling party of Zimbabwe since independence in 1980.
[342] The mission had been established by the Reverend Robert Moffat in 1859. It is situated some 75 kilometres north-north-east of Bulawayo. Moffat was a member of the London Missionary Society, which had been established in England with the aim of spreading the knowledge of Christ among heathen and unenlightened nations.
[343] A local word meaning animals or wildlife.

poach rhino. This act earned Sipho considerable kudos among many sectors of Zimbabwean society, particularly among enlightened black citizens from various tribes who were motivated to protect the country's wildlife from the tyranny of poaching and greed.

In addition to its environmental credentials, Mhuka Ranch had greatly improved the quality of life for its employees, their families, and the surrounding rural peasant community in and around Chiredzi. Farai was certain that if a senior employee and shareholder like Sipho were killed under suspicious circumstances, the political and legal repercussions would be significant.

Finally, Farai had ordered a clandestine reconnaissance of the ranch. This reconnaissance indicated that the ranch was very well defended and protected. Its defences included a squad of extremely well-trained and armed rangers, robust perimeter fencing around all key assets, and high-mast antennas, indicating an extensive radio communications network. Successfully attacking the ranch would require a large assault group and comprehensive planning. Even with such planning, any assault was likely to result in casualties.

Given these factors, Farai absolutely ruled out a military assault on the ranch or orchestrating Sipho's demise through a nefarious misadventure or accident. There had to be another, less risky way.

As he contemplated the dilemma, Farai realised that Sipho himself was not the problem — the real issue was his relentless quest for justice over his parents' murder. Farai began to wonder if there might be another way to address Sipho's need for justice. As he thought about it, a plan of action slowly started to take shape in his mind. However, this plan was certainly controversial and would require approval from key ZANU-PF figures.

To facilitate this, Farai spent nearly a week drafting a top-secret report outlining his plan and rationale. He then met with the assistant director of the CIO's internal security branch to discuss it. The meeting was promising, but the assistant director advised he would need to seek approval from *'the top'* for the plan, codenamed

'*Operation Kushamisika* [344]', to proceed. He requested time to arrange this.

A few days later, on Friday, 25th October, Farai received a call from the assistant director, informing him that the *'big chief'* had approved his proposal but had strictly stipulated that only those persons mentioned in the report were to be privy to the operation.

---

[344] *Kushamisika* is a Shona word meaning *to be surprised*. It conveys the sense of being taken aback or experiencing a sudden unexpected turn of events.

Chapter 35 – Planning Operation Kushamisika

The first phase of Operation *Kushamisika*[345] was led by Farai Mutasa himself. There were considerable rumours within the 5th Brigade regarding the truth of what occurred during the raid on the mission on 2nd August 1984. Farai's initial task was to separate fact from fiction.

Using his authority as a senior intelligence officer with the CIO[346], Farai was able to establish that the raid had been commanded by an individual named Major Tawanda Nyati. Subsequently, he was granted permission to interview the Major. During the interview, Major Nyati was cautious but reasonably cooperative. Farai informed him that the CIO was exploring ways to protect members of the 5th Brigade from criminal or civil prosecution for any excesses committed during the *Gukurahundi*[347] campaign. This protection would involve legislation granting immunity, though with some limitations. Farai advised that the CIO was particularly keen to safeguard those who had acted decisively against military or political dissidents in defence of the current government and its leader, Robert Mugabe.

---

[345] *Kushamisika* is a Shona word meaning *to be surprised*. It conveys the sense of being taken aback or experiencing a sudden unexpected turn of events.
[346] Zimbabwe's Central Intelligence Organisation.
[347] *Gukurahundi* is a Shona word which roughly translates as '*the early rain that washes away the chaff before the spring rain'.*

Farai explained to the Major that one of the most difficult cases he had encountered involved a raid at Inyati Mission School in August 1984, during which he believed the Major had shot and killed two individuals. This matter was particularly sensitive because the deceased, Mandla[348] and Nandi[349] Pukelo, were employed by an educational institution owned by the Council for World Mission[350], which was well known for its support of black nationalist parties during the Rhodesian Bush War. The Council was now using its resources and reputation to oppose alleged human rights violations by the government against Ndebele tribespeople. Additionally, their son, Sipho[351] Pukelo, was an employee and shareholder of Mhuka Ranch, renowned globally in wildlife protection circles for its rhino conservation efforts. Moreover, Duncan Oliver, a prominent businessman and the largest shareholder of Mhuka[352] Ranch, was currently working with a Bulawayo-based law firm to investigate the killings.

Farai assured Major Nyati that the interview would be off the record and that nothing would be recorded. However, he warned Nyati that if any falsehoods were uncovered, the immunity legislation would not apply to the events at Inyathi Mission on 2nd August 1984. Based on Farai's explanations and assurances, Major Nyati provided a detailed account of the events of that date. Farai found Nyati's account credible and sufficient for his purposes.

*****

On Tuesday, 12th November 1985, a week after Farai's interview with Major Nyati, the receptionist at Webb, Low, and Barry received an

---

[348] Mandla is a Ndebele boy's name meaning Power and Strength.

[349] Nandi is a Ndebele girl's name meaning Sweetness.

[350] The Council is a worldwide community of mainly Protestant Christian churches. The organisation works to spread the knowledge of Christ throughout the world and to strengthen their members in their mission work by sharing their resources of money, people, skills, and insights. It was formerly named the London Missionary Society.

[351] Sipho is a Ndebele boy's name meaning Gift.

[352] A local word meaning animals or wildlife.

anonymous call from a man with a strong Shona accent requesting to speak with Mr Bheki Mpofu.

Mr Mpofu took the call. The caller was brief, stating he was phoning from Bulawayo and understood that Mr Mpofu was investigating the 5th Brigade's involvement in the raid on Inyathi Mission School in August 1984. He claimed to be a member of the raiding party and said he knew who had shot and killed the two mission employees, as well as who had shot a young woman through the knee. He explained that shortly after the raid, he had been unfairly dismissed by the 5th Brigade, prompting him to now blow the whistle on what had happened that day. According to him, the raiding party was under the command of Major Tawanda Nyati, who had shot and killed the two employees. The caller claimed that Nyati had received intelligence indicating that the two employees were dissidents collaborating with armed ZIPRA[353] renegades. He also stated that a young woman who attempted to escape had been shot in the knee by one of Nyati's corporals.

Mr Mpofu attempted to elicit more details, asking, "Thank you for this information. It will help us to bring the perpetrators to justice. Could you provide any additional details, or perhaps your name and contact information?"

The caller replied, "No, I cannot. That would be too dangerous for me."

"I understand," said Mr Mpofu. "But can you tell me why Major Nyati believed the two employees were dissidents, and do you know what happened to their bodies?"

The caller said, "The Major had good intel[354] that the two employees were visited by their son, a former RAR[355] *masodja*[356], a few weeks before they were killed. Villagers stated that Mandla and Nandi

---

[353] Zimbabwe People's Revolutionary Army. ZIPRA was the military wing of ZAPU.
[354] Intelligence information (often military in nature).
[355] Rhodesian African Rifles.
[356] Masodja is the Africanised word for soldier.

Pukelo, along with their son, were helping armed ZIPRA dissidents trying to overthrow Robert Mugabe's Government. Nyati hence viewed them as traitors who needed to be dealt with under the *Gukurahundi* objectives. The son wasn't in the village at the time, so he escaped. The bodies of his parents were thrown into an old mineshaft about 20 kilometres north of the mission."

Mr Mpofu sensed the caller was about to hang up. To obtain more information, he asked, "You mentioned you were unfairly dismissed by the 5th Brigade. Can you tell me the nature of your dismissal?"

The caller replied, "I was dismissed for questioning Major Nyati on why the 5th Brigade continued to kill suspected dissidents instead of handing them over to the police for proper investigation and trial. He reported me for insubordination and failure to follow orders. I hope you can bring him to justice. He is a dangerous man who believes he is above the law."

With that, the line went dead.

"Damn," Mr Mpofu muttered. He quickly made notes about the caller's statements and then went to consult with the senior partner, Mr Robert Holdman. Fortunately, Mr Holdman was available, and they discussed the call in detail. Both men were thrilled by this new information. Their investigations had almost stalled, but they now believed their inquiries would gain momentum.

Mr Holdman suggested Mr Mpofu phone Sipho to update him on the latest news. Later that morning, Mr Mpofu called Mhuka Ranch and spoke with Sipho, disclosing little over the phone but saying they had received intriguing new information about the raid on Inyathi Mission and inquiring when Sipho could come to Bulawayo to discuss the matter further. They agreed to meet at Webb, Low, and Barry on Monday, 18th November 1985, at 12:00 noon.

Just before ending the call, Sipho heard sharp static that hurt his ear, causing him to rub it instinctively. Unknown to Sipho, the static was caused by an illegal tap on the Mhuka Ranch telephone line. A CIO operative had monitored the entire call and later relayed a transcript of the call to Farai Mutasa. Upon receiving the transcript, Farai rubbed his hands in glee and muttered, "So far, so good. Operation *Kushamisika* is going according to plan. I hope it continues this way."

****

Sipho arrived at the offices of Webb, Low, and Barry just before midday. Prior to this, he had informed Duncan Oliver that the law firm investigating the killing of his parents by the 5th Brigade had received further credible information and now needed to meet with him to share this intel. Duncan was pleased with the update and gladly granted Sipho a few days' leave to travel to Bulawayo for the meeting.

The offices of Webb, Low, and Barry were located in Bulawayo's CBD[357]. Upon arrival, the receptionist asked Sipho to take a seat and then informed Mr Mpofu of his arrival. Shortly after, Mr Mpofu appeared and led Sipho into the boardroom.

In the boardroom, Sipho met two white men. He recognised one as Robert Holdman, the senior partner at the law firm. Mr Holdman warmly shook Sipho's hand and introduced him to Mr David Dumart, a new lawyer at the firm with a strong interest in human rights who was already investigating several other matters related to the *Gukurahundi* massacres. Mr Holdman suggested that Mr Dumart's expertise would be helpful in the management of Sipho's case, subject to Sipho's agreement.

Mr Mpofu confirmed that he had fully briefed Mr Dumart on Sipho's case and agreed that Mr Dumart's involvement would be advantageous. Sipho had no objections to this arrangement.

Mr Dumart opened the meeting, saying, "As you know, Sipho, our investigations into your parents' murder have, to date, yielded very little. The 5th Brigade has been uncooperative, aided by the government. Attempts to compel the provincial magistrate to address our inquiries have been thwarted by the chief magistrate,

---

[357] Central Business District.

who has prohibited all magistrates apart from himself from investigating 5th Brigade matters. Similarly, political pressure has put the case off-limits to the ZRP[358]. While there may be other possible remedies, pursuing them in the current political climate will be challenging and protracted. However, last week we received an anonymous phone call that could potentially change everything. Mr Mpofu took this call, so I'll ask him to update us."

David Dumart looked at Bheki Mpofu. "Over to you, Bheki."

Bheki replied, "Thank you, David. On Tuesday, 12th November, we received an anonymous phone call from a man with a strong Shona accent. He claimed to have been part of the 5th Brigade assault squad that raided Inyathi Mission on 2nd August 1984. The caller stated that the squad was under the command of a Major Tawanda Nyati and that this officer was responsible for shooting and killing your parents."

Bheki paused and continued, "I asked the caller why Major Nyati had targeted your parents. The caller claimed that Major Nyati had received credible reports that your parents had been visited a few weeks before their deaths by their son, a former member of the RAR. Sipho, I assume this refers to you. According to the caller, your parents, along with you, were believed to be aiding and abetting armed ZIPRA dissidents who were planning to overthrow Robert Mugabe's government. Major Nyati thus considered the three of you were traitors deserving elimination under the *Gukurahundi* objectives. He mentioned that if you had been in the village at the time, you would have been killed alongside your parents. The caller also claimed that your parents' bodies were dumped in a disused mineshaft about 20 kilometres north of Inyathi.

"The caller also stated that during the raid, a young woman attempted to escape. While trying to apprehend her, a corporal shot her in the knee. Based on what we now know, this woman is likely to be Jabulile, whom Mr Viljoen interviewed at Mpilo Hospital on 27th

---

August 1984. Although the caller's account does not entirely match Jabulile's testimony, the consistencies suggest that he was indeed part of the assault party. It seems he may have altered certain details to protect himself. Jabulile's testimony is more reliable, though she could not identify Major Nyati. However, we now know his identity."

Mr Dumart interjected, "We should also note that the caller mentioned you had visited your parents around two weeks before their deaths. This detail was only disclosed during the raid, making it reasonable to assume that the caller was present at the time. He also claimed to have come forward now because he had recently been unfairly dismissed from the 5th Brigade. The information he provided corroborates other known facts, suggesting that his story is genuine and not merely fabricated retaliation for his dismissal."

A heavy silence filled the room. Sipho finally said, "What the caller said about us helping ZIPRA dissidents is a lie. But I still can't forgive myself for what happened. If I hadn't visited my parents at the mission after coming back from the UK, they might still be alive."

Mr Dumart rose from his chair and placed a reassuring hand on Sipho's shoulder. "You cannot blame yourself for their deaths, Sipho. It's natural for a son to visit his parents, especially after an overseas trip."

"Maybe you're right," Sipho said. "But perhaps it was wrong for me to join the RAR back in 1972. If I had not enlisted, the 5th Brigade would have had no reason to target my parents."

Mr Dumart offered compassion once more. "Sipho, your parents were targeted because they were Ndebele, not because you were a former member of the RAR. The real issue lies with the actions of the 5th Brigade, not your own. Our focus now is to bring Major Nyati to trial. The caller's information has proven invaluable. We've confirmed the existence of an individual named Major Tawanda Nyati, who serves with the 2nd Battalion of the 5th Brigade. Additionally, we now have a general location for where your parents' bodies were dumped. With any luck, we might even be able to recover their remains. This new information should help us compel the police to conduct a thorough investigation, despite any further attempts by the government to obstruct our efforts."

Sipho smiled and leaned back in his chair. "Good work, gentlemen. I'm glad we're finally making progress. I was starting to think we'd never find out who was responsible."

Mr Mpofu added, "Yes, this information certainly changes things significantly. Let's hope that matters will now progress quickly."

Chapter 36 – Executing Operation Kushamisika

Timeline – November 1985

The next phase of Operation *Kushamisika*[359] was perhaps the most difficult. However, Farai was supremely confident that with appropriate planning and a modicum of good luck, this leg of the operation would be successfully completed.

To assist in the operation's success, Farai had liaised with one of the leading anaesthetists at Bulawayo's Mpilo General Hospital, Dr Felix Chigumba. Dr Chigumba was a loyal ZANU-PF[360] supporter. He had not been present during the Rhodesian Bush War, as he had been studying in the UK at that time, where he obtained his medical degree from Cambridge University's Medical School. This degree spanned six years, with the final three, known as the clinical years, spent at King's College Hospital in London. Following the completion of his medical degree, he undertook his internship at the nearby Guy's Hospital.

---

[359] *Kushamisika* is a Shona word meaning *to be surprised*. It conveys the sense of being taken aback or experiencing a sudden unexpected turn of events.
[360] Zimbabwe African National Union – Patriotic Front. ZANU-PF is a political organisation that has been the ruling party of Zimbabwe since independence in 1980.

Dr Chigumba was an outstanding medical student, and his excellence had been recognised by all his tutors and clinical mentors. Encouraged by them, following the completion of his internship at Guy's Hospital, he successfully applied for specialist training in anaesthesia. This marked the beginning of a further six-year period of intense study and clinical experience at various teaching hospitals in and around London. At the end of 1980, he completed his specialty training and passed the FFARCS[361] exams. Following this, he returned to the new Zimbabwe, driven by a passion to not only offer his clinical expertise to the newly independent nation but also to help ZANU-PF build a meaningful and lasting legacy in the country.

Upon his return to Zimbabwe, he secured a senior position in the Department of Anaesthesia at Mpilo General Hospital, a position he still held when contacted by Farai Mutasa in November 1985.

Prior to contacting Dr Chigumba, Farai carried out research into sedatives that could be used to incapacitate an individual. Based on his findings, he decided that diazepam[362], a drug widely used for its sedative and muscle relaxant properties, seemed to be best suited to his needs. When Farai phoned Dr Chigumba, he introduced himself as a senior research student at the University of Zimbabwe, stating that he was conducting research into the use of diazepam in Zimbabwe and wanted to know whether it was commonly used at Mpilo General Hospital. Dr Chigumba confirmed that diazepam had been a staple in medical practice at the hospital for many years and had proven to be a highly effective sedative.

Armed with this information, Farai collaborated with a forensic scientist in the CIO[363] to determine how diazepam could be discreetly administered orally to an unsuspecting adult male victim, as well as the dosage required to incapacitate him for up to two hours. Despite

---

[361] Fellowship in the Faculty of Anaesthetists of the Royal College of Surgeons of England.
[362] Diazepam, sold under the brand name Valium among others, is a medicine of the benzodiazepine family that calms the central nervous system.
[363] Zimbabwe's Central Intelligence Organisation.

the obvious risks associated with non-clinical persons administering the sedative, they concluded that the most effective way to do so without detection was to dissolve it in sweetened tea, which would mask its bitter taste. They calculated that to incapacitate an adult male weighing 90 kg, approximately 30 mg of diazepam, dissolved in a standard mug of tea, would be needed. They estimated that the diazepam would take effect about 15 minutes after administration.

Next, he escalated the matter to the Director of the CIO, requesting that 30 mg of diazepam be requisitioned from the medical stores at Mpilo Hospital in tablet form, which could then be crushed into powder form. A week later, he received the required diazepam tablets.

He was now ready to execute the next phase of Operation *Kushamisika*.

Armed with the required diazepam tablets, Farai then co-opted the services of another trustworthy CIO intelligence officer named Chipo Sithole. Farai advised Chipo that the CIO had been commissioned by the Zimbabwean leadership to eliminate a black man who had become a significant embarrassment to the country. Farai explained that the mission was top secret and that he was not at liberty to disclose the name of the individual concerned. He did, however, advise that if the mission was successfully executed, he would be rewarded handsomely by the government. Chipo, a true party man, took no convincing and pledged an oath, on pain of death, to keep all details of the mission secret.

Farai then contacted Major Nyati again. He advised the Major that he needed to ask him some supplementary questions regarding the killing of the two alleged dissidents, Mandla[364] and Nandi[365] Pukelo, at the Inyathi Mission School. He requested to meet the Major at a CIO safe house located in the Bulawayo suburb of Entumbane.

---

[364] Mandla is a Ndebele boy's name meaning Power and Strength.
[365] Nandi is a Ndebele girl's name meaning Sweetness.

Major Nyati was well-acquainted with the suburb of Entumbane, the site of the Battle of Entumbane, which took place in February 1981. During this battle, the nascent ZNA[366], with assistance from the RAR[367] and other white-commanded elements of the former Rhodesian Security Forces, successfully quelled a significant uprising involving renegade groups of ZANLA[368] and ZIPRA[369] cadres. This battle served as a wake-up call for ZNA's hierarchy, as, without the support of the RAR and other white-commanded forces, a major tribal-based civil war could have erupted in the newly independent Zimbabwe. The performance of the ZANLA and ZIPRA troops, who had transitioned into the ZNA, was abysmal, while the actions of the RAR and other white-led elements were exceptional. ZNA military instructors now used the Battle of Entumbane as a case study to illustrate the dangers of poor leadership, confused command, insufficient intelligence, and inadequate planning in warfare.

Major Nyati was immediately wary of the request to meet with Farai again. He was concerned that his sanitised version of the deaths of Mandla and Nandi Pukelo had somehow been exposed and that some form of sanctions might now be imposed on him. He therefore asked Farai whether his lawyer could be present at the meeting. Farai said that would not be necessary, as the meeting was simply to discuss the finer details of the immunity legislation that the government was working on. In particular, the person who had drafted the legislation wanted to road-test it against the events that had resulted in the deaths of Mandla and Nandi Pukelo, to ensure that the relevant immunity provisions were adequate.

Somewhat reluctantly, Major Nyati agreed, and the meeting was set for noon on Monday, 2nd December 1985.

---

[366] Zimbabwe National Army.
[367] Rhodesian African Rifles.
[368] Zimbabwe African National Liberation Army. ZANLA was the military wing of ZANU.
[369] Zimbabwe People's Revolutionary Army. ZIPRA was the military wing of ZAPU.

Following the conclusion of the phone call, Farai contacted the Director of the CIO, asking him to urgently arrange for a draft of the fictitious immunity legislation to be prepared. This draft copy was delivered to Farai three days later.

*****

Farai and his colleague, Chipo, visited the safe house on Sunday, 1st December, to prepare it for their meeting with Major Nyati the following day. The house was ideal — a nondescript, basic two-bedroom concrete-block property with a flat asbestos-sheeted roof, located in a high-density area of Entumbane. The meeting would take place in the dingy kitchen at the rear of the house, which had a small window overlooking a scruffy backyard. Farai and Chipo brought mugs, tea, sugar, milk, and biscuits, with them and stored these in the kitchen before securing the house and leaving.

On the following morning, Farai and Chipo arrived at the safe house around 11:00 am. Farai carried three draft copies of the fictitious immunity legislation and the diazepam tablets, which had been crushed into powder. Both agents were armed with Soviet Tokarev semi-automatic pistols concealed beneath their jackets. While waiting for Major Nyati, they rehearsed their plans, including contingencies should anything unexpected happen.

Just after noon, Major Nyati arrived at the house, parking his dusty Land Rover behind the Peugeot 404 station wagon that Farai and Chipo had arrived in. He sat in his car for a moment, looking around. Down the street, he noticed a couple of mangy-looking stray dogs and two young boys kicking a football in the dusty roadside verge. Everything seemed normal, yet an uneasy feeling gnawed at him. He patted the underarm holster containing his Enfield revolver, concealed beneath his camouflage jacket, before stepping out and walking up to the front door, which stood ajar.

Farai greeted him and introduced him to Comrade Chipo Sithole, whom he said worked for the Legal Drafting Department in the Attorney-General's office. They went into the kitchen, where Farai thanked the Major for attending and summarised the progress which had been made in drafting the legislation, which, subject to certain limitations, would grant immunity to members of the 5th Brigade who might have committed excesses during the *Gukurahundi*[370] campaign. He explained that he would like to provide a copy of the draft legislation for the Major's review before it was reviewed by the Cabinet.

At this point, Major Nyati raised his hand and said, "I am not a lawyer. I would need my lawyer to look at the draft legislation."

Farai replied, "I completely understand, Major. The document in front of you is a copy of the draft legislation, and you are free to take it with you to discuss with your lawyer. However, I have asked Comrade Sithole to be present today to explain the overall structure of the draft legislation, its main provisions, and its limitations. From your perspective, it's crucial to pay close attention to the limitations to ensure they protect you from any accountability that you might otherwise have for believing the two Inyathi Mission employees were dissidents and that your orders necessitated their elimination."

Major Nyati picked up the document and began to leaf through it.

Farai said, "Comrade Sithole will now explain the draft legislation for us. But before he begins, let's have a cup of tea."

He stood up, walked over to the bench near the sink, and switched on the kettle. As it heated up, he opened the packet of biscuits and placed it on the kitchen table.

Farai asked the Major how he took his tea. The Major replied, "With milk and two spoons of sugar, please."

Comrade Sithole chimed in, "Same for me."

The Major's chair had been carefully positioned to face away from the kitchen table, allowing Farai to prepare the tea without being observed. As Farai made the Major's tea, he surreptitiously poured in

---

[370] *Gukurahundi* is a Shona word which roughly translates as *'the early rain that washes away the chaff before the spring rain'*.

the powdered diazepam tablets and two spoons of sugar, and gave it a good stir.

Farai placed the mugs of sweetened tea in front of each of them. The Major had already taken a biscuit from the packet and, as was customary, dunked it into the hot tea.

Comrade Chipo then began to carefully guide Major Nyati and Farai through the draft legislation. Surprisingly, the Major did not struggle with the legal language and occasionally asked insightful questions.

After about 15 minutes, the Major yawned, rubbed his eyes, and stood up to stretch his legs. He walked over to the kitchen window to get some fresh air. As he did so, he stumbled and fell to the floor. His survival instincts kicked in, and he fumbled beneath his jacket to draw his revolver, but Farai was already next to him and easily restrained him. The Major struggled weakly for a few seconds before collapsing into an unconscious heap.

After checking that the Major's revolver was still in its holster, Farai turned to Chipo and said, "You will need to help me move him into the back of the station wagon."

The two men struggled with Major Nyati's weight but managed to drag him to the front door. Before carrying his comatose body out of the house, Farai checked down the street for any passers-by. Fortunately, the two young boys who had been playing soccer had disappeared, and the street was now empty.

Farai unlocked the station wagon, and the two men lugged the unconscious Major to the back of it, then hauled him into the rear section. They placed a cushion beneath his head and a blanket over his body.

Farai retrieved the keys to the Major's Land Rover from Nyati's pocket and handed them to Chipo.

Farai and Chipo returned to the house, where Farai placed the three draft copies of the fictitious immunity legislation into the briefcase he had arrived with. They carefully washed the mugs and poured the unused tea and milk down the sink, then gathered the remaining items into a small garbage bag, which they stowed in the front of the Peugeot. After conducting a quick inspection of the house to ensure no incriminating evidence was left behind, they exited the building.

Farai got into the Peugeot while Chipo got into the Major's Land Rover. They then headed towards the Matobo Hills, which were some 55 kilometres south. En route, they passed a lay-by where Farai disposed of the garbage bag into the lay-by's rusted rubbish bin. They then continued south along the Matopos Road.

Just before Matopos Road reached Matobo[371] National Park, they turned sharply left onto a well-graded dirt road that steeply wound around a kopje[372] before continuing into the distance. The road's ascent to the top of the kopje was followed by a rapid descent along a straight stretch of road of about 100 metres, after which the road rounded a sharp bend. This bend was unprotected by guard rails, so if a vehicle was unfortunate enough to have an accident at that point, it would tumble into a steep, well-treed ravine, through which a dry riverbed snaked its way.

Farai brought his Peugeot to a dusty stop at the summit of the road, with Chipo following closely behind. The two men stepped out of their cars and scanned the area for any signs of vehicles or people, but found none. After putting on leather gloves, they carefully carried Major Nyati's unconscious body from the Peugeot to the driver's seat of the Land Rover. They straightened his clothes, ensured his seatbelt was fastened, and checked that his Enfield revolver was still securely in his underarm holster. Farai then went to the rear of the Peugeot station wagon and retrieved a 20-litre jerry can, provided by the assistant director of the CIO's internal security branch. For authenticity, the jerry can bore the 5th Brigade's insignia. Farai unlatched its metal cap and placed it upright on the back seat of the Land Rover.

---

[371] Prior to 1982, this was known as the Matopos National Park.
[372] The word kopje is derived from the Afrikaans word koppie, which means a small hill.

Chipo restarted the Land Rover's engine and shifted the gear stick into neutral. Together, he and Farai pushed the vehicle back onto the dirt road, pointing the front down the steep descent toward the sharp, unguarded bend about 100 metres ahead. Chipo opened the passenger door and slid up against Major Nyati's body. He depressed the clutch with his right foot and shifted the vehicle into first gear. Then, with the clutch still depressed, he rested the Major's foot onto the accelerator pedal.

As he released the clutch, the Land Rover lurched forward, slowly rolling down the incline. Chipo steered the vehicle into the middle of the road, then quickly slid into the passenger seat and exited through the passenger door, slamming it shut behind him.

The vehicle continued its downward journey, gradually picking up speed as it travelled down the steep road. The engine whined louder, straining against the top speed of first gear. By the time the vehicle reached the bend, it was travelling at about 40 km/h.

As the vehicle rounded the bend, it veered off the road and careened into the steep ravine. It flew down the slope, gaining momentum, while the unlatched jerry can toppled over, spilling petrol onto the rear seat. When the Land Rover hit the bottom of the ravine, it crashed with a loud thud, flipping end over end twice before coming to a crunching halt.

For a moment, there was silence, then a bang erupted as the spilled petrol ignited from the crash. The jerry can, still containing some petrol, exploded with a thud, followed shortly by a much louder blast as the fire spread to the vehicle's main fuel tank.

Meanwhile, Farai and Chipo used branches to brush away any evidence of footprints and tyre marks at the spot where the Land Rover had been parked before they loaded the Major aboard. They then drove the Peugeot down the road to the point where the Land Rover had left the road.

Parking in the middle of the road, they walked to the edge and peered down at the twisted wreckage of the Land Rover at the bottom of the ravine. The smashed vehicle was ablaze, as was the surrounding bush. They exchanged broad smiles, shook hands, and returned to the Peugeot, making sure to erase their footprints with a branch from a nearby bush.

After driving another kilometre down the dirt road, they executed a U-turn to head back toward the summit and onto the Matopos Road, proceeding north to Bulawayo.

Chapter 37 – The staged accident is investigated by the ZRP

Once Farai was back in his CIO[373] office in Bulawayo, he phoned Superintendent Max Chaora of the ZRP's[374] Bulawayo Provincial Traffic Section. Superintendent Chaora was a close friend of Farai Mutasa, who, like Farai, had advanced quickly from the rank of sergeant within the ZRP following the country's independence in 1980. Although Chaora was a diligent and effective member of the police force, his rapid advancement was due more to his connections with the wider Mugabe family than his effectiveness as a policeman. These connections had significantly advanced Superintendent Chaora's career. As a result, Chaora was an avid admirer of Prime Minister Robert Mugabe and a loyal member of ZANU-PF[375].

In the weeks leading up to the supposed road traffic accident in which Major Tawanda Nyati was killed, Farai Mutasa had met with Max Chaora on three separate occasions. During these meetings, Farai had explained that the CIO needed to stage a road traffic accident to eliminate a black man who had become a significant nuisance to Robert Mugabe and his inner circle. Farai emphasised

---

[373] Zimbabwe's Central Intelligence Organisation.
[374] Zimbabwe Republic Police.
[375] Zimbabwe African National Union – Patriotic Front. ZANU-PF is a political organisation that has been the ruling party of Zimbabwe since independence in 1980.

that while the accident would need to be investigated as usual, the conclusion should point to excessive speed and loss of control as the cause of death. The two men also agreed that the operation would be given the code name *Operation Smoke Screen*.

Farai dialled Max's direct number. After a couple of rings, Max picked up the handset, saying, "Superintendent Chaora here. How can I help you?"

Farai replied, "Hi Max. I hope you are well. I am just calling to let you know that *Operation Smoke Screen* has commenced. You will find the vehicle on a dirt road just before the Matobo National Park[376], at the bottom of a steep ravine. The locstat[377] coordinates are 20.39 degrees south and 28.52 degrees east."

"Roger that," said Max. "It's already after 6:00 pm, so it's too late to send out the *fix-it team* today. But I will ensure they are deployed first thing tomorrow to investigate."

Before Superintendent Chaora left work that evening, he phoned the leader of the *fix-it team* to inform him that they were to be deployed first thing the following morning. He instructed the leader to ensure that he and the two other team members reported for duty at the ZRP offices of the Bulawayo Provincial Traffic Section at 6:00 am the following morning.

The *fix-it team* comprised three experienced inspectors employed by the ZRP, who also received secret monthly retainers from the CIO. They were discreet about the team's existence and unquestioning of any orders given to them, which typically were issued by way of a short phone call from Superintendent Chaora. The inspectors followed these instructions implicitly and without question.

As required, all three men were present at the ZRP offices of the Bulawayo Provincial Traffic Section well before 6:00 am the next day. The first to arrive was the leader of the team, a man called Dixon.

---

[376] Prior to 1982, this was known as the Matopos National Park.
[377] Ordnance survey map reference.

Despite being early, Superintendent Chaora was at the offices before Dixon. He handed Dixon the keys to a police squad car and advised him that the *fix-it team* was required to investigate a road traffic accident that had occurred the day before near Matobo National Park. Superintendent Chaora provided the locstat of the crash site, together with a detailed ordnance survey map of the area. He advised Dixon that one male adult had been killed in the accident and that no other vehicles or persons had been involved. He instructed Dixon that the *fix-it team* was to investigate the circumstances surrounding the crash and that their final report should conclude that the accident had been caused by the driver's excessive speed.

Superintendent Chaora then departed. A short time later, the other two members of the *fix-it team* arrived, and together they left in the supplied squad car, heading south towards the Matobo Hills area.

Upon arrival, the inspectors quickly located the crash site using the locstat coordinates and the ordnance map provided. The fire that had started when Major Nyati's Land Rover careened down the ravine had burnt itself out. The three inspectors clambered down to the charred wreckage at the bottom of the ravine, where the driver's body was still securely strapped in his seat By now, rigor mortis had set in. They took a series of photographs of the crash site, the burnt body in the car, and the path the vehicle had taken as it left the road and hurtled down the steep ravine.

While searching the body, they found a wallet in the inside pocket of the partially burnt camouflage jacket. The contents allowed them to identify the body as belonging to Major Tawanda Nyati, a serving member of the 5th Brigade. They also located his Enfield revolver in his underarm holster. Carefully, they removed the wallet, revolver, and holster, and placed them into evidence bags. Afterward, they radioed base to request another vehicle and three additional policemen to assist in retrieving the body from the car, carry it back up the ravine to the road, and transport it to Bulawayo's central morgue.

It was apparent that there had been no witnesses to the crash, and accordingly, no witness statements needed to be taken. The inspectors did retrieve a burnt-out jerry can lying in the back of the Land Rover. This was removed and placed into the squad car to be disposed of. No mention was made of this in their final report.

Surprisingly, no photographs were taken of the spot where the Land Rover had left the dirt road, crossed the verge, and entered the ravine. Had they been taken, a keen observer might have wondered why there were no skid marks on the dirt road. Similarly, there were no photographs of the vehicle's gear stick, which might have raised questions about why it was still in first gear. Additionally, no attempt was made to conduct post-mortem toxicology tests on the corpse to identify the presence and concentration of foreign substances, particularly alcohol. Had such tests been performed, they likely would have found no evidence of alcohol but would have detected traces of drugs from the benzodiazepine family, specifically diazepam[378].

Within a fortnight, the final report produced by Inspector Dixon's team was completed. It concluded that Major Nyati of the ZNA's[379] 5th Brigade had been killed in a road traffic accident on Monday, 2nd December 1985, at approximately 3:30 pm. No other vehicles or persons were involved. The report stated that excessive speed had caused the Major's car to leave the dirt road it was travelling on and plunge down a steep ravine. At the bottom of the ravine, the vehicle had burst into flames, resulting in Major Nyati's instantaneous death. There were no suspicious circumstances surrounding the incident.

The report was internally checked and reviewed by senior personnel within Bulawayo's Provincial Traffic Section. Copies of the final report were then released to the 5th Brigade as well as to Major Nyati's family. Additionally, given the Major's relatively high rank within the 5th Brigade, the police issued a press statement summarising their

---

[378] Diazepam, sold under the brand name Valium among others, is a medicine of the benzodiazepine family that calms the central nervous system.
[379] Zimbabwe National Army.

findings. A copy of this statement was specifically sent to the editor of Bulawayo's leading daily newspaper, *The Chronicle*[380], which published a short article on page five on Monday, 23rd December 1985, just before Christmas.

---

[380] *The Chronicle* was published in Bulawayo and mostly reported on news affecting the Matabeleland area in the south of the country. It was first published in 1894.

Chapter 38 – The end justifies the means

Timeline – January 1986

It was the day before Christmas 1985, and everyone at the offices of Webb, Low, and Barry was in high spirits. The holiday break was just around the corner. Many of the more affluent staff members would soon be heading south for their annual holidays in South Africa, while others looked forward to spending time at home with their children, family members, and friends. For a brief moment, the difficulties the country was facing and the recent trauma that many Ndebele families in Matabeleland had suffered at the hands of ZNA's[381] 5th Brigade would be eased and replaced by a festive Christmas spirit — a short period during which many Zimbabweans really did try to love their neighbours as themselves.

Just before 11:00 am, the receptionist at the law firm received a phone call from a man who did not identify himself but asked to be put through to the lawyer in charge of the investigations into the deaths of Mandla[382] and Nandi[383] Pukelo. The receptionist immediately connected the call to Mr David Dumart, who had recently assumed responsibility for this matter.

---

[381] Zimbabwe National Army.
[382] Mandla is a Ndebele boy's name meaning Power and Strength.
[383] Nandi is a Ndebele girl's name meaning Sweetness.

The phone rang in David Dumart's office. "Good morning, David Dumart here," he answered.

There was a brief silence on the other end.

"Can I help you?" David Dumart prompted.

From the other end of the line, a male voice with a strong Shona accent said, "Yes, good morning, Mr Dumart. Can you confirm that you are the person handling Webb, Low, and Barry's investigations into the killings of Mandla and Nandi Pukelo?"

"Yes, that is correct," replied David Dumart.

"Well, I was wondering if you have seen the article on page five of yesterday's edition of *The Chronicle*[384]," said the voice.

"Hmm, I don't recall reading that article," said David Dumart.

"In that case, I suggest you get a copy of yesterday's paper. I am sure you will find the article of great interest."

With that, the line went dead.

David Dumart scratched his head in thought for a few moments. Then he called out to his personal assistant, "Penny, please bring me yesterday's copy of *The Chronicle*."

Five minutes later, Penny arrived with yesterday's paper, which had not yet been microfilmed and archived.

David quickly thumbed through to page five. His eye was drawn to a headline on the top right of the page, which read *5th Brigade Officer Killed in Road Crash*. He read the short article, which reported that Major Tawanda Nyati had been killed in a road accident near the entrance to Matobo National Park. The article stated that the accident had been caused by excessive speed. The vehicle had left the road and crashed down a steep ravine, bursting into flames on

---

[384] *The Chronicle* was published in Bulawayo and mostly reported on news affecting the Matabeleland area in the south of the country. It was first published in 1894.

impact. Major Nyati had died instantly. No other vehicles or persons were involved.

David Dumart muttered to himself, "How very convenient. This sounds very suspicious."

He debated whether to phone Sipho[385] Pukelo and draw his attention to the article. Given that the Christmas holiday season was about to commence, he was reluctant to address the matter immediately. However, he decided he was duty-bound to inform Sipho as soon as possible. He rang Mhuka[386] Ranch. Jenny Oliver answered and informed him that Sipho was indeed at the main homestead. She called him to the phone, and David conveyed the news to Sipho, who was stunned.

There was a long pause. Then Sipho asked, "Are you telling me that Major Nyati, the thug who murdered my parents, has been killed in a road accident?"

"That is what it appears," said David. "I only have the details as reported in yesterday's newspaper. I will follow up on this matter after Christmas, but I thought you should know. Our firm will be closed between Christmas and New Year and will re-open on Monday, 6th January 1986. I will call you shortly thereafter to arrange a meeting to discuss how we will progress our case against Major Nyati and the 5th Brigade in light of these developments. How does that sound to you?"

"I guess that will be fine. But I must say, the whole thing sounds a bit mysterious. Do you believe the story in the newspaper?" asked Sipho.

"Well, that is all we know at the moment. But I agree it sounds too convenient. I am certainly going to keep an open mind until we have thoroughly investigated the matter," replied David.

---

[385] Sipho is a Ndebele boy's name meaning Gift.
[386] A local word meaning animals or wildlife.

"Okay," said Sipho. "In the meantime, I will also do some investigations of my own."

"Right then. We will talk again in the new year. I wish you and the rest of the fine people at Mhuka Ranch a very happy Christmas."

With that, David Dumart hung up.

*****

It was Friday, 27th December 1985, and Farai Mutasa found himself in a dilemma. On one hand, he was pleased with his efforts in orchestrating the road traffic accident that had led to Major Nyati's demise. He knew without hesitation that the senior leadership of the country, especially Prime Minister Mugabe, would be pleased that this troublesome matter had been resolved without further political damage to himself or his government.

On the other hand, Farai remained troubled by the investigations into the deaths of Mandla and Nandi Pukelo, which were being led by their son, Sipho Pukelo, with assistance from the Bulawayo-based law firm of Webb, Low, and Barry. Farai knew that neither Sipho nor the law firm would allow the matter to rest, even though the individual responsible for Sipho's parents' deaths was now deceased. From Farai's perspective, Operation *Kushamisika*[387] could not be deemed a success unless and until Sipho could be persuaded to abandon his investigations. This would require Farai to implement the final phase of the operation.

This involved Farai phoning Sipho Pukelo at Mhuka Ranch. He had carefully rehearsed the contents of this call and decided to make it at lunchtime that day, being Friday, 27th December 1985.

Farai phoned Mhuka Ranch just before noon. He was fortunate that the call was answered by Sipho himself. "Hello, this is Sipho Pukelo. How can I help you?"

---

[387] *Kushamisika* is a Shona word meaning *to be surprised*. It conveys the sense of being taken aback or experiencing a sudden unexpected turn of events.

Farai replied, "Good afternoon, Sipho. I am glad I was able to catch you. My name is Farai Mutasa, and I work for the CIO. If you have some time to spare, I would like to discuss the deaths of your parents on Thursday, 2nd August 1984."

There was silence on the other end of the line. After a long pause, Sipho said, "I am listening. What would you like to talk about?"

Farai paused before replying, then slowly said, "I suppose you have heard that the person most directly involved in your parents' deaths, a man by the name of Major Tawanda Nyati from the 5th Brigade, was killed in a road traffic accident on Monday, 2nd December 1985."

Sipho replied, "Yes, so I understand."

Farai then slowly and deliberately said, "Well, Sipho, you have probably also heard that the accident occurred on the Matopos Road, near Matobo National Park[388]. No other vehicles or persons were involved. According to the police report, the accident was caused by the excessive speed of Major Nyati's vehicle."

"I am not aware of the details of the accident," said Sipho.

"Well, I am intimately aware of the details," said Farai. "I know that this was no accident. The crash was meticulously staged by the CIO to appear as one. Major Nyati's body was found in the driver's seat of his wrecked vehicle, but he was heavily sedated at the time of the crash and had no control over the vehicle. In fact, he was murdered, but the crash was made to look like an accident."

There was a long silence on the other end of the phone. Sipho's mind was racing as he tried to make sense of what he was being told.

"So, are you telling me that Major Nyati was, in fact, murdered by the CIO and that the crash was an elaborate hoax?"

"Yes, that is correct," Farai said solemnly.

---

[388] Prior to 1982, this was known as the Matopos National Park.

"And why would the CIO[389] want to kill Major Nyati?" asked Sipho.

"His death was authorised by the Prime Minister himself. Major Nyati had become reckless in the performance of his duties under the *Gukurahundi*[390] campaign. He had become an embarrassment and a liability to the government. He had to be taken care of!" said Farai.

Sipho was stunned. "I find it hard to believe this story you're telling me," he said. "If Major Nyati had become a liability to the government, why wasn't he simply arrested, relieved of his duties, and tried in court?"

"That's a very good question," replied Farai. "Let's just say it was more expedient to have him eliminated. The government didn't want his excesses against the Ndebeles investigated and made public."

Sipho was dumbfounded. "Are you saying the government found it easier to kill this man rather than take the matter through the courts?"

"That is correct," said Farai.

"Well, I am horrified. I am obviously no fan of Major Nyati, but there is no way the government can simply order his death and get away with it," said Sipho.

Farai said, "Well, I'm here to tell you that it can do exactly that and will get away with it. Similar actions were taken against the black community by Ian Smith's former white RF[391] government, and they escaped accountability. The current government has simply learned from the RF government. However, whereas those past actions were white against black, today they are black against black."

---

[389] Zimbabwe's Central Intelligence Organisation.
[390] *Gukurahundi* is a Shona word which roughly translates as '*the early rain that washes away the chaff before the spring rain*'.
[391] Rhodesian Front.

With an accusatory tone, Sipho asked, "Why are you telling me this? What has allegedly happened is highly illegal. I am duty-bound to report this matter to the police or to the media, or both."

"That would be highly dangerous and foolish," said Farai threateningly.

"And why is that?" asked Sipho.

Farai replied, "You need to be careful. The CIO has already avenged your parents, and the police have found that Major Nyati's death was an accident. Even if they re-open the case, they'll still find it was just a road accident. The key thing is, Nyati's dead. It's better for you to leave it alone. If you don't, it'll cause you a lot of trouble."

"What kind of trouble?" Sipho asked.

"The list of problems you will face is a long one," replied Farai. "For starters, Mhuka Ranch will lose its rhino conservancy status. The Olivers will also face difficulties, like strikes from their workers. International visitors won't get permits or visas. Everything you and the Olivers have worked so hard to build will be at risk — all because you won't let Nyati's death go.

"We also know you served in the RAR[392] with a man named Nick Sinclair. You and Sinclair were involved in a firefight at Mhuka Ranch in August 1981, where three poachers were shot and killed. We understand you acted in self-defence, but we could reopen that case, just to make sure the police didn't miss anything."

Farai paused, then went on. "But if you stop digging into your parents' deaths, everything at the ranch will stay the same. Think carefully before you do anything foolish. I'll call you again early in the New Year to confirm your decision. However, make no mistake — if you keep pushing, the future of Mhuka Ranch, the Olivers, and yourself will be destroyed."

---

[392] Rhodesian African Rifles.

With that, Farai hung up. Sipho was breathing heavily, and his hand was shaking. He hung up the receiver and stood silently staring at the phone for many long minutes.

*****

The next few days were extremely tough for Sipho. He became withdrawn as he pondered his next move. He was both outraged by the audacity of what Farai Mutasa had said to him and acutely aware that, unless he dropped his investigations into his parents' deaths, the government could and would destroy Mhuka Ranch, along with his and the Olivers' businesses. Additionally, he dreaded the potential consequences if the ZRP[393] were to reopen the case into the shooting of the three white poachers in 1981.

It didn't take him long to realise that, in reality, he had no choice but to cease further investigations into his parents' deaths.

On Monday, 6th January 1986, he phoned David Dumart at Webb, Low, and Barry to inform him that, in light of Major Nyati's death in the road traffic accident on Monday, 2nd December 1985, he wished to discontinue the investigations into the circumstances surrounding his parents' deaths in August 1984.

David desperately tried to dissuade Sipho from abandoning the investigations, especially now that they knew who the alleged killer was, but his pleas were in vain. Consequently, the file on this matter was closed at Webb, Low, and Barry, and the case was archived, never to be reopened.

---

[393] Zimbabwe Republic Police.

Chapter 39 – The price of silence

Timeline – February to April 1986

As you've heard before, Sipho[394] often found he did his best thinking when alone, gazing out over the beauty of the African bush from the decking of his house on the banks of Ingwe[395] Dam. This location epitomised everything he had come to love about the expanse of land known as Mhuka[396] Ranch — sublime beauty, ever-changing horizons, the rawness of nature, and the persistence of those working at the ranch to overcome any challenge that came their way.

His recent decision weighed heavily on his mind, gnawing at his conscience. Abandoning the investigation into his parents' murders had not been an easy choice. He had wrestled with this decision for many weeks, torn between his duty to his family and heritage and the harsh realities of the dangerous political landscape.

The elimination of Major Nyati, the key figure in his parents' killings, should have brought a sense of closure. Yet the manner of Major Nyati's death — a staged car accident orchestrated by ZANU-PF[397] itself — left Sipho stunned by the audacity and impunity of the

---

[394] Sipho is a Ndebele boy's name meaning Gift.
[395] Ingwe is a local word meaning leopard.
[396] A local word meaning animals or wildlife.
[397] Zimbabwe African National Union – Patriotic Front. ZANU-PF is a political organisation that has been the ruling party of Zimbabwe since independence in 1980.

Mugabe regime. Their breathtaking arrogance and unchecked power made him feel sick. What else, he wondered, were they capable of?

His Ndebele heritage called to him, reminding him of his ancestors who would rather die than betray their principles. His parents, too, deserved justice. They had been brutally murdered by the 5th Brigade, with their deaths hidden behind a façade of lies and buried beneath a stony wall of silence. Sipho knew that the country needed to know the truth about the *Gukurahundi*[398] campaign and the government's role in orchestrating these atrocities. Without some form of accountability, the government would become even more ruthless, while the families of the victims would forever be tormented by the horrific, unacknowledged wrongs done to their loved ones.

But pursuing this truth would have dire consequences. Persisting in his investigations would probably achieve little other than inviting retribution from a powerful and merciless regime. Moreover, it would put Mhuka Ranch, its businesses, and the rhino conservancy at risk. There was also the lurking fear that reopening the investigation into the deaths of the three white poachers in 1981 could spell further personal trouble for him and his brother-in-arms, Nick Sinclair.

Reluctantly, Sipho had succumbed to the CIO's[399] threats and agreed to keep quiet. The CIO kept its word — in return for his silence, they left him and the ranch alone. However, they ensured he knew they were still watching. Every two or three months, an anonymous document detailing major events that had occurred at the ranch during the previous period would arrive addressed to him personally. The accuracy of these reports astounded Sipho, serving as a chilling reminder of the CIO's meticulous surveillance through its expansive network of spies and informers.

---

[398] *Gukurahundi* is a Shona word which roughly translates as '*the early rain that washes away the chaff before the spring rain'*.
[399] Zimbabwe's Central Intelligence Organisation.

Despite his resolve to remain silent, Sipho could not withhold the truth from Nick Sinclair, his trusted friend, who was now happily married and living in the UK with his wife, Rachel. Sipho phoned him on a couple of occasions, revealing the grim details of his parents' murders, the role played by Major Nyati, and the CIO's subsequent elimination of the Major. He explained how Nyati's death had been sanctioned by Mugabe's inner circle as part of the broader campaign to cover up the *Gukurahundi* atrocities. Despite Nick's busy work schedule, he took time to listen to Sipho's anguish and help him work through the issues.

Nick was staggered by Sipho's revelations. This new information, coupled with his suspicions about what had happened to Jonathon Khumalo, deeply concerned Nick about Zimbabwe's future. The regime's willingness to silence dissent through murder and manipulation was terrifying.

Nick understood the personal risks involved in stirring up these issues. He knew that digging into the past could jeopardise his own safety. Despite this, he felt compelled to act. The weight of the truth pressed heavily upon him. He decided he needed to return to Zimbabwe to meet with Sipho face to face to discuss what they should do next.

He discussed his feelings with Rachel. Despite her concerns that Nick could be exposing himself to unnecessary danger by returning to Zimbabwe to meet with Sipho, Rachel knew that this was a matter Nick needed to face and resolve himself. Accordingly, she agreed and encouraged Nick to return to the land of his birth to meet with Sipho.

In subsequent discussions, they agreed that the trip should take place shortly after Easter. This would allow Nick to spend Easter in the UK with Rachel and her family before flying to Zimbabwe to enjoy the delightful early autumn weather of the lowveld.

Chapter 40 – Searching for solutions

Nick flew out from London on a British Airways flight departing from Heathrow on the evening of Monday, 7th April 1986, and landed at Harare Airport early on Tuesday morning. His mother, Brenda Sinclair, collected him from the airport, overjoyed to see him again, although she expressed sadness that Rachel, his wife, had not been able to accompany him on this occasion.

Nick was set to spend a few days in Harare, staying with his parents at their home in Ballantyne Park. On Friday, he would drive approximately 450 kilometres south to Mhuka[400] Ranch via Masvingo[401], using a Toyota Land Cruiser his father had generously provided for the trip.

Nick spent a few relaxing days at his parents' home before departing for Mhuka Ranch. One evening during dinner, he was taken aback when his parents mentioned an unsettling incident that had prompted them to seriously consider leaving Zimbabwe. While still weighing up their options, they had firmly ruled out migrating to South Africa and were now contemplating either the UK or Australia.

When his father mentioned the UK, Nick assured them that he and Rachel would do whatever they could to help. He also reminded his

---

[400] A local word meaning animals or wildlife.
[401] Masvingo was previously known as Fort Victoria. The name changed in 1982.

father of the generous offer from Rachel's parents to provide support as well.

The incident that had deeply unsettled Nick's parents had occurred a few weeks earlier while Matthew and Brenda were returning from a canoeing safari on the Zambezi River. Just outside Chinhoyi[402], a small rural town north-west of Harare, a young black girl had suddenly emerged from the long grass by the roadside and ran directly into the path of their car. Later, Matthew learned that the young girl had been trying to catch up with friends who were ahead of her. At the point where the foot path she was running along crossed the road, she had dashed out onto the bitumen road without looking for oncoming traffic. At 120 kph, Matthew had no chance to avoid her, and she was severely injured.

Fortunately, an ex-army medic had arrived on the scene shortly after the accident. The medic helped Matthew place the injured girl into his car, and they then rushed her to Chinhoyi's public hospital. It was a Sunday afternoon, and the hospital had no doctors on duty — only one nurse. Additionally, the hospital's X-ray machine was inoperable because no one knew how to use it. It took 24 hours for the girl to be seen by a doctor and another 24 hours to arrange for an X-ray. She was hospitalised for six weeks and was fortunate to survive. Meanwhile, Matthew and Brenda faced intense questioning by the local police. With corruption increasing in the mid-80s, the police attempted to extort a bribe from Matthew, but he refused, which only prolonged and intensified their interrogation.

The incident had deeply unsettled Matthew and Brenda. While health facilities in Harare and Bulawayo remained relatively functional, health care in smaller regional towns was a different story. Matthew was alarmed by the thought that he and Brenda might have received the same inadequate care and treatment if they had been involved in an accident outside Harare and taken to a small regional hospital.

---

[402] Chinhoyi was previously known as Sinoia. The name changed in 1982.

As planned, Nick travelled to Mhuka Ranch on Friday, 11th April. He had timed the trip to coincide with a visit from some wealthy British entrepreneurs who had already contributed significantly to the Afro-Asian Humanity and Wildlife Foundation (the Foundation), which was chaired by Stewart Sinclair, Rachel's father and his father-in-law. These entrepreneurs were keen to involve more colleagues in the Foundation and had come to the ranch to better understand its work. Nick was eager to meet them to advocate not only for the ranch but also for the Foundation and RQI[403].

Nick also wanted to share with Duncan and Sipho[404] some preliminary ideas he and Stewart had discussed about transferring the land comprising the rhino conservancy into a trust. This trust would be established to safeguard against any potential attempts by the Zimbabwean government to seize the land. The idea had arisen after Sipho revealed that the CIO[405] had pressured him to halt further investigations into his parents' deaths by threatening to revoke Mhuka Ranch's licence for its rhino conservation work.

Nick's road trip to Mhuka Ranch was uneventful and pleasant. He arrived at the main homestead just after 4:00 pm and was greeted by Sipho. The two of them enjoyed a cup of tea together before Nick made his way to his allocated bedroom in the guest wing. He had a short nap followed by a shower to freshen up before joining Sipho and the Olivers for dinner in the guest wing's dining room.

Over dinner, he enjoyed lively conversation with Sipho, Duncan Oliver, and Mark and Jenny Oliver. Jenny shared the joyful news that she was now heavily pregnant with her and Mark's first child, due in early June.

The Olivers and Sipho brought Nick up to speed with all the news from the ranch. Things were going from strength to strength as a result of the capital that had been injected into the business

---

[403] Rare Quest Imports.
[404] Sipho is a Ndebele boy's name meaning Gift.
[405] Zimbabwe's Central Intelligence Organisation.

following the sale of one-third equity interests to each of Sipho and RQI. The rhino conservancy project was thriving, as were the big game hunting and photographic safari arms of the business. In addition, Mitch, the manager they had recruited from Mexico to run the cattle ranching and big game hunting arms of the business, had fitted in extremely well and was now making a valuable contribution to the ranch's overall business success.

Over dinner, Sipho opened up to the Olivers about why he had decided not to pursue his investigations into the role the 5th Brigade had played in his parents' murder. He explained that Major Tawanda Nyati, a 5th Brigade officer, had commanded the squad that raided Inyathi Mission School, and it was Nyati who had shot his parents in cold blood. Sipho also shared what he had learned about the CIO's involvement in orchestrating the staged road traffic accident in which Major Nyati was killed. Nyati's supposed death in the accident had, in fact, been a murder ordered by the government and arranged by the CIO, as Nyati had become an embarrassment to Mugabe. This embarrassment arose because Nyati had unquestioningly followed the baseless orders issued to him as part of the *Gukurahundi*[406] campaign against suspected ZIPRA dissidents and Ndebele citizens — orders that were not only morally despicable but also devoid of any legal foundation.

Sipho also shared the dire threats that the CIO had made against him and Mhuka Ranch if he continued with his investigation into the 5th Brigade's role in his parents' deaths. He emphasised that he had no doubt these threats would be carried out unless he complied.

For his part, Nick shared with them his acquaintance with an exiled Zimbabwean citizen now living in London and working as a human rights lawyer with Amnesty International[407]. The man, Jonathon

---

[406] *Gukurahundi* is a Shona word which roughly translates as *'the early rain that washes away the chaff before the spring rain'*.

[407] Amnesty International is an international non-governmental organisation focused on human rights, with its headquarters in the UK. It was founded in 1961 with the mission of campaigning for a world in which every person enjoys all of the human

Khumalo, claimed to be a member of the royal House of Khumalo[408] in Zimbabwe. Interestingly, Jonathon was planning to return to Zimbabwe to re-establish this royal line and to draw global attention to the wrongs and injustices that the government of Zimbabwe had inflicted on the country's Ndebele citizenry.

Nick recounted how Jonathon had arranged the secret meeting between the two of them and Joshua Nkomo in the English countryside outside London, sharing what Nkomo had revealed about the threats to his life during their meeting. He also informed them of Jonathon's tragic death in a hit-and-run incident in West Croydon, London, which Nick suspected was orchestrated by Zimbabwe's CIO as well. Throughout Sipho and Nick's descriptions, Duncan, Mark, and Jenny remained silent, spellbound by the depth of duplicity and evil perpetrated by the senior leadership of their country.

Over the following week, Nick spent many hours with Sipho, Duncan, Mark, and Jenny exploring what needed to be done to try and curb the current excesses exhibited by Mugabe and his government.

However, despite their best efforts to develop effective strategies that could be pursued internally in Zimbabwe, it soon became clear to Nick that, in the short term at least, it was unlikely that Mugabe's current grip on power could be weakened via the ballot box.

This was primarily because voting patterns in the independence elections in April 1980 and in the subsequent general elections in 1985 had been largely tribally based.

---

rights enshrined in the Universal Declaration of Human Rights and other international human rights instruments.

[408] The House of Khumalo is the continuing royal family of the former Mthwakazi Kingdom (modern day Matabeleland). The Mthwakazi Kingdom was founded in 1823 and ended in 1894 with the First Matabele War. The House has endured to the present day.

ZANU-PF[409] remained immensely popular among the Shona and related tribes, who constituted approximately 70% to 80% of the population. In the short to medium term, these groups were likely to continue their strong support for the ruling party.

Although many Ndebele people did not support Mugabe or ZANU-PF, they only represented about 15% of the population. Moreover, the recent and brutal *Gukurahundi* campaign against Ndebele citizens living in Matabeleland had left many terrified, resulting in a reluctance among some Ndebele to vote for ZAPU, the main opposition party.

Whites comprised around 2% of the total population. While 20% of the seats in the 100-seat House of Assembly had been disproportionately reserved for whites in the 1980 independence elections, this provision was set to end by 1990, or possibly earlier. After that, all seats would be contested based on the principles of majority rule and equal representation, regardless of race.

Furthermore, Mugabe's politicisation of the defence forces, police, judiciary, and administrative arms made it relatively easy for him to enforce draconian policies that might otherwise be deemed unconstitutional.

These factors painted a grim picture, indicating that unless the international community could be persuaded to exert significant pressure on Mugabe's Government, its repressive, dictatorial, and brutal tendencies were likely to worsen.

Sipho, Duncan, Mark, and Jenny questioned Nick on whether he believed he could mobilise political opinion, particularly in the UK, to exert diplomatic pressure on Mugabe. Nick admitted he could do little alone, but through his work and family ties with Stewart Dixon, he hoped to achieve something. He pledged to prioritise this upon returning to the UK.

---

[409] Zimbabwe African National Union – Patriotic Front. ZANU-PF is a political organisation that has been the ruling party of Zimbabwe since independence in 1980.

Nick left Mhuka Ranch on Friday, 11th April, driving back to Harare where he spent a few days with his parents before flying back to the UK on Tuesday, 15th April.

On his flight back to the UK, Nick reflected on his brief visit to the land of his birth. Despite the short duration of the visit and his growing awareness of the dangers posed by Zimbabwe's current regime, he still felt inspired and invigorated by the country. With its immense potential, he believed that under the right leadership and policies, Zimbabwe could become a beacon for other newly independent African nations. Determined to contribute to the country's journey toward realising its true potential, he resolved to do whatever he could to help, albeit from abroad.

Chapter 41 – Concern for the Povo

Nick arrived back in the UK on Tuesday, 15th April 1986. Though tired from his flight, the sight of the smiling and ever-radiant Rachel in the arrivals hall at Heathrow immediately lifted his spirits.

Rachel had driven to the airport, and during the hour-long return trip to their home in Medstead, Nick gave her a complete rundown of his trip to Mhuka[410] Ranch. She was delighted to hear about the ranch's success, but the best news of all was that Jenny was pregnant with her and Mark's first child, due in early June. On Rachel's two previous trips to the ranch, she had grown particularly fond of Jenny, who had a contagious laugh, a quick wit, an endearing passion for Zimbabwe, and a sacrificial love for her family — qualities that Rachel admired and aspired to replicate.

On the journey home, Nick took some time to explain to Rachel the complex political and economic challenges facing Zimbabwe, which were being exacerbated by Robert Mugabe's relentless pursuit of power. He noted that with ZAPU's[411] political influence waning and the white community's limited capacity to impact Zimbabwe's politics coming to an end, it was likely that the country would soon become a one-party state under Mugabe's leadership. Nick added that, given the current political climate and the lack of effective internal

---

410 A local word meaning animals or wildlife.
411 Zimbabwe African People's Union.

opposition to ZANU-PF[412], it was improbable Mugabe would ease his harsh policies without substantial external pressure on him and his party.

At this point, Nick turned to Rachel and said, "Honey, I don't quite understand it, but I really feel compelled to try and do something to help the black people in Zimbabwe. By this, I mean the ordinary black populace. Mugabe will look after the political elite, while the wealthy and educated will look after themselves, but I feel for the *povo*[413], both Shona and Ndebele. No one will worry about them."

"What does *povo* mean?" asked Rachel.

"Sorry," replied Nick. "It's a Zimbabwean slang word derived from the Portuguese word '*povo*', which means people or populace. In Zimbabwe, it generally refers to the rural people and the working classes. Zimbabweans use the word to distinguish between those with political or economic power and those without."

"Well, I applaud you for worrying about the *povo*," said Rachel.

There was a pause. Then Nick asked, "I would like to approach your Dad to see if he can help me discern what I might be able to do to improve things for the Zimbabwean *povo*. Do you think he would be open to that?"

Rachel replied unhesitatingly, "Absolutely, Nick. At his core, Dad is a philanthropist, especially motivated to help the poor and powerless in African and Asian nations. That's something he has tried to cultivate in me as well. I'm sure he will help if he can."

With that, she took her left hand off the steering wheel and placed it on his thigh. Nick took her hand, squeezed it, and said, "Thanks,

---

[412] Zimbabwe African National Union – Patriotic Front. ZANU-PF is a political organisation that has been the ruling party of Zimbabwe since independence in 1980.
[413] This is a Zimbabwean slang word used to describe the rural and working class people of Zimbabwe. It is used to distinguish between those with political or economic power and those without.

honey. Now, best you keep both hands on the steering wheel. I'll give you a real thank you once we're home."

Rachel grinned. "I can't wait. I've missed you."

Nick cheekily quipped, "That makes two of us. As my Mum would say, '*Absence makes the heart grow fonder.*' I can't wait to get home to show you just how fond I can be!"

They both laughed. Medstead was now only ten miles away!

Chapter 42 – The murky world of global politics

Time line – April to August 1986

Upon his return to the UK, Nick re-immersed himself in the hustle and bustle of business life at RQI[414]. His role had grown significantly, and he was now managing all of RQI's contracts with its key British customers. With the successful completion of his induction period, Stewart Dixon, the managing director, was strategically exposing Nick to more of RQI's work in southern Africa.

Nick had already been involved in some of RQI's ventures in the region, including finalising the company's acquisition of one-third of Mhuka[415] Ranch's share capital. Additionally, he had played a pivotal role in helping the South African Government circumvent the UN arms embargo, facilitating clandestine arms deals between South Africa and the British arms industry to support South Africa's fight against guerrilla incursions.

In June 1986, Nick found himself once again involved in such activities. This time, the South African government sought RQI's assistance in Angola, where the civil war between the Soviet and

---

[414] Rare Quest Imports.
[415] A local word meaning animals or wildlife.

Cuban-backed MPLA[416] and the Western-aligned UNITA[417] and FNLA[418] was raging. The Cold War was still in full force, and South Africa's concerns about communist influence in southern Africa meant they were keen to support the anti-communist factions of UNITA and FNLA in Angola. Although South Africa itself was under a UN arms embargo, Nick soon realised that the embargo was not strictly enforced if the arms were claimed to be destined for UNITA or FNLA. The fact that some of these weapons remained in South Africa was largely overlooked by UN enforcers.

Nick's ability to exploit these ambiguous political stances by the UK and USA governments had led to significant arms sales for British manufacturers and substantial profits for RQI. Yet, even with his focus on these deals, Zimbabwe remained at the forefront of Nick's mind.

Nick was eager to consult Stewart on the situation in Zimbabwe, but first, he wanted to map out potential scenarios that might benefit the country. His instincts told him that many older Britons still held a degree of sympathy for the former Rhodesia, particularly for its significant sacrifices in the World Wars and its economic progress before 1980. Many of these individuals struggled to understand why the British Government had so quickly supported unproven black nationalist parties with communist ties, overlooking Rhodesia's economic advancements and historical links to the UK.

---

[416] The People's Movement for the Liberation of Angola. The MPLA fought against the Portuguese Army in the Angolan War of Independence from (1961 to 1975). In the ensuing Angolan Civil War (1975 to 2002), it defeated the joint forces of UNITA and FNLA.

[417] The National Union for the Total Independence of Angola. Founded in 1966, UNITA fought alongside the MPLA and FNLA in the Angolan War for Independence (1961 to 1975). In the ensuing Angolan Civil War (1975 to 2002) it fought against the MPLA.

[418] The National Front for the Liberation of Angola. The FNLA was an anti-colonial movement that fought against the Portuguese Army in the Angolan War of Independence from (1961 to 1975). In the ensuing Angolan Civil War (1975 to 2002), it fought against the MPLA with support from the United States and other Western countries.

Nick saw this sentiment as a potential opportunity to sway British policy towards Zimbabwe, though he knew it would be difficult. The Thatcher Government's neoliberal policies of deregulation and privatisation were the order of the day, and its stance towards Zimbabwe was deeply influenced by both global and domestic considerations.

To gain further insight, Nick requested RQI's analyst team to investigate the British Government's current thinking regarding Zimbabwe and to summarise their findings in a report. Their findings, delivered in early July 1986, painted a bleak picture for individuals like Nick, who were hopeful of fostering British intervention in Zimbabwe. The analysts outlined that the current British Government, under Margaret Thatcher, was leaning firmly towards a hands-off approach to Zimbabwe's internal affairs.

The report highlighted several reasons for this stance. Economically, maintaining stable relations with Zimbabwe was seen as essential to safeguarding British investments in the region, particularly in the country's rich mineral resources like gold and chrome. In terms of global stability, Britain was cautious about destabilising southern Africa, which might have wider implications, potentially drawing in neighbouring countries and leading to broader conflicts.

The Cold War still loomed large in Britain's calculations. The Thatcher Government likely believed that a non-interventionist stance would prevent Zimbabwe from aligning itself more closely with the Soviet Union or other communist influences. A direct challenge to Mugabe's regime could push Zimbabwe further into the Soviet sphere of influence, something Britain sought to avoid.

Diplomatically, Britain was also mindful of its place within the Commonwealth. Zimbabwe, as a fellow Commonwealth member, held symbolic significance, and any actions that jeopardised Britain's relations with Mugabe's Government could undermine the unity of the Commonwealth, something that Thatcher was keen to preserve. Additionally, the government had to reconcile its colonial legacy with the post-colonial reality. While some in Britain still took pride in the country's colonial past, the political climate demanded sensitivity to the decolonisation narrative that had dominated global discourse for decades.

Domestically, the report pointed out that there was limited public appetite for intervention in Zimbabwe. Thatcher's Conservative Party was focused on free-market principles and non-interference, leaving little room for interventionist strategies. Regionally, Britain also supported the Southern African Development Coordination Conference (SADCC), an organisation focused on reducing economic dependence on apartheid-era South Africa. The SADCC[419], of which Zimbabwe was a founding member, adhered to non-interference in internal affairs of member states, a policy Britain appeared to respect.

Despite these justifications for non-intervention, the report also outlined the potential drawbacks. Human rights concerns were becoming more prominent, with increasing reports of political repression and violence under Mugabe's rule. Britain might face criticism for turning a blind eye, with some arguing that, as the former colonial power, it had a moral responsibility to ensure the well-being of Zimbabwe's people and governance.

There was also the issue of Britain's declining influence in southern Africa. By adopting a hands-off approach, the Thatcher Government risked ceding ground to other powers, such as the Soviet Union, China, or even South Africa. If conflict in Zimbabwe escalated, it could destabilise the region and threaten British interests in both economic and security terms.

Internationally, the UK's reputation was also at stake. Britain was widely regarded as a promoter of democracy and human rights, and

---

[419] The Southern African Development Coordination Conference (SADCC), the forerunner of the Southern African Development Community (SADC), was established to promote regional economic development and reduce dependence on apartheid-era South Africa. It was formally launched with the signing of a declaration in Lusaka, Zambia, on 1st April 1980, by a group of southern African countries.

some in the Commonwealth might see the government's non-interventionist stance as a failure to uphold these principles.

After reading the report, Nick was left with a dilemma. The findings suggested that pursuing an interventionist approach would be difficult, if not impossible, given the current political climate in Britain. The cautious tone of the report urged against any significant attempts to influence Zimbabwe's internal matters, and Nick knew he could not dismiss the analysts' conclusions lightly.

Before making any decisions, Nick decided to discuss the matter with Rachel. He knew her insights, given her understanding of her father and his connections, would be invaluable as he weighed his next move.

Chapter 43 – No knight in shining armour

Nick sat at the dining table, the contents of the RQI[420] analysts' report weighing heavily on his mind. The early morning light filtered through the curtains, casting a soft glow across the room. Rachel entered, carrying two mugs of tea, and placed one in front of him. She took a seat opposite, her face radiant in the soft light.

"You look troubled," she said gently. "What's going on?"

Nick pushed the report across the table. "Remember I asked RQI to assess Britain's approach to Zimbabwe? Well, this is it. They've concluded that Britain is staying hands-off. The risks of intervention are too high. There's no way your Dad would support anything that even hints at interference in Zimbabwe's internal affairs, especially after reading this."

Rachel glanced at the report, then back at him. "I understand. You know how much my father values the findings of his analysts."

Nick sighed, running a hand through his hair. "But I promised Sipho[421], and the Oliver family. They're counting on us — on me. I thought I could make a difference."

Rachel reached out, resting her hand over his. "You've already done more than most would. But this isn't about us stepping in and fixing

---

[420] Rare Quest Imports.
[421] Sipho is a Ndebele boy's name meaning Gift.

things for Zimbabwe. Their future has to be determined by Zimbabweans. You've said this yourself."

Nick met her gaze, searching for reassurance. "I know — but it feels like I'm abandoning them."

"You're not," Rachel replied softly. "You're helping in the best way you can. By ensuring Mhuka[422] Ranch thrives, you're giving stability and hope to the community around Chiredzi. But we can't fix an entire country's problems, especially not by imposing solutions from the outside. These changes have to come from within Zimbabwe."

Nick nodded slowly, the weight of her words sinking in. "You're right. It's just hard to accept."

Rachel took a deep breath. "There's something else we need to talk about." She hesitated, then said, "I'm pregnant, Nick."

Nick's eyes widened. "Pregnant? That's amazing!" He stood, pulling her into a tight embrace. "How long have you known?"

"A few weeks," she admitted, her voice muffled against his shoulder. "I wanted to wait until the right time to tell you."

Nick pulled back, his face lit with joy and a hint of worry. "This changes everything."

"It does," Rachel agreed. "Which is why we need to focus on our family now. We have responsibilities here in England. And you need to help your parents as they decide whether to leave Zimbabwe. Whether they choose the UK or Australia, they'll need our support."

Nick sank back into his chair, his emotions swirling. "I've been so consumed with Zimbabwe that I didn't see what was right in front of me."

Rachel smiled softly. "It's time to look ahead, Nick. We can still care about Zimbabwe, but our priority has to be our family. And by supporting Mhuka Ranch, we're still doing our part."

---

[422] A local word meaning animals or wildlife.

Nick exhaled slowly, a growing sense of clarity settling over him. "You're right. I need to let go of trying to solve Zimbabwe's problems. The country has to find its own way."

Rachel nodded. "Yes, it's up to them now. No knight in shining armour is coming to rescue Zimbabwe. They need to find their own solutions, just as we have to find ours."

As they sat together in the growing morning light, Nick felt a deep sense of peace. The journey ahead, with Rachel by his side and a new life on the way, filled him with hope. Though the broader struggles of Zimbabwe were beyond his control, he could still make a difference — however small — by supporting Mhuka Ranch and the people around it. In time, he hoped, that Zimbabwe, a land which he still loved, would find its own heroes and its own path to peace.

For now, however, Nick's focus, alongside Rachel, would be on nurturing their families and careers here in the UK while embracing the impending arrival of their new child. Together, they would work to build a brighter future not only for themselves but also for generations to come.

Perhaps one day, if circumstances permitted, future generations of the Sinclairs could return to Zimbabwe to live in peace and happiness alongside Sipho's children and grandchildren, in a country free from the cancer of corruption, racism, and tribalism, yet still rich in nature's abundant treasures.

Epilogue

From the dawn of independence in 1980 to the present day, November 2024, Zimbabwe's hopes for democratic reform and prosperity have been met with the harsh reality of ZANU-PF's unrelenting grip on power and a steady decline in national wellbeing.

Summary of ZANU-PF Strategies to Retain Power:

1980-1987: Initial Changes

Constitutional Changes: The 1980 Constitution initially included 20 reserved seats for whites to ensure minority representation. However, by 1987, these seats had been removed prior to the expiry of their ten-year term. This removal marked not only the erosion of white representation but also set the stage for ZANU-PF's long-term dominance, unencumbered by political opposition.

1987-1999: Consolidation of Power

Unity Accord (1987): The signing of the Unity Accord between ZANU-PF and ZAPU integrated ZAPU into ZANU-PF, effectively creating a one-party state and consolidating Mugabe's control.

Executive Presidency: Mugabe assumed the role of Executive President, merging the functions of Head of State and Head of Government to exert direct control over the executive branch.

Politicisation of Security Forces: The Zimbabwe Defence Forces, Central Intelligence Organisation, and Zimbabwe Republic Police were increasingly politicised to ensure loyalty to Mugabe and ZANU-PF.

Land Reform Rhetoric: Early land reform policies, initially intended to address colonial injustices, were also used to gain rural support and suppress opposition. This land redistribution not only decimated agricultural productivity but also shattered the livelihoods of countless farm workers, leading to widespread hunger and displacement.

2000-2009: Economic Turmoil and Political Repression

Fast-Track Land Reform (2000): The aggressive redistribution of white-owned farms led to economic collapse and international isolation while solidifying rural support.

Suppression of Opposition: Violent crackdowns on the Movement for Democratic Change (MDC) and other opposition parties, and the use of state-sponsored militias and repressive laws like the Public Order and Security Act, were employed to crush any meaningful opposition.

Control of Media: State media was tightly controlled, and independent journalists faced harassment to silence dissenting voices.

2010-2017: Power Struggles and Economic Decline

Indigenisation Policies: Policies requiring foreign companies to cede 51% of their shares to black Zimbabweans aimed at economic empowerment but led to further economic decline.

Electoral Manipulation: Electoral fraud, intimidation, and manipulation, notably in the 2013 elections, ensured continued ZANU-PF victories despite allegations of rigging.

Factionalism within ZANU-PF: Internal strife increased, particularly between factions loyal to Grace Mugabe and those aligned with Emmerson Mnangagwa. Amidst economic turmoil, ZANU-PF faced increasing internal rifts. These factional struggles reflected the party's growing reliance on loyalty over governance, with devastating consequences for Zimbabwe's economy.

2017-2024: Mnangagwa's Era

Military Intervention (2017): The military coup led to Mugabe's resignation and Mnangagwa's ascension, initially portrayed as a move towards democracy but effectively a reorganisation of ZANU-PF control. Mnangagwa's ascension was initially seen as a potential turning point. However, hopes for real democratic reforms soon faded, as ZANU-PF's entrenched interests reasserted themselves under his leadership.

Re-engagement and Reforms: Mnangagwa's efforts to re-engage with the international community and introduce economic reforms faced setbacks due to ongoing corruption and lack of genuine political reform.

Continued Repression: Repressive tactics persisted, with the military and police used to suppress opposition and dissent. The judiciary remained under executive influence to legitimise questionable outcomes and stifle challenges.

Electoral Tactics: Electoral manipulation and gerrymandering ensured ZANU-PF's dominance, with the 2023 election remaining disputed.

Economic Control: Key economic sectors were controlled, and patronage networks secured loyalty from business figures and political elites.

Surveillance and Intimidation: Surveillance capabilities expanded, maintaining a climate of fear to deter dissent and activism.

Conclusion

From 1980 to November 2024, ZANU-PF has used a blend of political manoeuvring, economic policies, and repression to maintain its grip on power. Under both Mugabe and Mnangagwa, the party has adeptly adapted its strategies to shifting circumstances while ensuring that power remains firmly within its grasp.

Glossary of Terms

1RAR	1st Battalion of the Rhodesian African Rifles.
3RAR	3rd Battalion of the Rhodesian African Rifles.
4WD	This is an acronym for four-wheel drive. 4WD vehicles are typically used in off-road or other challenging driving conditions.
A-Levels	A-Levels were the Advanced Level of school examinations. It was conferred as a school leaving qualification to senior school pupils as part of the Cambridge International General Certificate of Education.
African Unity Square	Prior to 1981 this was known as Cecil Square.
AHWF	Acronym for *Afro-Asian Humanity and Wildlife Foundation*.
AK-47	The AK-47 was developed by the Soviet Union and was the preferred light automatic rifle of the ZANLA and ZIPRA forces. After the end of the Rhodesian Bush War, it became one of the automatic rifles used by the Zimbabwe National Army.
Amnesty International	Amnesty International is an international non-governmental organisation focused on human rights, with its headquarters in the UK. It was founded in 1961 with the mission of campaigning for a world in which every person enjoys all of the human rights enshrined in the Universal Declaration of Human Rights and other international human rights instruments.
ANC	This is the acronym for the African National Congress. The ANC is one of the oldest and most well-known liberation movements in South Africa. It was founded in 1921 and played a central role in the fight against apartheid.

Apartheid	Apartheid is the Afrikaans word for apartness. It was a system of institutionalised racial segregation that existed in South Africa and South West Africa (now Namibia) from 1948 to the early 1990s.
AWOL	Absence Without Leave.
Bishop Muzorewa	Bishop Abel Muzorewa served as the first and only Prime Minister of Zimbabwe Rhodesia. His election in April 1979 followed the Internal Settlement which had been concluded in March 1978 between the RF Government and other non-exiled black nationalist leaders. He held office for less than a year.
Bobotie	Bobotie is a spiced, baked minced meat dish topped with an egg-based topping. It's a Cape Malay dish with Indonesian and Dutch influences.
Boerewors	**Boerewors is a type of spicy sausage which originated in South Africa.**
BOSS	Bureau of State Security. This was the main South African intelligence agency from 1969 to 1980. In 1980 BOSS was significantly restructured and transformed to become the National Intelligence Service (NIS). The NIS is now, however, defunct.
Braai	Braai is the Afrikaans word for a BBQ.
Bulawayo Club	This had been established in 1895 as a gentlemen's club along the lines of similar gentlemen's clubs in London, Cape Town, and Johannesburg. It had moved to its current premises at the corner of 8th Avenue and Fort Street, in 1934.
CAZ	Conservative Alliance of Zimbabwe, formerly known as The Republican Front, and before that The Rhodesian Front. These House of

	Assembly members were elected by voters on the White Roll.
CBD	Central Business District.
Chibuku	Chibuku is a traditional African beer brewed from sorghum and/or maize.
Chinhoyi	Chinhoyi was previously known as Sinoia. The name changed in 1982.
CIO	Zimbabwe's Central Intelligence Organisation.
COIN	Counter-insurgency.
Council for World Mission	The Council is a worldwide community of mainly Protestant Christian churches. The organisation works to spread the knowledge of Christ throughout the world and to strengthen their members in their mission work by sharing their resources of money, people, skills, and insights. It was formerly named the London Missionary Society.
Dagga	Dagga is a local term used to describe the psychoactive drug cannabis.
DIY	Acronym meaning Do It Yourself.
Dumiso Dabengwa	ZIPRA's intelligence chief during the Rhodesian Bush War and for a short time thereafter. In 1982 he was charged with treason by the Mugabe administration and arrested.
Diazepam	Diazepam, sold under the brand name Valium among others, is a medicine of the benzodiazepine family that calms the central nervous system.
Eastern Highlands	The Eastern Highlands is a mountainous area on the border of Zimbabwe and Mozambique. It extends for about 300 kilometres from north to south and includes the Inyangani Mountains,

the Vumba Mountains, and the Chimanimani Mountains.

Emmerson Mnangagwa   Emmerson Mnangagwa was a senior member of ZANLA during the Rhodesian Bush War. Following Zimbabwe's independence in 1980, he was appointed the Minister of State Security in the President's office and oversaw the Central Intelligence Organisation. He would later become the 3rd president of Zimbabwe following the successful 2017 coup which ousted Robert Mugabe.

Entumbane uprisings   These had occurred in February 1981 in and around Bulawayo. During the uprising former ZIPRA guerrillas rebelled creating a situation that threatened to develop into a fresh civil war, barely a year after the Rhodesian Bush War. The uprising was quashed by the newly formed Zimbabwe National Army who used troops from the former RAR and other white-commanded elements of the Rhodesian Security Forces to eliminate the threat.

FFARCS   Fellowship in the Faculty of Anaesthetists of the Royal College of Surgeons of England.

FN   This was a light automatic rifle designed in Belgium and manufactured by FN Herstal. The FN had been the standard issue rifle for the Rhodesian Security Forces.

FNLA   The National Front for the Liberation of Angola. The FNLA was an anti-colonial movement that fought against the Portuguese Army in the Angolan War of Independence from (1961 to 1975). In the ensuing Angolan Civil War (1975 to 2002), it fought against the MPLA with support from the United States and other Western countries.

Fundi	This is a South African slang term meaning a person who has gained a lot of knowledge about a particular subject.
Great Zimbabwe Ruins	The Great Zimbabwe Ruins is the name of the stone ruins of an ancient city known as Great Zimbabwe. The ruins are located just outside Fort Victoria (now called Masvingo). People lived in Great Zimbabwe from around 1100 but abandoned it in the 15th century. The city was the capital of the Kingdom of Zimbabwe, which was a Shona trading empire. Zimbabwe means "stone houses" in Shona.
Gukurahundi	*Gukurahundi* is a Shona word which roughly translates as *'the early rain that washes away the chaff before the spring rain'*.
Gwelo	Gwelo was renamed Gweru in 1982.
Gweru	The name of Gweru during the colonial era had been Gwelo.
Hendrik Verwoerd	Hendrik Verwoerd was the Prime Minister of South Africa from 1958 to 1966. He is commonly regarded as the architect of apartheid.
House of Khumalo	The House of Khumalo is the continuing royal family of the former Mthwakazi Kingdom (modern day Matabeleland). The Mthwakazi Kingdom was founded in 1823 and ended in 1894 with the First Matabele War. The House has endured to the present day.
Induna	In Ndebele culture, an *induna* was a title meaning a great leader, headman, or commander of a group of warriors.
Ingwe	Ingwe is a local word meaning leopard.
Intel	Intelligence information (often military in nature).

Inyathi Mission	The mission had been established by the Reverend Robert Moffat in 1859. It is situated some 75 kilometres north-north-east of Bulawayo. Moffat was a member of the London Missionary Society, which had been established in England with the aim of spreading the knowledge of Christ among heathen and unenlightened nations.
Ishe	This is a term of respect used by RAR soldiers when referring to their officers.
Isilima	Isilima is a Ndebele word meaning idiot.
IZG	Independent Zimbabwe Group. These House of Assembly members were elected by voters on the White Roll.
IUCN	International Union for the Conservation of Nature. This is an international organization working in the field of nature conservation and sustainable use of natural resources.
Kopje	The word kopje is derived from the Afrikaans word koppie, which means a small hill.
King Lobengula Khumalo	King Lobengula Khumalo (1845 to circa 1894) was the second and last official King of the northern Ndebele people.
Knobkerrie	A knobkerrie is a wooden club with a large knob at one of its ends. Traditionally, they were used by South African tribespeople for throwing at animals or for clubbing an enemy's head.
Kushamisika	*Kushamisika* is a Shona word meaning *to be surprised*. It conveys the sense of being taken aback or experiencing a sudden unexpected turn of events.
Kyle National Park	This is now known as Mutirikiwi National Park.
Lake Kyle	This is now known as Lake Mutirikiwi.

Lamé	Lamé is a type of fabric woven with threads made of metallic fibre wrapped around natural or synthetic fibres like silk or nylon.
Lancaster House Agreement	In August 1979 the British Government invited the leaders of the ZANU and ZAPU, Bishop Muzorewa, and Ian Smith to participate in a Constitutional Conference at Lancaster House in London. The purpose of the Conference was to discuss and reach agreement on the terms of an Independence Constitution, to agree on the holding of elections under British authority, and to enable Zimbabwe-Rhodesia to proceed to lawful and internationally recognised independence, with the parties settling their differences by political means.
Lesotho	Lesotho was formerly known as Basutoland. Its name changed in 1966 when it gained independence from British colonial rule.
Locstat	Ordnance survey map reference.
Lookout Masuku	Lookout Masuku was the commander of ZIPRA during the Rhodesian Bush War. After independence, he served as deputy commander of the Zimbabwe National Army until his arrest in 1982 for allegedly plotting to overthrow Robert Mugabe.
Malva Pudding	A sweet and sticky baked dessert typically served warm and often accompanied by a creamy sauce or custard.
Mandla	Mandla is a Ndebele boy's name meaning Power and Strength.
Masodja	Masodja is the Africanised word for soldier.
Masvingo	Masvingo was previously known as Fort Victoria. The name changed in 1982.

Matobo Hills	Prior to 1982, these were known as the Matopos Hills.
Matobo National Park	Prior to 1982, this was known as the Matopos National Park.
Mhuka	A local word meaning animals or wildlife.
Mlimo	Mlimo refers to the ancestral spiritual leader of the Ndebele people. Mlimo is believed to possess supernatural powers and is revered by the Ndebele community as a guardian and protector, including seeking justice and avenging wrongdoings.
Mpilo Hospital	Mpilo Hospital, is the largest public hospital in Bulawayo, and second largest in Zimbabwe after Parirenyatwa Hospital in Harare. It serves as the referral centre for the Matabeleland North, Matabeleland South and Midlands provinces of Zimbabwe. The name *Mpilo*, means *life* in the Ndebele language.
MPLA	The People's Movement for the Liberation of Angola. The MPLA fought against the Portuguese Army in the Angolan War of Independence from (1961 to 1975). In the ensuing Angolan Civil War (1975 to 2002), it defeated the joint forces of UNITA and FNLA.
Mutare	The name of Mutare during the colonial era had been Umtali.
Nandi	Nandi is a Ndebele girl's name meaning Sweetness.
NIS	National Intelligence Service. The NIS was established in 1980, succeeding the Bureau of State Security (BOSS). Its primary role was to gather intelligence, conduct covert operations, and support the South African Government's counter-intelligence efforts.
Nookies	Slang terms for sexual intercourse.

Nyoko yemhumgo	Cobra snake.
OAU	The Organisation of African Unity (1963 to 2002). In 2002 the OAU was superseded by the African Union (AU).
Perrance Shiri	Perrance Shiri was distantly related to Rogert Mugabe. After independence, he commanded the 5th Brigade from 1983 to 1984. In 1992 he was appointed the commander of the Airforce of Zimbabwe. Shiri was influential in orchestrating the 2017 Zimbabwean coup d'état which removed Mugabe from power. On 30th November 2017, Shiri was appointed Minister of Agriculture by President Emmerson Mnangagwa.
Povo	This is a Zimbabwean slang word used to describe the rural and working class people of Zimbabwe. It is used to distinguish between those with political or economic power and those without.
Pro Bono	In a legal context, *pro bono* means the provision of legal services on a free or significantly reduced fee basis.
PW Botha	Pieter Willem Botha was a South African politician who was the last Prime Minister of South Africa from 1978 to 1984 and its first executive state president from 1984 to 1989.
Queen Lozikeyi Dlodlo	Queen Lozikeyi Dlodlo (c 1855 to 1919) was one of the favourite wives of King Lobengula and a senior queen until 1893.
RAR	Rhodesian African Rifles.
RF	Rhodesian Front.
Rhodes Scholarship	The Rhodes Scholarship was founded by Cecil John Rhodes. It is an international postgraduate award for students to study at the University of Oxford, in the UK.

RLI	Rhodesian Light Infantry. This was an infantry regiment and was one of the country's main counter-insurgency units during the Rhodesian Bush War.
RQI	Rare Quest Imports.
SAA	South African Airways.
SADCC	The Southern African Development Coordination Conference (SADCC), the forerunner of the Southern African Development Community (SADC), was established to promote regional economic development and reduce dependence on apartheid-era South Africa. It was formally launched with the signing of a declaration in Lusaka, Zambia, on 1st April 1980, by a group of southern African countries.
Sadza	Sadza is a thickened porridge made with white maize meal. It is one of the staple foods in Zimbabwe.
Salisbury	Salisbury was renamed Harare in 1982.
San	The San, often known as "Bushmen," are descendants of hunter-gatherers who have lived in southern Africa for tens of thousands of years.
Second Boer War	The Second Boer War, was a conflict fought between the British Empire and the two Boer republics (the South African Republic and Orange Free State) over the Empire's influence in Southern Africa.
Second Chimurenga	The Second Chimurenga, also known as the Rhodesian Bush War or the Zimbabwe Liberation War, refers to the guerilla war of 1966 to 1979 which led to the end of white-minority rule in Rhodesia.
Sipho	Sipho is a Ndebele boy's name meaning Gift.

Solomon Mujuru	Commander of Zimbabwe Defence Forces. His nom de guerre during the Rhodesian Bush War was Rex Nhongo.
South African Wildlife Foundation	This was founded in 1968. It later became the Southern African Nature Foundation and in 1995 was renamed the World Wildlife Fund South Africa.
South West Africa	South West Africa achieved its independence from South African administration on 21st March 1990, and was renamed Namibia.
The Acropolis	The Acropolis is now referred to as the Hill Complex.
The Chronicle	*The Chronicle* was published in Bulawayo and mostly reported on news affecting the Matabeleland area in the south of the country. It was first published in 1894.
The Two Ronnies	Mhuka Ranch's first two male black rhinos had been named the Two Ronnies after the British comedic duo consisting of Ronnie Barker and Ronnie Corbett which aired on the BBC in the UK from 1971 to 1987.
UANC	United African National Council.
Ubaba	Ubaba is the Ndebele word for father.
UCCSA	This is the acronym for United Congregational Church of Southern Africa.
UDI	Unilateral Declaration of Independence. On 11th November 1965, the Rhodesian Government unilaterally and illegally declared itself to be independent of Britain.
UK	The United Kingdom.
Ukuthula	Ukuthula is the Zulu word for calmness or silence.

Umama	Umama is the Ndebele word for mother.
UN	United Nations.
UNITA	The National Union for the Total Independence of Angola. Founded in 1966, UNITA fought alongside the MPLA and FNLA in the Angolan War for Independence (1961 to 1975). In the ensuing Angolan Civil War (1975 to 2002) it fought against the MPLA.
UV	Ultraviolet
VHF	Very High Frequency.
Vivienne Westwood	Vivienne Westwood was one of London's leading fashion designers and businesswomen.
Wankie Colliery	Wankie Colliery, which is now known as Hwange Colliery, was established in 1899 and is one of Zimbabwe's oldest and largest coal mines.
ZANU	Zimbabwe African National Union.
ZANU-PF	Zimbabwe African National Union – Patriotic Front. ZANU-PF is a political organisation that has been the ruling party of Zimbabwe since independence in 1980.
ZANLA	Zimbabwe African National Liberation Army. ZANLA was the military wing of ZANU.
ZAPU	Zimbabwe African People's Union.
ZIPRA	Zimbabwe People's Revolutionary Army. ZIPRA was the military wing of ZAPU.
ZNA	Zimbabwe National Army.
ZRP	Zimbabwe Republic Police.

About the Author

www.authormichaelchalk.com

Michael's novels invite readers to witness the seismic shifts in southern Africa's recent history, rendered through characters whose lives are marked by love, war, and political upheaval.

Born in Durban, South Africa, in October 1955 and raised in Rhodesia (now Zimbabwe), Michael experienced firsthand the complex dynamics that fuel his storytelling. After completing his education in Rhodesia and earning a Bachelor of Laws in Scotland, he returned to Rhodesia, where he worked as a prosecutor and served as a 2nd Lieutenant in the Rhodesian African Rifles. His experiences gave him a deep understanding of the era's conflicts and camaraderie — insights he brings to his books.

In *The Unravelling*, Michael captures the tensions of the 1970s and 1980s as Rhodesia's colonial rule collapses. Following two comrades, Nick and Sipho, through war and the challenging aftermath, the novel reveals the scars left on individuals and nations alike.

The story continues in *A Moment of Madness*, set amid Robert Mugabe's rise to power. As Nick and Rachel navigate life in the UK and grapple with Zimbabwe's brutal Gukurahundi campaign, they're drawn into dangerous political currents that put love, loyalty, and integrity to the test. With vivid portrayals of Cold War geopolitics and Zimbabwe's internal strife, Michael offers readers a gripping narrative of a country in turmoil.

In March 1990, Michael emigrated to Australia with his wife and two sons. Settling in Adelaide, South Australia, he worked in various senior roles in the private health sector for over 30 years.

Now retired and living in Adelaide, South Australia, Michael remains deeply connected to Zimbabwe. Through his writing, he explores the powerful intersections of history and personal destiny, inviting readers to uncover the untold stories behind Zimbabwe's transformation.

www.ingramcontent.com/pod-product-compliance
Lightning Source LLC
Chambersburg PA
CBHW070117120726
47909CB00002B/633